THE
Astronomer's
OBSESSION

A SWEET REGENCY ROMANCE

K. LYN SMITH

Epigraph Image: *William Herschel's Forty-Foot Telescope*. Bunce, J., & Walker, J. (2009). Available by the University of Cambridge, Institute of Astronomy Library under CC BY 4.0 license. Modified from the original version. https://www.repository.cam.ac.uk/handle/1810/218815

ISBN: 978-1-7376579-1-0

For small creatures such as we
the vastness is bearable only through love.

- Carl Sagan

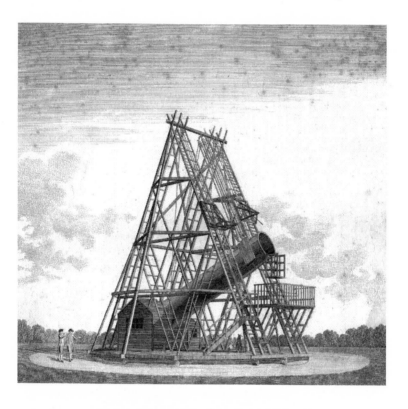

WILLIAM HERSCHEL'S FORTY-FOOT TELESCOPE

PROLOGUE

SEPTEMBER 1815
REDSTONE HALL, KENT

HARRY CORBYN STUDIED THE GREEN substance before him and pressed down a shiver. Chilled asparagus soup. How could any self-respecting Englishman call this food? Surely it must be an invention of the French.

An array of silver lay in formation next to his place setting. He straightened a spoon until it was perpendicular to the edge of the table.

How was a man to know which was the chilled asparagus soup spoon? His mother may have been the daughter of a country squire, but his father had been an innkeeper of limited means. They'd only ever needed one spoon.

He glanced up to find Lord Ashford's daughter watching him. Lady Celeste lightly touched a spoon

1

at her own place before lifting it to her bowl, the corner of her mouth turning up slightly. He found his matching spoon and dipped it into the green stuff.

"Do you enjoy the chilled asparagus soup, Mr. Corbyn?" Lady Grey spoke from his left. The mother of his old school mate, Julian, she'd merely tolerated her son's friendship with Harry when they'd been boys. Now that he was a frequent guest of Lord Ashford, whose estate bordered her own Fernwood, she'd thawed a bit.

"It's nice." He winced at the ridiculous adjective, but he'd found it effective to answer polite-but-meaningless questions. When Lady Grey turned to the gentleman at her other side, he glanced back toward the head of the table.

Although it had been a year since he'd seen Lady Celeste, they'd been acquainted for years. She likely knew exactly what he thought of the chilled asparagus soup.

She spoke with the vicar at her left. Despite what must be dull conversation, her eyes sparkled. She wore her cinnamon hair in a simple style, and though he couldn't see them from where he sat, light freckles dotted the bridge of her nose. Her pale skin gleamed against the white silk of her evening dress. Lady Celeste looked quite fetching.

His musings brought him up short. Despite the "Lady" before her name, he recalled her as always disheveled, often dirty, as they'd spent holidays tramping the woods between Fernwood Manor and Redstone Hall. His brows came together as he considered her. Didn't she usually wear her hair in braids?

————

CELESTE ASSESSED VICAR PITT WITH an artist's eye. Of average height, with average hair and unremarkable features, he was . . . muted, colorless, with hazy edges. His voice was as soft as his conversation was dull. There was nothing memorable about him. She supposed that, in and of itself, was memorable. She attempted to tease diverting conversation from him, but to no avail.

"Are you looking forward to the harvest festival? Do you think Mr. Pinkerton's cow will win this year?"

"I don't believe so, Lady Celeste."

To be fair, that had been two questions. Perhaps she'd confused him. She tried again.

"Did you have any interesting experiences while you were in London?"

"No, Lady Celeste. The weather was dismal. Although I did find time to visit the impressive monument to my cousin, The Right Honorable William Pitt. You'll recall we're related on my mother's side."

Celeste smiled tightly. When the vicar turned to

respond to a question from Miss Olive Miller, she sighed with relief. Miss Miller was everything Vicar Pitt was not. Tall and angular. Sharp-edged. Charitable acquaintances might call her handsome, although sometimes it was difficult to tell her from her twin, Mr. Roger Miller.

Celeste suspected the lady's unmarried state had as much to do with her mother as with Miss Miller's unfortunate resemblance to her brother.

Mrs. Miller led the Planning Committee for the annual harvest celebration, and engaging her in conversation always led to an unwelcome assignment. Arranging flowers for the assembly. Sewing bunting for the storefronts. Judging cows. Consequently, most people avoided the woman, and poor Miss Miller was a hapless victim by association.

A bark of laughter interrupted Celeste's thoughts and she turned. As Celeste watched, Miss Miller laid a hand on the vicar's dark sleeve, and he rested his own atop hers. Celeste's brows notched up at this intriguing development. She suppressed a smile and lifted another spoonful of asparagus soup to her lips.

Tonight was the midpoint of her father's week-long Round Table event. As it had for the past decade, the occasion brought eleven astronomers from across England to discuss their latest theories. While the scientific gentlemen enjoyed their discussions, the local gentry enjoyed the gentlemen.

Vicar Pitt and the Millers were just a few of the local guests tonight.

The Eleven, as they styled themselves, were "gentlemen astronomers," men of independent means with an interest in scientific study. Harry Corbyn, whose livelihood depended on educational grants, was the singular exception. She watched him push his spoon around his bowl for a bit longer before taking pity on him.

"Mr. Corbyn, tell us about your upcoming travels. You're to leave for Berlin at week's end?"

Several pairs of eyes turned toward Harry. He looked up from his soup with a relieved smile.

"Indeed, Lady Celeste. I've been corresponding with Herr Kraus on the subject of stellar parallax." He pushed his spectacles up. "We'll test several of my theories together in Berlin."

The Eleven nodded while other, non-scientific heads angled blank expressions his way. Harry clarified, "We're using the earth's various positions to calculate the distance to the stars."

"Bah!" Lord Knowles, a member of the Eleven, said. "Parallax is a fool's errand. There is *no evidence* the earth is in motion." He punctuated his statement with a broad slash of one hand then rested that hand on his planetary form.

Celeste watched Harry's fingers flex then settle on the table. She'd always admired his hands. While his posture and facial expressions might be restrained, his hands were always in motion, full of energy and purpose.

"With all due respect, my lord," Harry continued, "it's true we don't have definitive evidence of the earth's motion yet, but we have a duty to exhaust all possible avenues of investigation. If our theories prove out, the impact would be significant. The ramifications could alter the course of astronomical study."

"Quite right, Mr. Corbyn." This was from Lord Porter, another of the Eleven. The Voice of Reason. When another member spouted ridiculous theories about sun creatures or lunar towns of bat people, Lord Porter could be counted on to settle the discussion with science. "I've long thought we're on the cusp of an exciting era in astronomy," he said. "Mark my words, this will be a discipline in its own right before long."

Mrs. Miller sniffed and added, "Gentlemen would do well to mind more earthly concerns."

"Indeed," Lady Grey added, "it hardly seems appropriate to devote so much time to matters of no import. A gentleman should direct his energy to finding a wife and setting up his nursery." She directed this last toward her son, Julian, with a speaking glance at Celeste.

"But if they did that," Celeste added, "then we

would have no need for a Round Table event." As her father's Round Table was one of the few social events in Marshfield, the lady could hardly wish for its demise. Indeed, Lady Grey's mouth pinched as she struggled to refute Celeste's logic.

"I find Mr. Corbyn's work exciting," Celeste continued. "To travel and devote your time to something you feel so passionate about. How satisfying that must be!"

"You will find plenty of excitement soon enough," Mrs. Miller said, "with the Ladies' Society for the Advancement of Needlework Samplers."

"Have you decided to take up needlework, Lady Celeste?" Harry asked.

If he knew her at all, he knew no such decision had occurred. Celeste narrowed her eyes as Mrs. Miller answered for her.

"Why, yes, Mr. Corbyn. As Lady Celeste's mother remains on the Continent"—she paused significantly—"I'm taking it upon myself to see that she engages in appropriate pastimes."

Like a ball tossed in the air, conversation hung at the mention of Lady Ashford, and the room waited in heavy expectation. The only movement was her father as he slowly lifted a spoonful of soup to his lips. The room took a collective breath as Mrs. Miller continued.

"A lady should cultivate elegant accomplishments

to make her husband's life comfortable." She looked pointedly at Celeste then at her son, Mr. Roger Miller. "To that end, the Society has embarked on a most ambitious project. We aim to tell the story of Creation in embroidery, for our dear vicar to display in the parish church, of course."

"It sounds, er, ambitious indeed," Harry agreed.

Celeste was unclear how the story of Creation would improve a husband's comfort, but she remained silent as she'd little interest in becoming more clear.

"I've appealed to Lady Celeste to join us," Mrs. Miller continued. "She's understandably reticent, but I'm certain her contributions will be adequate." She then delivered a lengthy monologue on the merits of cross stitch versus *petit point*.

Celeste gripped her hands in her lap. She had no liking or talent for needlework. While she might have suffered through a single afternoon of stitching, if forced to it, there was no way she could endure *weeks* of embroidery. The Lord may have created heaven and earth, the sea and all that is in them in a mere six days, but she was certain the story of Creation could not be embroidered in anything less.

————

THE GENTLEMEN LINGERED OVER THEIR port before joining the ladies in the yellow drawing room. Harry had never understood the appeal. As a man with an aversion to spirits, Harry was forever a fish out of water in polite society. He had witnessed too many gin-shot nights with his father to see the attraction, so when the gentlemen lingered over their port, he merely swirled the tawny liquid in his glass.

When he entered the drawing room, Celeste was seated in a circle of ladies, hands folded before her. She looked about the room like a felon seeking escape. She'd never been one for idle chatter, and if the topic was needlework . . . well. He suppressed a smile.

Lord Ashford approached him in the drawing room with a hearty clap on the back. "Harry, my boy. I can't quite grasp that you're soon to leave England. Are your arrangements all set?"

"Yes, my lord." Harry smiled. "I believe everything is in order." Ashford, with his gruff, paternal manner, was more of a father than Harry's own sire had been. William Corbyn had never troubled himself with his son's aspirations, but Harry counted this as the third time Ashford had inquired about his travel plans.

Across the room, Celeste left the ladies to speak with Sir John and Lady Grey. He realized he'd been watching her when Ashford spoke. "I worry for Celeste," he said.

"Is she unwell, my lord?"

"She's well enough, but I fear she's bored.

Unsatisfied." Ashford sighed. "Sir John hinted that Julian would like to pay his addresses."

Celeste and Julian? Harry cleared his throat. He tried to imagine his friends married, with a family of their own. His mind couldn't form the image.

"I had hoped . . . Well, as much as I would like to have her close, I fear marriage won't be enough to satisfy her boredom. She's much like her mother."

Ashford rarely mentioned his wife and her nine-year holiday in Paris, but Harry occasionally caught a distant gaze in the man's eyes. A hint of loneliness that he would shake off before refocusing on the matter at hand.

Harry had never married, and he couldn't envision a wife for himself. His livelihood was uncertain, dependent as it was on research and educational grants. Marriage simply wasn't in the stars for him. How could he ask a lady to leave her home and family to join him in his scientific quests? Or to remain behind, waiting for him? He cleared his throat again and sought to turn the conversation.

"Tell me about your latest project, my lord. You're working on a catalog of binary stars, I understand."

"Indeed, indeed! I'd love your opinion on a theory of min."

After Ashford left him to speak with Lord Knowles, Celeste caught Harry's eye with a visible sigh. He smiled and watched her approach; it appeared her patience with social niceties was at an end.

"Harry," she said. "Won't you entertain me with a game of chess?"

His brows lifted. "I'll not let you win," he warned.

"Of course not. I wouldn't expect it."

He frowned but set his reservations aside and began setting up his half of the board. He studied Celeste's long, slender fingers as she placed her pieces, then he asked, "When did you leave off your braids?"

She stared at him for a beat before responding. "Harry, I haven't worn braids in four years."

He blinked. How had he missed that? He thought back to last year's Round Table, and the year before that, but he couldn't recall whether she had worn braids or not.

They began to play, and it was clear Celeste had something on her mind. He felt certain he would hear it soon enough. As his knight closed in on her king, she spoke.

"Harry, do you have a special lady in your life?"

Confused, he said, "You know my mother has been gone these past twenty years, and my sister and I are not close."

"No, I mean a *special* lady. Are you courting anyone?"

On the heels of his earlier thoughts on marriage,

her question came as a surprise. "No, I don't have time for courting. And it wouldn't be right to form an attachment with a lady since I'm leaving for Berlin soon."

She nodded and tapped her chin. Leaning toward him, she whispered across the board, "Harry, I've had a brilliant idea."

He shifted in his seat. That she'd had an idea, he was certain. That it was brilliant, he doubted. As children, Celeste had used similar claims to convince him and Julian to go along with one of her impulsive—but rarely brilliant—schemes.

The balloon incident had been but one example . . . After reading about a hot-air balloon ascension, she'd flipped her braid and snapped her fingers. "Harry! Julian! I have a brilliant idea! Let's make a balloon and fly!"

"Are you mad?" Julian had asked. "That's the most ridiculous notion I've ever heard." Julian was always one for hyperbole.

"You'll never get enough altitude for it to work." Harry, the pragmatist.

Celeste had been persistent, though. Although they were older and should have known better, the idea did sound intriguing.

When Ashford had spied his bed linens flapping from the parapet above Redstone Hall, he'd bellowed quite impressively. He ordered Celeste to her room then frog-marched Julian and Harry back to Fernwood. Ashford's disappointment had devastated ten-year-old Harry; he hadn't spoken to Celeste for at least a full week.

Given his vivid experience with Celeste's brilliant ideas, Harry should have been more prepared for her next words.

"Why don't I come with you to Berlin?"

———

HARRY DROPPED HIS KNIGHT AND it rolled beneath a nearby chair. He pushed his spectacles up and glanced around to see if anyone had overheard her outrageous statement.

"Are you mad? Of course not." That he sounded like Julian wasn't lost on him.

"I can be your assistant. I'm good with sums. Well, passably so. And my penmanship is excellent. I can maintain your notes." She grinned. All the image needed was her hands pressed together in supplication.

Although he was older and should know better . . . No.

"No," he said, ignoring the tiny slip of her smile. Surely this was a jest. He looked for Julian, to see if he'd put her up to it, but Julian was deep in conversation with Ashford and Knowles. He was clearly not watching Harry for a reaction.

Harry turned back to Celeste; she'd regained her

smile, her expression hopeful. He debated other responses and opted for silence.

"Harry," she whispered, "were you not attending at supper? Can you not see what's afoot? Mrs. Miller is *taking me under her wing*."

"A dastardly plot, to be sure."

"She plans to mold me in her image to be the future Mrs. Miller." She wrinkled her nose. "Now I think on it, there must be a shortage of unmarried ladies in Kent. Lady Grey has begun hinting at a match with Julian." She twisted her lips as she thought. "Surely, Harry, even you can see Julian and I are not suited."

"Even I? What does that mean?"

She waved her hand. "It's just that your attention is so often on your studies that you don't always notice . . . people."

He stared at her, prepared to defend himself, until she motioned to her hair.

"Braids?" she said.

Right.

She stood and bent to pick up his fallen knight. He quickly averted his gaze from her . . . Well. There were some things even he couldn't fail to notice.

She turned back to face him, and he regained the thread of the discussion.

"And you and Julian—" he said.

"It's not that Julian wouldn't make a good

husband. I find him quite agreeable. Handsome in fact. He's definitely filled out lately. Grown into his paws, don't you think?"

Was he supposed to answer that? She continued, so he assumed the question was rhetorical.

"But there's no, I don't know, *fizz* with Julian."

"Fizz?"

"That fluttery feeling you get inside, like champagne bubbles. Spark, flash, twinkle, hum. Call it what you will, but it's not there." Her forehead creased. "I think there's supposed to be fizz."

Did that mean she felt *fizz* with him? Heat rose on his neck. Fizz or no, it was simply out of the question for them to entertain such a possibility. She was an earl's daughter—his mentor's daughter, at that.

She sighed at his silence. Looked at him meaningfully. "Harry, if you don't take me with you, I shall never forgive you."

Well, that was hardly fair, and he told her so.

Celeste passed him the knight, her fingers grazing his. Even through the thin silk of her gloves, he felt the heat of her touch. He folded his own fingers over the ebony carving, the edges digging into his palm.

She studied his face for a beat then crossed her arms. When he didn't say anything, she turned away with a disappointed sigh and left him.

"Harry? Is everything all right?" Ashford asked.

"Yes, my lord. I think Lady Celeste just needed some air."

———

SHE WOULD NEVER SURVIVE THE Ladies' Society for the Advancement of Needlework Samplers. She would likely poke her eye out with her scissors and bleed all over Creation.

But the Ladies' Society was only the latest in a long string of Mrs. Miller's "improving activities." There had also been the Marshfield Fern Collectors Club. The Ladies' Alliance for Compassionate Benevolence. The Marshfield Pressed Flower Circle.

As Mrs. Miller continued to arrange ladylike pursuits and Lady Grey hinted at an alliance between herself and Julian, the weight of Celeste's future pressed heavily upon her.

She was certain this unease must be to blame for her artistic dry spell. She loved watching form and color come to life beneath her hand, but she'd not put brush to canvas in over six months. Her paintings had begun to feel flat, her enjoyment shallow. For her painting to grow, *she* needed to grow. She needed to experience more colors of life, but the options for a single lady were limited.

Over the last days and weeks, she'd contemplated the notion of marriage to gauge her feelings. It was the obvious next step for a lady of one and twenty. To many, it was the *only* next step.

She and Roger Miller had never exchanged more than ten words between them, so she couldn't envision marrying *him*. And though she liked Julian well enough, she didn't believe her future was with him, either. She was fairly certain he felt the same, his parents' hints to the contrary notwithstanding.

Then her father's Round Table had begun, and she'd had the unexpected notion of marrying Harry. And that idea, if only as a means to escape Marshfield . . . appealed. Harry spoke of his work with passion and intensity. She envied that vitality. She wanted it. What must it be like to feel such passion for something?

Marriage was a drastic step. She knew that. She wasn't completely *dicked in the nob*, as Julian had once accused. But she and Harry had always gotten on well. Once the idea flickered to life in her mind, the flame wouldn't be doused.

Her awareness of him had reached an annoying level after that. The dark slash of his brows as he contemplated something from one of the Eleven. The way his eyes shifted from smoky silver when he laughed, to icy-crisp shards when he was irritated. His passion for his field.

Over the past days, she'd cast numerous hints in his direction, encouraging him to see how well suited they were. But this was Harry, who was oblivious to subtlety, so tonight she'd taken a more direct approach.

She'd simply asked him to take her to Berlin.

Or had she told him? He and Julian had often accused her of being managing, so perhaps Harry's resistance wasn't to the *idea* itself, but to her delivery of it. She fiddled with a loose button on her sleeve as she replayed their conversation in her mind.

She'd tried reasoning with him. She didn't have much to offer in the way of astronomy assistance, but she could learn. But he, it seemed, had no need for an assistant.

She'd tried cajoling, and she may have even threatened him. All to no avail.

But she had one more card to play.

Harry was a male, and were not all males subject to the gentle art of feminine persuasion? She was not experienced in flirting—there weren't many opportunities in Marshfield, after all—but what did she have to lose?

———

IT HADN'T BEEN TOO DIFFICULT to avoid Celeste in the Hall's rambling corridors, but it seemed Harry's luck was at an end. As he made his way toward the guest wing the next evening, she emerged from a nearby hall. He bowed and prepared to step around her, but she took his hand. And he, foolish man that he was, allowed her to pull him into the conservatory.

"Celeste?" He looked around to be sure they hadn't been seen.

She closed the door and watched him over her shoulder. Candlelight from a single sconce outlined her profile. Part of his brain noted that, amid the humid fragrance of plants and flowers, she smelled of vanilla. Warm and spicy and slightly exotic. Not the damp scent of frogs and grass and pond water he expected.

As she moved closer, the light caught her eyes. They were an intriguing shade: neither blue nor green, but a unique blend of the two. How had he never noticed her eyes?

"Harry, you are decidedly difficult to run to ground. I'd almost say you've been avoiding me."

She blinked long lashes at him. Did she have something in her eye?

"Won't you at least consider my suggestion?" she continued. "We get on well together."

Her voice was throaty. Perhaps she was coming down with something. He swallowed. "Celeste, you know it would be improper for you to come to Berlin with me."

"Improper? Harry, you mistake me. I'm not suggesting anything untoward. Of course, we would marry." She bit her lip and moved closer still.

Had she just . . . *proposed* to him? He didn't expect to marry, but he thought a proposal should somehow be . . . more. He exhaled.

She stood close, too close. He could hear her

breath in the stillness of the conservatory. This new awareness of her unsettled him. Her eyes were large and dark in the candlelight, her lips unbearably close. He raised his hands to her shoulders, but whether to hold her from him or pull her near, he couldn't say. He was surprised to feel the heat of her skin beneath the fabric of her gown, the smooth slope of her shoulder beneath his thumbs.

The urge to close the distance between them shocked him with its intensity. Another tiny inch and he would know if her lips were as lush as they appeared. This was Celeste, he reminded himself. His friend. His mentor's daughter. Still, he felt his head lowering as his heart pounded a rapid staccato.

Voices sounded in the hall beyond the door, shattering the moment and restoring his senses. He released her and straightened with an inhale, eyeing her in the heavy stillness. Finally, mercifully, she stepped back.

He studied her, noting an anxiety about her eyes that he'd not seen before. As children, they'd passed hours talking and dreaming with one another, but it had been some time since they'd been children. He looked at her—truly looked at her. "What's this about, Celeste?"

She hesitated before saying, "You'll achieve greatness." He blinked, and she continued. "You'll be known for scientific discoveries that will shape the path of humankind, and they'll name *stars* after you."

Her eyes were more blue than green now. Bright. *Suspiciously* bright. He'd never handled her tears well. One hint of them and he waved a white flag. Gave her whatever she wanted just to avoid them. He averted his gaze.

"If I stay here," she whispered, "I will only be known as Mrs. Miller. Or Mrs. Grey, whichever the case may be. I want more, Harry."

She'd always had a penchant for the dramatic, but he felt her desperation as it thrummed a familiar chord in his chest. This was more than dramatic airs, but it didn't make the impossible possible. He tried once more to explain why her scheme wouldn't work.

"Celeste, you're an earl's daughter. You're meant for something noble. You deserve a better life than to be a scholar's wife, or . . . or an astronomer's assistant."

He waved a hand at the luxury around them, but it wasn't material things to which he referred. How could he make her understand she deserved a majestic, monumental life full of purpose and honor and worth?

"I know I must sound ungrateful. To have all this and still want more. I can't explain it, Harry. I just know I'm meant to be somewhere else, to *do* something else."

He nodded, understanding her need for purpose, for significance, as he felt the same himself.

"Then you need to find it, Celeste. Whatever *it* is that makes your life meaningful. Find it and hold on. Don't settle for an innkeeper's son with no future or fortune."

She smiled, a gentle curving of her lips, her hair sparking red and gold in the candlelight. "I'm sorry, Harry. It wasn't fair of me to ask this of you." She moved to exit, and he stepped aside.

"Celeste," he began. He lifted a hand to her then dropped it. He wasn't sure what to say, and she continued through the door.

He stood there after she left, head down. He rubbed the back of his neck as he tried to make sense of the evening. Of Celeste's attempts to leave behind a future that, by any standards, should have been a pleasant prospect. Of his newfound awareness of her.

He went to leave then noticed something shiny on the floor. He picked it up and held it close to the candelabra's light. It was an enameled button, painted with dainty rosebuds and edged in a delicate filigree. He put it in his pocket to return to her later.

———

CELESTE LEANED AGAINST THE CLOSED door of her bedchamber and pressed cool hands to her burning cheeks. Harry had always been independent, always alone, even in company. Of course, a wife was the last thing he wanted.

But his rejection wasn't what caused her cheeks to

burn and her stomach to tighten. She could handle his rejection—was accustomed to it, in fact, after all their misadventures as children.

No, what had caused her insides to melt was the kiss they'd almost shared. She'd intended to persuade him, to practice her—admittedly meager—feminine persuasion on him, but she'd only succeeded in flustering herself. With *Harry*, of all people.

As she'd stood there, the silk of her dress brushing the tops of his shoes, the smooth pads of his thumbs burning her shoulders through her silk, all thought had fled her mind. Her purpose, her goal of escaping Marshfield, her desire for something *more*—all had fallen away beneath the pull of his lips and the compelling grey of his eyes. She blew a shaky breath.

No. This would not do.

Harry was going to Berlin without her. She didn't need an ill-fated infatuation, one more thing to add to her restlessness. It would be best if they moved on from this incident. The next time they saw one another, she would likely be married anyway. Her heart thumped uncomfortably.

————

HARRY MISSED CELESTE. SHE HAD been polite in company since their encounter in the conservatory two nights before, but he didn't want polite. He wanted Celeste. He wanted the friend of his youth, who'd laughed and raced through the woods with him. Who hadn't made improper suggestions and tempted him with improper kisses. He wasn't sure how to return her button to her, much less repair things between them.

The Marshfield harvest festival would begin tomorrow. The entire household was abuzz with excitement. He, however, was packing to leave for his ship to the Continent. He wouldn't see Celeste again for some time. Months, for certain. Years, perhaps.

Maybe he could write to her while he was in Berlin. No, he sighed. That wouldn't do. A single lady didn't correspond with a single gentleman. He would simply have to seek her out to say his farewell and hope they could restore their easy friendship.

But she wasn't in the library, or the yellow drawing room, or the conservatory. He took a long walk in the gardens, but she wasn't there either. He entered the dining room, hoping to find her breaking her fast, but Ashford and Lord Knowles were the only people present. He could hardly come out and ask Ashford where he might find his unmarried daughter.

When he casually asked after her welfare, Ashford chuckled. "She's likely still abed if I know my Celeste. She's not much for mornings." Ashford then turned the conversation to Knowles' latest theory on the sun's inhabitants.

When the time came for Harry to leave, he mounted his borrowed horse with a heavy heart then patted the small, enameled button in his pocket. As he rode away, he thought a curtain moved at the third window, but he couldn't be certain. He turned in the saddle and continued down the drive.

———

HER MOTHER HAD INVITED HER to Paris. Again. Celeste studied the letter with its elegant script tightly inked across the page. She'd not planned to go. Her emotions surrounding her mother were a confusing mixture of sadness, anger, resentment and confusion.

She lived in color, *felt* in color. Joy and wonder sparked around her in yellow tones. Pain throbbed in hues of violet. Thoughts of her mother swirled in red, blue, violet and indigo. Anger, sadness, pain, loneliness. Richly hued ribbons twisting at the edge of her vision. Ribbons she wasn't sure she was ready to confront.

As a child, she'd believed everyone felt things as she did. At the age of seven, she'd fallen and hurt her knee. When her father asked what was wrong, she complained through her tears. "My knee—it's *purple!*" Confused, her father assured her it was not. After years of similar incidents, she'd finally accepted that she was different. She *felt* things differently.

But with Napoleon defeated once more and talks of a second treaty with Paris, there was no impediment to traveling. Paris would be a fine city in which to study and practice her art.

Paris also had the added allure in that it lacked a Mr. Roger Miller and a Julian Grey. There were no Mrs. Millers or Lady Greys. Creation could be embroidered without her. Perhaps a change was just what she needed.

Find it, Celeste. Whatever it *is that makes your life meaningful. Don't settle.*

She sat at the large bow window in the ladies' morning room. It was a clear day for traveling. She refolded her mother's letter then watched as Harry paused in the drive. He turned to look back, and she let the curtain fall.

CHAPTER ONE

FEBRUARY 1818
ROYAL PRUSSIAN ACADEMY OF SCIENCES,
BERLIN

Harry removed his spectacles and rubbed his eyes. The candles in his office had burned down to stubs again. He hadn't noticed the late hour until he caught himself squinting at the figures before him. Was that an eight or a three? He needed to work on his penmanship.

Tidy, squared stacks of books and papers lined his desk, and ink stained his fingers. A notebook lay open with sprawling equations and charts crossing the pages. Brass instruments and planetary models sat on shelves behind his desk, and the smell of dust surrounded everything. Harry took a moment to re-straighten a pile of journals, lining the leather edges with the lines of his desk.

The door flew open, and Herr Kraus advanced into the room with his usual exuberance. The older gentleman's hair, more salt than pepper, stood on end as he pulled off his hat and ran a hand through it.

"*Ach*, Mr. Corbyn, why are you still here? The hour grows late, and the stars, they are not going anywhere." He chuckled at his own joke.

Harry smiled. "I'm still working on this equation. I've almost worked out the constant."

"Your constant can wait. I'm collecting my sister and niece for supper at Hoffstein's. You'll join us, *ja*?"

"Thank you for the invitation, but I must decline. Perhaps another time."

Herr Kraus's sister, Mrs. Pepper, and her youngest daughter were visiting from Italy. Harry gathered from some rather oblique references that Miss Pepper had encountered difficulties with a suitor there. He suspected she and her mother were biding their time until a new scandal occupied curious minds. While the ladies were pleasant enough dining companions, Harry had *Plans* that didn't allow for distraction.

He had his eye on Britain's Transit of Venus expeditions, and he hoped his latest research would secure a lead position. The transit, when Venus would pass between the earth and the sun, was eagerly anticipated in astronomy circles. By measuring the transit from various points around the globe, astronomers hoped to measure the size of the solar system.

Britain's teams were but a small part of the larger international effort. In ten months, they would observe the transit from remote islands in the South Pacific and Indian Ocean as well as New Zealand and Egypt.

It was an ambitious endeavor, to say the least, and Harry's heart raced to think of the scale of the work and its potential. What it would mean for human understanding of the universe. His work of the past years was narrowing to this point, and he couldn't afford a misstep now.

Herr Kraus sniffed and read the direction of his thoughts. "The Commission would be foolish to appoint someone else to lead the Cairo expedition."

The man had become a staunch supporter—and friend—in the past three years. Harry appreciated his unwavering faith, but he knew how capricious the minds of men could be. Harry was a diligent scholar, but the profession was young and favored gentlemen of noble birth, not innkeepers' sons.

Nevertheless, he'd written countless letters to the organizing commission sharing his theories and opinions on research methods, hoping something resonated. He wasn't sure what he would do next if he weren't selected.

The Commission would make their final selections in the autumn. Harry would journey to London once his work in Berlin was complete. If he could meet with a few of the Commissioners before their selection was complete, he hoped to persuade opinion in his favor.

Lord Porter, in particular, was a fellow member of the Eleven. He would be in London for the Parliamentary session, as would many of the Commission members, and Harry thought his might be a receptive ear. It wasn't the strongest plan, but it was his only plan at this point.

"Thank you for your confidence, Herr Kraus. I hope it's not misplaced." He re-donned his spectacles, straightened the inkwell, then bent toward his paper once again. He barely heard the click of the door as Kraus left the room.

———

PARIS
LADY ASHFORD'S TOWNHOUSE

FOR DAYS, A STEADY RAIN had splashed icy drops against windows and stripped Paris of color. Celeste pulled a soft wool shawl of deep plum about her shoulders as she descended the marble staircase.

Remy, her mother's favored—and devastatingly

handsome—footman, greeted her with a wink and opened the doors to the green salon. She rolled her eyes at his cheek.

Surrounded by gilt and spring green furnishings, her mother defied the day's dreariness. Lily St. James sat draped in soft cream silk, shining like her namesake, newly opened and kissed by the sun. She wore her pale blond hair in the newest style, and she angled her head toward a dark-haired gentleman, Le Comte de Tourven.

Another finely dressed gentleman, Monsieur La Fleur, pursed his lips from a chair opposite. Celeste smiled. Monsieur La Fleur would not be pleased to share her mother's attentions with Le Comte.

Her mother was not unaware of the picture she made or the effect she had on the gentlemen; it was carefully constructed after all.

As Celeste entered the room, La Fleur's bouquet hit her like a wave. The man reeked of floral scent. Whether his own, or a lady love's, Celeste couldn't say. She resisted the urge to put a hand to her nose as she greeted her mother's guests.

Another gentleman stood near the window with hands clasped behind his back. With burnished gold hair falling artfully over a strong brow, Monsieur Alexandre Marchand was striking. He approached and bowed over her hand.

"Lady Celeste, you are a fine restorative for such

a dreary day." He paused then leaned in and whispered, "I hope I can persuade you to walk with me?" He spoke the words as a question, but the elbow he offered betrayed his confidence.

Given the wet weather, a turn about the garden wouldn't do. They settled instead for the long gallery that ran along the back of her mother's leased townhouse. As they stopped at each painting, Alexandre commented on the boldness of a stroke here, or the use of color there.

"Señor de Goya has a good mastery of light and shadow. Here," he pointed, "you can see how he uses the direction of the light to emphasize the curve of her cheek. It's magnificent."

Celeste sighed and considered the painting, noting the familiar lines and depth of color. It drew her in, and every time she studied it, a different nuance emerged. "I should like to have half his talent."

"You will," he said with emphasis. "You have an artist's instincts, and others are beginning to notice. You may not be ready for the Salon yet, but you will rule it one day. Until then, perhaps one of the ladies' exhibitions . . ."

"You know how I feel about that. The works in the ladies' exhibits are remarkable, indeed. But the exhibits, by their detached nature, devalue the diverse perspectives we should be honoring."

He held up an elegant hand. "Say no more, my lady. The world is not yet ready for your revolution." It was an old debate, and their respective arguments had not changed. Alexandre was right about one thing, though. Her paintings, despite his praise, were not ready for the Salon.

She was, however, eager to apply for admission to the Royal Academy. Again. She had already applied twice, with disappointing results. But few were accepted on their first or third application, so she would continue to apply. Women weren't permitted to attend the life drawing classes, but any Academy training would be a significant boon.

Her artistic dreams were proving to be costly. She was fortunate that Denton Manor, which comprised much of her dowry, was profitable. Her father was more progressive than most and allowed the small estate's income to support her independent lifestyle. It would serve until she had need of a dowry, as long as she was prudent.

She and Marchand turned and retraced their steps. "Have you decided on a subject for your own submission to the Salon?" she asked. Like many artists, he was very secretive about his painting, and she had yet to see his latest work.

He sighed. "*Non*, alas, my muse has deserted me."

She chuckled. "Monsieur Marchand, you are one of the most prolific artists I know. I've no doubt you'll settle on a subject soon."

He winced at her formality. "Have we not agreed that you will call me Alex?" he asked. "Or Alexandre, if you prefer."

She smiled. "We did. Old habits, I suppose. And I'm certain your muse will return when you least expect her, Alexandre."

"You're more confident than I, my lady. But I wonder if my barren soul might not be soothed if you were to provide an answer to my question."

Alexandre had proposed very prettily two days past. Celeste had hoped he would not press for an answer so soon. She studied his face. He was gilded perfection, with a wide mouth, smooth forehead and piercing amber eyes. Their children would be stunning if they had half his appeal.

She wanted to say yes. She would be four and twenty this year, well past the time when she should have married. Alexandre's wasn't her first proposal, but it was the first one she'd considered in earnest.

He was a talented painter. Celeste thought she might learn a great deal from him. Surely shared interests and goals could be a solid foundation for marriage. His personality was pleasant and his regard for her seemed sincere. And yet . . . she found herself reluctant to say yes.

Was something wrong with her? Was she broken? Why could she not form an attachment with a pleasant gentleman? While other young ladies tittered and whispered about their beaus, she felt . . . flat.

Unbidden, the memory of one almost-kiss sparked in her mind. A not-quite-there kiss that had felt decidedly . . . un-flat. She quickly forced it from her thoughts, certain her overactive imagination applied more dramatic emphasis than the barely-there moment warranted.

Alexandre watched her face. "*Non,* I can see that you are not yet ready to give your answer."

Ah, a gentleman waited for an answer to his proposal, and she was woolgathering. About a kiss that never even happened. "Alexandre—"

"Do not say no," he said. "Take more time to think on it."

She wasn't ready to say yes, but she wasn't ready to say no, either, so she agreed.

———

CELESTE LOOKED UP FROM THE page she'd been reading and refolded it with shaking hands. "Odette, where is *Maman*?"

"She's in the green salon, my lady. That odious Monsieur La Fleur is here. Again."

Celeste placed the letter in her pocket then pinched some color into her cheeks. Pressing a hand to her stomach, she tried to suppress the anxiety roiling there. After the front door closed behind La Fleur, she ventured into the green salon. Her mother must have seen something in her expression.

"Dearest, what is it? You have the look of someone whose prized mastiff has died." As her mother's stables housed three of the breed, she spoke with authority.

"*Maman*, I'm afraid I need to borrow Odette." Celeste rolled the edge of her shawl between her thumb and forefinger. The quizzical look on her mother's face encouraged her to continue. "I must return home. Peters, Father's steward—"

"Yes, I recall Peters."

"Well, Peters writes that Father has been extremely ill. A fever of some sort." Celeste pulled the letter from the pocket of her skirt and handed it to her mother. Lily unfolded it, forehead creasing delicately as she read.

"But dearest, what of Alexandre? You won't want to miss his exhibit at the Salon, and I'm sure he's eager to receive your answer to his proposal." A question tipped her voice up on the last bit; clearly, her mother wished to hear Celeste's decision as well.

Celeste shook her head. "I will write to Alexandre and let him know of the situation. It can't be helped."

"But what can you do for your father? Certainly, a doctor is tending him."

"Julian Grey—you'll recall him from Fernwood— he's Father's doctor now that Doctor Smythe has retired. I'm sure he must be competent, but Father needs his family at a time like this. I must go."

Her mother sighed. "Yes, of course. You're right. Although I can't like you traveling all that way. Odette may accompany you. Take Remy as well. They're a matched pair, you know, and a lady can always use a strong footman to assist with the travel things."

Celeste rolled her eyes and squeezed her mother's hand. Lily appreciated a well-formed physique. The fact that Remy was head-over-arse for the pretty maid didn't lessen her mother's regard for his handsome appearance.

Lily's lips curved in a sad half-smile, and she pulled her hand away to cup Celeste's cheek. "You always did have a soft spot for your father. When you came to me nearly three years ago, I counted myself fortunate. I meant to enjoy your company for however long you cared to stay. I always expected you would return to him."

"I'm not staying there, *Maman*. I'll return to Paris as soon as Father is improved." Peters hadn't provided much in the way of a prognosis, but she had to believe her father would improve. She was sure of it.

Lily stood and tugged the bell pull. In a matter of seconds, she transformed from comforting mother to commanding general. She called for Odette to begin the packing and sent Remy off to book their passage. Over the next day, Odette carefully folded Celeste's wardrobe into her trunks, while Celeste settled her paints and sketch pads. She was willing to leave the packing of her silks and satins to others, but she secured her paints herself.

Her mother spoke little of her father or his illness. Lily had left England when Celeste was twelve. Celeste had remained behind, confused by her mother's absence and resentful of her father, who'd not stopped her from leaving.

Celeste suspected her mother's energy had simply been too much for the placid pace of life at Redstone Hall. Lily sparkled and thrived in the *bohémien* life she'd created for herself in Paris, so when the day of Celeste's departure arrived, she was surprised to see her mother's trunks stacked next to hers.

"Dearest, I've decided to join you."

Celeste stared at her mother for a beat, but she couldn't discern either her current intention or emotion. Her mother misread Celeste's hesitation.

"Fear not, dearest. Odette has already packed my things, so I won't delay your departure."

"*Maman*, of course I'm happy to have your company, but you must know it's not necessary. I'm perfectly capable of making the journey on my own." If traveling with two servants could be considered "on one's own."

"Of course you can, dearest. But if I'm to be a widow soon, I find I'd like one last chance to greet your father." She said this last without any malice or ill intent, but as a statement of fact. "Contrary to what others may believe, I don't harbor ill thoughts of your father. I truly hope he's been happy these last years with his . . . papers and contraptions." Her nose wrinkled with these last words.

Celeste smiled. If her mother only knew . . . In Celeste's fourteenth year, her father had turned the expansive blue drawing room into his personal laboratory. When she'd seen it last, most surfaces had been buried beneath journals and books. Telescopes and sextants and planetary models. Her mother, who'd spent months decorating the space, had already left for Paris by then; she'd never seen what had become of her beloved room.

"*Maman*, I don't mean to upset you, but have you considered that Father may not welcome your visit?" she asked.

"Bah, I'm married to the man. I assure you I've seen him at his worst."

"But what if your presence upsets him? Or causes his condition to worsen?"

"Dearest, you overestimate my effect on your father. I promise, if my presence is distressing to Edmund, I shall return home straightaway."

Celeste sighed and pulled on her own gloves. She could hardly prevent her mother from attending her own husband, even if she doubted the wisdom of such a course. "Very well, then. Shall we go?"

CHAPTER TWO

THE CARRIAGE RIDE FROM DOVER was an improvement over the pitching waves of the Channel. Celeste, who'd never tolerated sea travel well, had spent the duration of the crossing hunched over a wooden bucket. But now, as they advanced inland, the salty bite of sea air gave way to the verdant scents of the countryside. While Paris smelled of antiquity, Kent was redolent of chalk and grass and sunshine.

Celeste didn't want to like it, but she couldn't deny the magnificence of a Kent spring. High clouds skipped over a sapphire sky, and a hundred shades of green painted the valleys with a soothing palette of sap, moss, and olive. Chalky scars highlighted the steeper slopes, and a brisk wind blew across the Downs. In summer, wild orchid, poppy and gentian would dot the landscape like random splatters from a painter's brush.

Her mother sat next to her, serene and seemingly unaffected by their return, although her gloved hands tightened on the string of her embroidered reticule.

The action drew Celeste's eye to the bag's small enameled clasp, a forgotten relic of her miniatures era. Tiny rosebuds decorated the button, and a delicate gilt filigree wrapped the edge. She'd long since lost its mate, and the lone button had found a new home on her mother's reticule. It was but one of dozens of miniature florals, landscapes, and fruit that she'd painted before moving on to her exotic bird era.

That phase, the year she'd turned nineteen, had endured for an entire six weeks, during which she must have painted two hundred birds. The colors were complex, and she loved anything with an exotic flair, but, well . . . birds. Her interest had quickly shifted to something else; the fact that she was currently between eras was not unusual.

As the carriage rounded the final curve, she anticipated the sight to come. Redstone Hall sprawled in the valley behind a thick cluster of sentry trees. Begun in the thirteenth century, the rambling estate was solidly constructed of red stone, its name a testament to the Ashford earls' lack of creativity. There was nothing exotic about the pile at all. It felt . . . comfortable.

Celeste glanced at her mother to measure her reaction. Lily's face was impassive. There was not a quirk to her brow or a curve to her lip, nothing to give away her thoughts.

"*Maman*? How do you feel about returning"—she caught herself before saying *home*—"to Redstone Hall?"

Her mother hesitated before responding. "It looks much the same as when I left. I daresay your father hasn't made any changes."

Celeste wasn't sure how to interpret that. As they neared the entrance to the drive, she saw the edge of a domed tower behind the main structure.

"I wouldn't say *nothing* has changed. Look there." She pointed to where the tower came more fully into view through the trees. "Father said he was going to complete the observatory. That must be it."

Celeste squinted to assess the structure further. Jutting off the manor's northwest corner, the tower rose about twenty feet, and a metal dome capped the structure. Celeste smiled to think how proud her father must have been to complete it, then her smile slipped as she thought of him here alone, pursuing his dreams with no one to witness his successes.

"*Mon Dieu!* What is that?" Her mother pointed ahead, and Celeste craned her neck to see. She caught glimpses of a wooden structure through the trees, nestled atop the estate's highest point. Bellamy Hill was but a short distance from the main house and had the best view of the North Downs where one could see the patchwork farms for miles.

"I—I haven't any notion," Celeste said. A winding path led to the top of the Hill from the Hall's back gardens, branching off to Fernwood Manor halfway up. A small pond lay between the two estates where she had often spied Harry and Julian swimming, but the Hill itself had been nothing but trees and grass when last she'd seen it. There certainly hadn't been a structure built atop it.

The carriage crunched over gravel as it entered the circular drive. Her father's staff were well-trained, but Celeste was still unsure what type of welcome they would receive. When they slowed in front of the manor's large double doors, there was a reassuring flurry of activity. The butler and housekeeper appeared with several footmen and house maids lining the entrance.

Remy climbed from his seat next to the driver and reached in to hand down first her mother, then Celeste. His rich navy livery was a dark contrast to the ruby-red coats of her father's staff.

Lily eschewed the tradition of bewigging her footmen, so Remy's gilded locks were on full display, along with a broad smile, a well-muscled calf and a twinkle in his eye. Celeste didn't miss the glare from her father's first footman, who'd also stepped forward to open the carriage door.

Jenkins greeted them along with the housekeeper, Mrs. Gilkerson. The butler's stiff manner was as likely due to rheumatism as it was to any disapproval for their absence.

"Lady Ashford," he said with stately dignity. "Lady Celeste. Welcome home."

"Jenkins, it's good to see you," her mother said as if she'd not been gone for more than a decade. "How are you and your lady wife?"

The old retainer's face remained impassive as he replied. "As well as can be expected, my lady. Thank you for asking. We celebrated our twelfth great-grandchild last winter."

"Congratulations, Jenkins. Please extend my felicitations to your family."

Jenkins nodded, his face stoic as he escorted them inside.

The familiar smells of aged oak and lemon and beeswax—of home—washed over Celeste. Much was the same, but she noted little changes. Extra wear on the rug. A new scratch on the hall table to mark the passage of years. She swallowed and handed her bonnet to the butler.

"Jenkins, how is my father? I'd like to see him."

"Of course, Lady Celeste. However—" He paused and cut a glance at Mrs. Gilkerson.

"Yes?"

"Your father has . . . disappeared."

"Disappeared?" her mother said, stepping forward.

"Yes, my lady," Jenkins responded apologetically. "His fever broke a few days ago, and he's been improving slowly. A maid took a tray to him some hours past, but when she went to retrieve it, Lord Ashford was gone from his rooms. We were just gathering the staff to begin a search when you arrived."

Jenkins had been his normal, unflappable self upon their arrival, but Celeste could now see signs of strain around his eyes, and his stoop was more pronounced than she remembered.

"That is just like your father," Lily said. "He must have known we were coming, and he made a point to be elsewhere."

Celeste suppressed a sigh. "*Maman,*" she whispered, "you know Father has done no such thing."

Jenkins awaited their direction, his butler mask firmly in place. Lily blew a sigh and pulled her gloves off with jerky movements.

"Jenkins, I'm sure you have things well in hand, but let's check with the grounds staff to see if anyone has seen him outside. Mrs. Gilkerson, please organize the house staff to check the upstairs rooms as well."

"Yes, Lady Ashford. Lady Celeste." Jenkins bowed and left them.

After checking with the grounds staff, the kitchen

staff, and the footmen, everyone agreed. No one had seen Lord Ashford since Tillie took him his meal. He was not in the library, or the conservatory or the blue drawing room. His observatory was vacant. The staff checked rooms below stairs and in the attics, as well as the unused guest chambers. The hour grew late, and Celeste grew concerned. The day's earlier chill had sharpened as the sun began its descent.

"Jenkins, tell me about the structure atop Bellamy Hill. Would he have gone there, perhaps?"

"That's your father's latest project." Jenkins paused then shook his head. "But it's too far for him to have walked in his condition."

"We'll have to check. Have some of the men bring lanterns and meet me beyond the terrace." Remy fell into step beside her as she stepped through the library doors and onto the terrace. Her mother and Mrs. Gilkerson remained behind to continue searching the house.

Once the footmen arrived with extra lanterns, they set off for the path beyond the walled garden. The sun was low and cast the trees along the path in ragged silhouette as dusk settled.

As Celeste led the way, she noted more evidence of time passing. The ditch was deeper where rains had eroded the edge, and a storm had thinned out several trees on one side. But all in all, the path to the Hill remained as it had been when she'd raced Harry and Julian to an imagined castle at the top.

When they neared a curve halfway up, she heard rustling beyond a clump of shrubbery. Then a thump and a soft, "Blast."

Everyone stopped and listened. "Father?"

A pause. "Celeste?"

She rounded the shrubbery and found her father sprawled on the ground. "Father! What's happened? Help me, Remy."

It took two footmen to help her father out of the shrubs and onto unsteady feet. Once up, he listed to the side until they righted him again. He wore only his shirtsleeves, a sure sign he was not himself. Her father never went out without his waistcoat and coat.

"I need to check the telescope."

Celeste checked the ground around them but didn't see anything but flattened yellow gorse. "How did you end up in the shrubs? Are you all right?" She looked him over for injuries. He seemed to favor his arm.

"I'm fine, I'm fine." He brushed her worry aside and continued mumbling about a telescope.

She took a moment to study him in the waning light. It had been nearly three years since she'd last seen him. At seven and forty, Edmund, Lord Ashford, was still quite handsome. He wore his full head of silver-dusted brown hair brushed back from his forehead. Sideburns framed his cheeks, and his eyes crinkled when he talked. But he'd lost weight, and deep grooves framed his mouth in parentheses.

"Father, you mustn't wander off. What if we hadn't found you?"

He ignored her admonishments. As they returned to the path, he lurched to the side to continue climbing.

"Oh, no you don't," Celeste said, guiding him back down the hill. "We are returning to the house."

"I must check the telescope," he said again.

"Father, we've just arrived after a very long journey and have spent the better part of the afternoon looking for you. I think it's best if you allow Dr. Grey to check you for injuries. We're returning to the house for tea. And a warm bath."

Her words stopped him. He looked directly at her, seeing her for the first time. "Celeste, m'dear. Welcome home. It's wonderful to see you."

She smiled against the sting in her eyes. "And you as well. I've missed you."

"Did you say 'we'?"

She drew a breath and slowed their descent. Better to tell him now than wait for him to find out later. "Yes, Father." She squeezed his hand. "*Maman* joined me for the journey home. We're both worried for you."

"Lily—" He stopped. "Your mother is here?"

She watched his face to measure his reaction. His

blue eyes narrowed and his forehead creased. Was he angry? Irritated? Or was that . . . hope?

They rounded the final bend and approached the garden wall. Her mother waited inside the gate, flanked by Jenkins and Mrs. Gilkerson, and her stern expression was unmistakable, even in the fading twilight. Her father's frame stiffened.

No, his was definitely *not* the posture of hope.

CHAPTER THREE

"JENKINS, PLEASE SEND FOR DR. Grey. My father appears to have injured his arm."

"Yes, Lady Celeste. The physician has already been summoned." At her father's glower, Jenkins added, "As a precaution, of course."

"I'm fine," her father grumbled. "There's nothing that boy-doctor can do that I can't do for myself."

Her mother stood aside as they moved through the garden to the terrace. She watched her husband, studying, not reacting.

As they passed, her father paused then bowed to her. "Lady Ashford. Welcome home."

She nodded, flattened her lips and turned to Celeste. "Where did you find him?" she asked.

"I was on my way to my telescope," her father answered before Celeste could respond.

"Hmm. I can see you haven't changed. Still obsessed with your contraptions."

"*Maman*, perhaps now is not the time."

Her mother drew a deep breath then nodded. They entered the house and turned toward the large staircase that led to the family quarters.

Her father scowled and shook off Celeste's arm. "I can see myself to my own room."

His tone, sharper than his familiar grumble, startled Celeste. She nodded and kissed his cheek. "I'll have supper sent up and will check on you later."

Julian—or rather, Dr. Julian Grey—arrived shortly from Fernwood. He'd completed his medical apprenticeship two years before, and Celeste was certain he must be competent, despite her memories of him as a brash boy with a perpetual cowlick. While he visited with his patient, Celeste joined her mother in the yellow drawing room.

"I never liked these dry biscuits." Lily's nose wrinkled as she passed a biscuit and a cup of tea to Celeste.

"Yes, well, they're English. You never liked anything English."

"This is true." A heavy pause hung in the air before she spoke again. "Your father seems . . . well enough. He's hardly the infirm I expected when we learned of his illness."

"I'm relieved to see he's recovered somewhat, although he appears weakened. I suppose that's to be expected."

"Well, as that is the case, I shall return to Paris."

Celeste could not have heard her mother correctly. "Return? But we've only just arrived. You can't mean to come all this way only to return so soon."

Her mother's hands tightened in her lap. A reaction, barely there, but still a reaction. "You were right, dearest. It was a mistake for me to come. Your father will fare better without my presence to distract from his recovery."

"*Maman*, I cannot think that is the case. Please, stay for a little while at least. Assure yourself that he is truly well before you leave." Regardless of their words and posture, Celeste had seen emotion—carefully banked—in both of her parents' faces. She didn't know if her mother's presence was for the best, but neither did she think her leaving would help.

"If I go now, I can reach Paris in time for Lady Silverton's annual masquerade." She turned to pour herself another cup of tea, thought better of it, and set her cup down.

Before Celeste could respond, Jenkins showed Dr. Grey into the room. He approached and bowed. "Lady Ashford. Lady Celeste."

Celeste greeted her old friend. "Dr. Grey, how is my father?"

"He is well enough. He has a contusion on his elbow and some scrapes, but no other injuries from his misadventure." Julian glanced down and rubbed his chin. "He's much improved since his illness, but he's not yet regained his strength, and he has moments of confusion. It's not unusual for a patient to take months to recover from a fever as grave as his, so I'm not overly concerned with his physical recovery. I am troubled by his low spirits, however. Since his fever, I've found him to be anxious and melancholy."

Celeste shook her head. "That doesn't sound like my father. He's always been very genial and optimistic."

Julian cleared his throat and continued. "I recommend rest and a moderate diet. He should take gentle exercise—nothing too strenuous—to improve his strength. Send for me if his condition changes and watch for excessive irritability or a general malaise. I've also advised him to abstain from wine and spirits as they can have a depressing effect on the psyche."

"Should we be concerned?"

"I don't think so, but it's better to be overly cautious. Troubled spirits could cause a relapse of the fever. Can I count on one of you to see my instructions carried out?" He looked from Celeste to her mother and back again.

Celeste looked pointedly at her mother.

"*Bien*," Lily grumbled. "I will do it."

"Thank you, Dr. Grey," Celeste said as she

walked with him toward the drawing room's double doors. They were no longer children, but the formality of his address sounded odd on her tongue.

He must have thought the same as he leaned toward her and said, "Surely, we've known one another too long to stand on ceremony. 'Julian' is fine."

She nodded her agreement as he accepted his hat and gloves from Jenkins.

After Julian left, Celeste returned to her mother. "You cannot leave now," she said. "You have instructions from the good doctor to carry out. And what if your leaving upsets Father?"

"I can hardly stay, dearest. My staying is much more likely to upset him than my leaving."

As a girl, Celeste had dreamed often of her mother's return. Her dreams had never gone quite like this, but her mother *had* returned. And although her parents weren't reunited, they were in the same country. That had to count for something.

In the end, she and her mother negotiated a compromise. Lily agreed to stay through the end of the month, or until Edmund threw her out.

———

THE NEXT MORNING, CELESTE DONNED sturdy half-boots and descended to the Hall's ground floor, intent on learning more of her father's telescope.

He'd been agitated and anxious the previous day, and she was curious to know if his mutterings were an effect of his illness, or something else altogether.

As she passed the ladies' morning room, she stopped. Morning sun streamed in the bright and spacious bow window—the same window where she'd watched Harry leave for Berlin. Where, years before that, she'd watched her mother leave for Paris.

She'd been twelve then—no longer a child, but not quite a woman. That morning had also been sunny, but warmer with the added scent of new apple blossoms drifting on a soft breeze. It had been a morning full of deceptive promise.

————

TWELVE-YEAR-OLD CELESTE pressed an ear to her mother's paneled door and balanced her stance to avoid making a noise. The aged wooden floor made creeping about difficult. She knew she wasn't supposed to listen at doors, but her mother's French curses were educational and altogether impossible to ignore. Celeste jumped back when something heavy, and probably expensive, shattered against the oak.

When the butler's distinctive tread sounded on the stairs, she raced on her toes to an alcove and tucked herself behind the curtain. The gap between the wall and the heavy damask allowed a slim view as Jenkins turned the corner to the family wing. He raised his hand to knock at her mother's door then hesitated when something hit the wood from the other side. But, mustering his courage, he straightened his coat and gave two quick raps.

A long silence passed, then the door cracked. Her mother stood in the opening, touching an elegant hand to still-perfect hair. She looked at Jenkins inquiringly. He murmured something, and she responded. Celeste couldn't hear their entire exchange, but the words "carriage" and "Paris" were clear enough.

As soon as Jenkins left, Celeste scrambled from the alcove and tapped on her mother's door. Lily opened it again, and after a taut moment, stepped back for Celeste to enter.

"Are we going to Paris, *Maman*?"

"I've told you not to listen at doors, dearest." Her mother began pulling dresses from her wardrobe and flinging them onto the bed.

"I wasn't at the door," Celeste assured her, "but I heard you say something to Jenkins about Paris. Are we going?" Her mother had often spoken of taking her to Paris "once this abominable war ends."

Her mother's lips thinned, and she shook her head. The ghost of a single tear's trail lined her cheek. Her mother had always been a beautiful crier, unlike Celeste, whose face turned cherry-red whenever she even thought about crying.

"I'm going to visit my cousin, dearest. You've heard me speak of Amelie. You'll stay with your father."

"But I want to go with you," Celeste said.

Her mother stopped and placed an armful of dancing slippers on a delicate Queen Anne chair. Fanny, her mother's maid, entered and eyed the haphazard pile of dresses on the bed and the open trunk at the foot. Her eyes widened at the atrocities being inflicted upon the poor silk, then she jerked into motion. One by one she smoothed and folded the garments before placing each into the trunk.

Lily placed her palms on Celeste's cheeks. "*Ma pauvre.* You are becoming such a lovely young woman." Celeste felt a very un-womanly urge to stamp her foot. Her mother continued. "One day you will understand. Sometimes, a lady must take drastic measures to secure her love's affections."

"What do you mean?" Celeste whispered. "Papa loves you."

"*Non*, dearest. Your father loves his papers and contraptions." Her lips thinned on the last word.

Celeste didn't know what to do. Her mother intended to go to Paris without her. She turned on the soft carpet and left, slamming the door on her mother's sigh. She found her father in the library, surrounded by the papers, journals and contraptions her mother so despised. His gaze narrowed on the page before him.

"Papa? Papa!" She called to him twice more before he looked up. Another moment passed before his blue eyes cleared and he saw her.

"What is it, m'dear?"

"*Maman* is leaving. She's going to Paris."

Her father's eyebrows bunched together in a scowl as he looked again at the journal he was reading. "Don't be ridiculous, Celeste. Of course, she's not leaving. She's merely put out with me at the moment."

"Tell her not to go. You have to make her stay."

Her father looked up again and rubbed his eyes. "Your mother is a grown woman, Celeste. If she wants to go to Paris—"

Celeste had stood at the expansive bow window as the Ashford traveling carriage pulled into the drive. Watched in confusion as a ruby-liveried footman held the door for her mother. Then she'd spun from the window and hurried after the carriage as it pulled away, while her father did nothing.

Somewhere, a maid dropped a bucket and Celeste jerked back to the present with a start. Straightening, she turned her back on the room and her memories and resumed her course.

She entered the library and stepped through French doors into the crisp March air. Crossing the terrace that ran the length of the house, she entered the Hall's walled garden. When spring was in full bloom, it would be rich with the warm scents of roses and apple blossoms, but now, branches with early buds scraped her cloak as she walked.

The gate opened on oiled hinges, and she ascended the path. She passed the brambles where they'd found her father, and the fork that led to Fernwood and the pond between the two estates. As she neared the top of the Hill, treetops gave way to blue sky and the silhouette of a large structure — the structure she and her mother had glimpsed from the road. She rounded the last curve in the path and stopped short. And stared. Her father had been busy indeed.

She'd seen his telescopes before. Constructed of brass, they varied in length from four to eight feet long. This was no such telescope.

An unfinished wooden scaffold sat atop a round platform. The height of eight or nine men, it was conical in shape, round and wide at the base. A massive iron tube lay in the grass. She bent and peered in one end. It was large enough to crawl through.

Her mind turned over her father's ambition as she returned to the Hall. She was no scientist, but she knew a telescope would require mirrors. And mirrors that size . . . there was no conceivable way this would work. How could he possibly position the iron tube on the scaffolding? What was her father thinking?

When she entered the breakfast room, she was surprised to find both of her parents. In the same room.

She paused to take in the scene while Remy held a chair for her. She sat, and Remy lifted a silver pot to pour her chocolate. Her mother eyed his well-formed arm, and her father cleared his throat noisily.

Remy would need to procure some proper Ashford livery if they were to stay any length of time. It was a shame, as he looked delicious in navy. Goodness, now she was behaving like her mother.

"Father," she began. He looked up, and the wrinkles on his forehead cleared. Guilt pinched her ribs for the years he'd been alone. "I visited your telescope project."

Her mother's brows drew together at that, while her father went still.

Finally, he nodded. "It's a design I conceived some years ago." He drew a long breath and blinked. "I thought to complete it for the next Round Table, but it was foolish to think . . ." His words trailed off and he stared into his tea.

She squeezed his hand where it rested on the table, unsure how to ease him. "I—I'm certain the Eleven will understand."

He swallowed and took a slow sip of tea. "I'm sure you're right, m'dear."

The Round Table's next gathering would be in . . . what? Seven months? Seven months or seven years, she didn't see how the massive structure could be completed. But then she thought of Julian's concern for her father's low spirits. Could this telescope provide some much-needed purpose for his days, at least until he'd recovered more fully?

"Perhaps," she began then hesitated. "Perhaps, I could help you."

"Dearest, don't encourage him."

Her father ignored her mother and looked at her. "How do you mean?" he asked.

"Well, if you designed it, you must have notes somewhere. I can help direct the work while I'm here. With your assistance of course." The more she talked, the more certain she was that he needed something with which to occupy his time. "Denton Manor's not far. Let's send for some of the staff to help."

His eyes widened and he shook his head. "No, no. I'm afraid there's not enough time, m'dear." And with that, he stood, grasped his cane, and trundled out of the room.

CHAPTER FOUR

C ELESTE STOPPED IN THE DOORWAY of the blue drawing room, eyes wide. Her father's papers and journals and instruments from three years before had multiplied. They covered every surface, in haphazard stacks that teetered atop tables and desks. She stepped across the threshold slowly, hesitant to disturb the delicate balance.

The only traces left of her mother's blue drawing room were the Wedgwood blue walls and dark patterned drapes. The original furniture had been removed, and tables, desks, shelves and cabinets filled the room. A pile of astronomical charts sat on one table next to several planetary models. Instruments of all shapes and sizes lined a shelf along one wall.

Cooling embers glowed in the fireplace, the fire having long since died out. A chill crept across the room from the floor-to-ceiling windows on the far wall. Her father sat in a deep leather chair before the failing fire, a glass of brandy in one hand.

"Father?"

He looked up, and she noted again the tired lines of his face. He made a visible effort to clear his expression and focused his gaze on her.

"Celeste. I was about to review my correspondence." He motioned to the stack of letters on a small table at his elbow. She rang for a footman to tend the fire then took the chair next to him.

"I've been thinking we should sell Denton Manor," he said.

That was unexpected.

"You've no use for the residence," he continued, "and we could invest the proceeds for you."

"Do—do you think that's best?" she asked. Aside from her father, Denton Manor was her only connection to England. There had been a time when she longed to be free of all restraints. But now, the thought of selling the small estate, of cutting one more tie to home, caused a lump to form in her throat.

"Yes . . . no. I don't know." He sighed.

She turned then, and the wall opposite the windows came into view. She gasped. "Father! What—?"

Paintings covered every inch of the wall. *Her* paintings, in new gilt frames. He must have had her canvases brought down from the attics. There was no rhyme or reason to the arrangement. Landscapes hung next to portraits, next to charcoal drawings, next to still life fruit. Miniatures were tucked here and there to fill the gaps, as were her exotic birds.

"The paintings remind me of you, m'dear."

"But . . . they're terrible! Why would you—"

They were the paintings of her youth. The colors were muddy, the compositions all wrong. Her technique had been juvenile at best.

"They're lovely," he said, taking another sip from his brandy.

She turned from the wall, thankful he no longer entertained in the blue drawing room. Thankful he had chosen an interior-facing wall, visible only from inside the room.

"You're my father. You're supposed to say that." Then she narrowed her eyes on the glass in his hand. "And I believe Dr. Grey advised against taking spirits." She held her hand for his glass.

He looked at her mutinously.

"I recall you making me take my medicine when I was ill," she said. "Consider this your medicine." She lifted her hand expectantly and quirked a brow at him.

"Ha! That's exactly what this is." He held the glass up to illustrate his point, but at her continued silence, he placed it in her palm with a twist to his mouth.

She turned to the pile of letters on the table, thinking to distract him. Thumbing through them, she said, "Here's a letter from your cousin in Bath, and another from Lord Knowles."

He reached out and plucked the latter from her fingers and scowled at the heavy black script.

She paused, uncertain. "Would you like me to leave you with your correspondence?"

"No." He tucked the letter inside his coat. "What else do you have there?"

She continued. "Here's one from Mr. Horatio Corbyn." It took her a moment to make the connection. "Harry?" Her stomach performed a traitorous little flip.

Her father smiled at the mention of Harry's name. That was positive.

"Shall I read it to you?" she asked.

He nodded and leaned back, crossing his hands over his middle.

"My lord," she began. She read the first lines, which detailed the weather in Berlin with a scientist's exacting precision. "He's awfully specific regarding the weather. Oh, and he writes of Herr Kraus's sister, Mrs. Pepper, and her daughter Anna. They've recently arrived in Berlin," she continued.

"He says Miss Pepper 'has a fair countenance, an agreeable manner, and a pleasing figure.' Oh, my. Perhaps I shouldn't . . ." She blushed and trailed off.

Her stomach gave an uncomfortable twist to go with its earlier flip. Surely, she shouldn't be reading

Harry's personal remarks regarding another lady, but she scanned ahead anyway. Her father grinned at her hesitation and motioned for her to continue.

"No, that was the worst of it," she said, relieved. "He hesitates to form a lasting attachment with any lady, as he hopes to travel to London soon. Then he writes of Mr. Blenkinsop's steam locomotive."

She chuckled as she related Harry's tale of trying out the iron horse, which ran along a circular track in the foundry's yard.

"Harry has always enjoyed new discoveries." There was pride in her father's voice, a fond smile on his face, as he said the words.

A gasp from the doorway drew their attention. Her mother stared wide-eyed at the room's disorder. "What have you done to the blue drawing room?" Her head swiveled from side to side, taking in the towering piles.

"It's my laboratory now," her father said. His voice dared her to argue.

"*Mon Dieu*. This room—" Her hand fluttered at the chaos until she regained her speech. "Let me have Mrs. Gilkerson send some maids to at least . . . straighten things."

"You will do no such thing. No one is to touch my laboratory." Her mother sniffed at his words then left, back straight as a queen's.

"Your rudeness to *Maman* was undeserved,"

Celeste chastised him. He harrumphed and motioned for her to read the next letter.

———

THE YEARS CELESTE HAD SPENT in Paris couldn't erase her traditional English upbringing. She knew it was inappropriate to write an unmarried gentleman, even if it was only Harry, but her father's reaction to his letter had been encouraging. She should inform Harry of her father's illness and request that he write again soon.

Perhaps propriety could be maintained if she wrote on behalf of her father and kept the tone of her letter formal. Business-like. Not the least bit proposal-like.

Would he recall their last encounter in as much detail as she did? She swiped her hesitation aside and settled at her writing desk.

~~Harry~~ *Sir,*

I write to inform you that my father was taken ill some months ago. I hasten to add that Dr. Grey's prognosis is favorable, but my father's disposition, which you know to be cheerful, has been brought low by these circumstances.

He was pleased to receive your letter of 4 March, which I shared with him. Please write again as you're able; your words have had a restorative effect on his psyche. He is eager for news of your latest experiments.

I also wonder if you're aware of my father's telescope project. His illness has understandably delayed the work, and he has become quite anxious over it. If you've any notion how I might help further his endeavor, I await your advice.

Yours respectfully,
Celeste St. James

Celeste read and re-read her words. Satisfied they were not overly familiar, she sealed the letter and left it with Jenkins. As she went down to dinner, she wondered, for her father's benefit, how quickly letters traveled between Berlin and Kent.

———

CELESTE SPENT THE NEXT DAYS with her father, telling tales from her time in Paris or reading to him, while her mother avoided him. When her father ventured to the drawing room, Lily retired to the morning room. If her father went to the garden, her mother retreated to the library.

Whether her father was aware of Lily's maneuvering, she couldn't say, but Celeste grew exhausted watching them.

Her mother had told Julian she would see his instructions carried out. And she did.

She consulted with Mrs. Gilkerson on her father's favorite dishes, to encourage his appetite.

She consulted with Cranston, her father's valet, to confirm he was taking "gentle exercise."

She asked Jenkins to remove the brandy from the blue drawing room—she refused to call it the laboratory. Jenkins had balked at that, so Lily prevailed upon Celeste to do the deed.

Remy had become her father's shadow, despite Edmund's gruff refusals of the Frenchman's aid. Celeste suspected the footman's new duties were at Lily's direction. So yes, her mother saw Julian's instructions were carried out, but never to the extent of personally engaging with Ashford herself.

As she and Lily spent an afternoon on their correspondence, her mother mentioned returning to Paris once again. "Your father seems well enough. My presence is surely not needed."

"Nonsense, *Maman*. You agreed to stay until the end of the month. It's only Thursday. Of the first week."

The sharp clearing of a throat startled them both, and they looked up to see her father in the doorway, a scowl on his face. His brows crouched over his eyes in an angry slash, until he spun on his heel and left.

Celeste's stomach sank. He must think they didn't

wish to be at Redstone Hall.

As one week became two, her father's spirits sank lower. His cheeks drooped, his shoulders stooped, and he leaned more on his cane. She caught her mother watching him with a speculative glance more than once before turning her attention elsewhere.

Her father spent more and more time in his laboratory reading his papers and making notations in a leather notebook. He became agitated if Celeste interrupted him for tea. And more than once, she caught him gazing toward Bellamy Hill and his telescope, a bleak expression in his eyes. Celeste looked forward to another letter from Harry, if only to ease her father's poor spirits.

CHAPTER FIVE

ARRY TURNED THE ENAMELED BUTTON in his pocket and studied the morning's post. He'd received a letter with Lord Ashford's frank, but the tidy handwriting was unfamiliar. Bold yet feminine.

He had no reason to expect it, but he was certain it must be from Celeste. Although why she would write, he couldn't fathom. He knew a moment of anxiety. Had something happened to Lord Ashford?

He broke the seal and read the letter.

He was troubled to hear of Ashford's illness and his low spirits. The man had recognized a fellow scientist in Harry when he was but a lad. Ashford had been a mentor, taking time to teach and encourage Harry when he'd spent his holidays with Julian. Harry had, in fact, spent as much time at Redstone Hall as he had at Fernwood Manor.

He recalled a cold afternoon before Christmas

when he'd been seventeen. A stout fire had danced in the grate, and feeble winter light tapped at the windows.

While Ashford and Harry played chess, Celeste painted. She'd recently taken up miniatures—portraits and landscapes painted on tiny canvases. She'd been quite good, in fact, although he was no judge.

Ashford had shared his plans for a grand telescope, finer and more exacting than any others.

"It will far surpass, Herschel's, mark my words, Harry." Ashford referred to Sir William Herschel's forty-foot reflecting telescope. Due to problems with Herschel's mirror, the mammoth instrument was rarely used, but Ashford had conceived a much-improved device.

"There's much to learn in the black unknown of the universe. We can only shine our light so far into the abyss, my boy. A better, stronger telescope will help us cast a wider beam."

His enthusiasm was contagious. He sought Harry's opinion, which few rarely did at his tender age. They debated aperture and concave versus convex lenses. They discussed chromatic aberration until darkness threatened and Harry had to return to Fernwood.

It had been one of his most memorable afternoons. In many ways, Ashford had been more than a friend, more than a mentor. Harry suspected Ashford had *saved him*. From a life lacking in intellectual stimulation and promise. From a life barren of wonder and the joy of discovery. He owed Ashford . . . everything.

He turned his attention to the rest of the letter. She'd signed it "Celeste St. James." She'd not married then. He knew she and Julian hadn't wed; Julian would have told him. But he assumed she would have found someone in Paris. Why her unmarried state should catch his attention—and why it should lighten his heart—was beyond him. As an earl's daughter—as his mentor's daughter—she was well beyond his reach.

And yet, his stomach tightened at the memory of their last encounter, when he'd very nearly pressed his lips to hers in the conservatory.

He could still smell her whispery vanilla scent and feel her heat. *Fizz.* From a phantom kiss. He rubbed his mouth then sat to pen a response.

Lady Celeste,

Thank you for your letter. Please accept my regret for your father's recent illness. His is a strong constitution, bolstered by a joyful temperament, and I'm optimistic he'll prevail.

Some years ago, he related plans for a grand telescope. I regret, however, that he has not mentioned his recent endeavors to me. Indeed, I'm most intrigued.

I've enclosed another missive for your father. It would be my pleasure to reconnect with him and learn more of his project. If your father is willing, perhaps I shall visit Redstone Hall when I journey to London next month.

Your servant,
Horatio Corbyn

CHAPTER SIX

CELESTE RE-READ HARRY'S LETTER, AND her heart triple-timed in her chest. *Perhaps I'll visit Redstone Hall.* She'd not expected to see him during her stay in Kent, but his simple words sent an unexpected rush of heat through her veins.

She pulled out a fresh page and placed it on her writing desk. Stared at the blank expanse of paper for a long moment before dipping her pen in the ink. Formal, she reminded herself. Business-like.

Mr. Horatio Corbyn,

Thank you for your words of encouragement. You have the right of it. My father has always been strong and hale, and I remain positive he will recover fully in time. Your letter detailing your recent calculations on stellar parallax quite piqued his interest. He is eager to learn more of your theories, and to see you as you travel to London, if your plans permit.

Did I mention my mother has returned with me? You may not remember her, as she left for France when I was twelve. You would have been fourteen at the time, and determined to ignore me, I'm certain. You and Julian had too much consequence to be bothered with a girl still in braids.

Please write again soon and tell us how your work in Berlin progresses.

Your Friend,
Celeste St. James

P.S. I can hardly credit you've never shared your given name. I don't think Horatio suits you. You are definitely a Harry. Do you have a middle name? I suppose you'll tell me it's Algernon.

Celeste propped her chin in her hand and re-read her words. She'd had true intentions of keeping her tone proper and reserved—indeed, she'd started out well—but it would seem her pen had other thoughts. She considered tossing the page onto the grate and starting over but stopped. She'd missed her friend, and it felt good to return to their youthful familiarity.

———

HARRY'S REPLY WAS GRATIFYINGLY SWIFT. Celeste lifted it from the salver Jenkins presented and was pleased with how casually she walked to her room, where she closed the door and broke the seal.

Lady Celeste,

Your letter was a pleasant relief, as the weather in Berlin has had a depressing effect. The skies have rained for days on end. There's a lingering chill that belittles the promise of spring and settles in the bones. I've taken to logging each day's temperature variation, rainfall amounts and barometer readings in an attempt to predict when the sun will return. My results are inconclusive.

Of course, I recall your mother. I remember one summer evening when she played for us on the pianoforte. She doted on you quite thoroughly. You were fortunate to have Julian and I to tease you, else you would have become spoiled.

I've enclosed another letter for your father detailing the latest developments in my work with Herr Kraus. Allow me to apologize for the dull nature of the account, but I assure you, your father will be most diverted.

Your servant,

Horatio William Corbyn

P.S. Horatio is a fine and dignified name. I imagine your middle name suits you perfectly. Perhaps . . . Prudence? No, I'm certain that can't be right. It must be something more vigorous. Gertrude? Hildegarde?

Celeste bit her lip and smiled at Harry's teasing. She reminded herself their correspondence was solely for her father's benefit. She'd almost convinced herself of the fact, even as she stored Harry's notes in her desk drawer and enjoyed the slight masculine scent of his pages. Warm and solid and slightly mysterious, it put her in mind of amber and oak.

She forced herself to wait an hour . . . maybe two, before bending her head to pen a response.

CHAPTER SEVEN

ARRY'S CHEST TIGHTENED AS HE studied the latest letter from Redstone Hall, and he savored the anticipation.

Celeste's tidy yet bold script stood out amid his other correspondence. Its vitality pulsed in a sea of serious letters from staid scientists. Her soft vanilla scent clung to the paper, despite its miles-long voyage across land and sea. He imagined her wide smile and blue-green eyes laughing at him as she penned her thoughts.

This, he thought, was a slippery slope he trod, but he eagerly ran a finger along the edge of the paper and lifted the seal.

Mr. Horatio William Corbyn,

Thank you for recognizing the fact that I am not spoiled. And for your restraint regarding my mother's pianoforte skills. Or lack thereof. As lovely as she is, she has no ear for music. I do not speak out of turn, as she'll be the first to admit the flaw.

I was sorry to hear of the unfortunate weather you suffer. It seems cruel to tell you spring has painted the fields and valleys of Kent with a radiance unlike any I've seen before. I'm reminded of the holidays you spent with Julian.

Do you recall the summer we built a raft and sailed across the pond like Robinson Crusoe? I don't think Julian's gardener ever knew what became of his fencing. It was such a shame when our vessel sank at the halfway point. It required all my creativity to explain what happened to that dress.

My father's recovery has been slower than any of us would like, although he has seen small improvements in his strength. He needs something with which to distract his mind so his body can heal. I read to him the account of your work in Berlin, and he was most appreciative, despite my stumbling over the more scientific words and phrases. I am certain my poor recounting did not do your work justice.

Your friend and shipmate,
Celeste St. James

P.S. You may tease and bully all you like. I shall
not tell you my middle name.

Harry smiled. If she had fond memories of the pond, then perhaps she'd forgotten about the frogs. On a dare, Celeste had shed her slippers and stockings to wade into the pond.

Harry and Julian had snickered behind their hands and plotted. They were boys, after all. While she squealed over the mud oozing between her toes, Julian put frogs in her stockings. The screech when she discovered them was unholy.

They had all received a scolding when her put-upon governess tracked down her muddy charge, and Harry had waited expectantly, anxiously, for Celeste's response. Julian told him he was being missish—she was only a girl, after all—but Harry knew better.

She left them (him) to suffer for two weeks before she took her revenge. Harry and Julian had risen early to swim. She'd never been an early riser, so it was an easy matter to evade her. But when they returned to the sunny bank for their shirts, green snakes slithered through the folds. He *still* had an aversion to snakes.

Dear Lady Celeste,

I'm certain your tender recounting of my letter added levity and color where there was none.

My work in Berlin is coming to an end sooner than expected. Herr Kraus and I leave for London presently and should like to stop in Kent to visit your father. It is my hope that this letter reaches you before I do. However, one can never tell with the unreliable nature of the mail packets.

Your friend,
Harry Corbyn

CHAPTER EIGHT

THAT WAS IT? CELESTE READ Harry's letter a second and third time. Like all his missives, it was brief—he was a man of few words—but he was coming to Redstone Hall. Her father would be pleased to hear it.

She checked the date on the letter. Two weeks ago. That didn't leave much time to decide how she felt about seeing him again. It was all well and good to exchange letters. Letters provided distance. But now that he was coming . . . well.

The Kiss That Wasn't replayed in her mind. She had kissed and been kissed before. She was almost four and twenty after all. But no actual, truly-happened kiss had even come close to what she'd felt with that near-kiss.

Had Harry felt it as well? And what if he had? An attraction between them was bound to disappoint. She would return to Paris, and he to . . . wherever he would go next. And besides, it seemed Harry had developed a fondness for his Miss Pepper. Her stomach dipped on the thought and a moody blue haze tinted her vision.

———

HARRY WOULD ARRIVE ANY DAY. On Tuesday, Celeste went to the garden to cut flowers, but realized she'd forgotten her basket and shears. Wednesday, she walked into the library to find a book, but then couldn't recall why she was there. And when she sat to sketch on Thursday, she found herself gazing into empty space. Annoyed with herself, she went searching for her father instead.

"Father, why don't we take a turn about the gardens? It's a fine day, and the exercise will do you good."

When Celeste called for Remy to accompany them, her father grumbled and crossed his arms. "I'll not go if he goes." And so, a ruby-liveried footman trailed them instead, ready to assist should her father require it.

Celeste suspected her father's dislike of Remy stemmed from her mother's overt admiration of the man. But surely he could see their footman only had eyes for Odette. No matter how pleasant it was to watch Remy, he and the maid were shamelessly in love with one another.

By the time they returned to the house, she'd

almost forgotten about Harry. But then Jenkins informed them that Lady Ashford entertained visitors. Harry had arrived. And Herr Kraus, she presumed.

She patted her hair and checked her skirts in the hall mirror while her father watched her curiously. She avoided his eye.

Was everything in order? Of course not. A stray curl dangled on her left side, and her face was pink. She'd forgotten her bonnet again. She debated returning to her bedchamber to right herself, but this was Harry. He'd seen her muddy and disheveled through the years. Her eagerness to see him trumped her pride.

She entered the drawing room on her father's arm. Harry stood before the windows, sunlight pooling at his feet. Her eyes went to him first, before noting the others in the room.

He was as she remembered, only . . . different. More, somehow. His frame seemed taller, his bearing more certain. His coat was not in the latest style, but his shoulders were solid and well proportioned. From an artist's perspective, his form was well made.

She completed her painter's inventory: His dark hair was soft and ruffled, as if he'd run a hand through it. His nose, straight and masculine. Afternoon stubble darkened his angular jaw and her stomach flipped. And his lips . . . his lips were imminently kissable. She swallowed.

His grey eyes pulled at her from across the room.

She drew a slow breath to clear her mind and forced her gaze to an older gentleman with thick, greying tufts of hair. He stood behind the sofa where a handsome dark-haired woman of middle years sat.

And next to her, a pretty lady perched on the edge of the damask cushion, soft hands folded in her lap. She had fetching blond ringlets arranged carefully atop her head and a delicate bow mouth. China doll skin and not a hair out of place. Celeste was instantly suspicious. Such perfection did not come without moral deficits.

Harry approached her father and bowed. "My lord, it's a pleasure to see you again. Allow me to introduce my traveling companions." He smiled as he presented Herr Johann Kraus, Herr Kraus's sister Mrs. Pepper and his niece Miss Anna Pepper. Ah. So this was Miss Pepper, of the "fair countenance, agreeable manner, and pleasing figure."

Celeste felt a wobbly, sinking sensation in her stomach. She fixed a serene smile on her face and tried not to think about her dangling curls.

————

HARRY'S BREATH FROZE IN HIS chest as he watched Celeste from the corner of his eye. Words swirled around him as Herr Kraus and the Pepper ladies shared stories of their travels. He tried to attend the conversation, but he couldn't think of anything sensible to add. Herr Kraus and Miss Pepper watched him, wondering at his silence he was sure, but nothing could persuade his brain to work.

Celeste's hair—the not-quite-brown, not-quite-red shade he recalled—framed her blue-green eyes with soft curls. A tendril danced along her neck to tease her collarbone, and a delicate flush stained her cheeks. The dusting of freckles across the bridge of her nose, which had made her appear impish as a child, was charming on her now.

He couldn't help looking at her soft lips. The memory of them was a vivid picture that lived on the edge of his mind, always there, never gone. He still didn't know what they felt like. What they tasted like. She smiled brightly at the newcomers but avoided his eye. Why was she avoiding him?

He turned the button in his pocket. The smooth enamel and the faint texture of the painted rosebuds teased his fingertips. It had become a talisman, an object of idle motion. It usually allowed him to filter out external distractions and focus on the task at hand, but he was having difficulty thinking on anything other than Celeste. His fingers twirled the button faster.

When tea arrived, Lady Ashford passed around delicate china cups and plates of seed cakes. Celeste wandered to the bank of windows overlooking the terrace, and he followed.

"You're looking well, Lady Celeste." With the top of her head passing his chin, she was taller than most ladies of his acquaintance. Not that he was acquainted with so very many.

"As are you, Mr. Corbyn. It seems Berlin agrees with you."

They were Lady Celeste and Mr. Corbyn now? What had happened to the carefree banter of their youth? Of their letters just weeks past? He turned the button in his pocket again and thought of returning it to her. He almost pulled it out, but it would be silly to return something so trivial after this much time had passed. It was unlikely she even remembered it and would think him daft for keeping it.

"Miss Pepper seems very agreeable," she said.

"Yes, she and her mother are pleasant companions. Herr Kraus sees little of his family as they've all left Berlin. He won't admit it, but their visit has been a comfort to him."

She studied him for the length of two heartbeats, and he thought she might persist with idle pleasantries. Then she gave him a small smile and linked her arm with his. "It's good to see you, Harry."

He sighed, relieved, and the tension in his shoulders eased. "Your mother appears well."

"To be honest, I thought she would have returned to Paris by now. She agreed to stay a month, and no more, but that was six weeks ago."

"She's in her element." They looked to where Lady Ashford entertained her guests, laughing and drawing conversation from each in turn. Ashford wore a morose expression on his face as he watched her hold court. Harry wasn't about to ask how her father was taking his wife's return. That was a conversation no gentleman wished to initiate.

"She does enjoy . . . everything. People, society, life. I've always envied her vitality."

Her words surprised him. Celeste's spirit was genuine, unaffected. Impulsive at times, but she had . . . fizz. She didn't have anything of which to be envious. How could she compare herself to her mother? He didn't know how to put his thoughts into words, so he said instead, "Tell me about your father's telescope project."

Her eyes widened, and she squeezed his arm. "Harry, it's the most impossible thing." Her voice dropped to a whisper. "I don't know how he hopes to complete the work, but he wishes to unveil it at the Round Table. He becomes agitated when we speak of it, and Julian worries his low spirits could cause a relapse of his fever."

"Is it so impossible then?"

"I'm not an expert, but I don't see how it can be done." Her eyes widened. "The tube is tremendous; I don't see how it can be placed into position, much less maneuvered into place. And the mirrors ... I can't even imagine the size of the mirrors that will be needed."

Harry rubbed his jaw. All problems had solutions if one looked hard enough. He wouldn't be staying long—he would leave for London soon to meet with the Transit Commission. But Ashford's plans for his improved telescope intrigued him. He didn't want to raise false hopes, but what if—

"Can you show me the site?" he asked. "I don't know what can be done, but maybe we can determine if there's any help for it."

"Are you talking about my telescope?" They started at Ashford's question. They'd not heard his approach, but now he leaned on his cane and watched them both, an intense expression in his eyes.

"Father—"

"It can be done," Ashford insisted, punctuating his words with taps of his cane. "My designs are complete. If anyone can execute them, Harry, you can." He narrowed his eyes as he stared at Harry.

Execute? "My lord, I'm only here for a short while before I continue to London—" He halted at the look on Ashford's face. He well understood the fervor that came with the thrill of discovery, but Ashford's expression was one of desperation rather than eagerness. "But perhaps I can offer a suggestion or two," he finished.

Ashford's face cleared. "Celeste, you're holding Harry much too closely." He nodded at her hand, which still gripped Harry's sleeve. Celeste dropped his arm, and he felt the loss of warmth where her hand had been.

"What's this about a telescope?" Miss Pepper asked.

She sidled next to Harry, her head not quite reaching his shoulder. She placed her hand on his other arm and gazed at him through the thick fringe of her eyelashes. Her flirting had grown more overt over the last weeks, and his attempts to deflect it more uncomfortable. He'd looked forward to escaping her when he left Berlin, until Herr Kraus had informed him the ladies, who were traveling to London as well, would join them.

He didn't wish to offend Herr Kraus, but he also didn't wish to find himself married to Miss Pepper.

He pulled his arm free and patted her hand before explaining how telescopes worked. He'd found, quite by chance, that the best deterrent to her flirtation was a lengthy scientific explanation. Her eyes narrowed on him before he even got to the difference between refractive and reflective instruments.

When he finished, it took her a moment to catch up, then she clapped her hands and said, "Oh, but we must organize a party to see this telescope."

———

JENKINS ARRIVED IN THE DOORWAY and announced three new, not wholly unexpected, arrivals: "Vicar and Mrs. Pitt. Mrs. Miller."

Celeste had been intrigued to learn Miss Olive Miller had married Vicar Pitt. The two were as incongruous in appearance and demeanor as they'd been three years before. Vicar Pitt—soft, dull and drab. His wife—hard and angular. Their pairing had seemed an unlikely one.

The couple had a disturbing talent for materializing whenever an unfamiliar equipage passed through Marshfield. It was as if they'd strung a bell wire at the vicarage to alert them to new arrivals. Celeste imagined it must be labeled *Marshfield Road* next to *Pantry* and *Dressing Room*. The couple had visited shortly after Celeste and her mother had returned to Redstone Hall, and now, Harry's arrival must have rung their bell.

Miss Olive Miller's marriage had had the unfortunate side effect of making her Olive Pitt. Celeste pressed her lips and waited for the precise moment when Harry made the calculation. He didn't disappoint; his own lips twitched, and he watched her from the corner of his eye.

Mrs. Miller was still active in the Ladies' Society for the Advancement of Needlework Samplers, but she'd relinquished her other social responsibilities to her daughter. Mrs. Pitt, it seemed, was fast becoming

Marshfield's chief organizer. Indeed, to hear her reports, she was already hip-deep in planning for the harvest festival, and it still some four months away.

At the lady's mention of the Society, Miss Pepper engaged her in a lively debate of the alternating basketweave versus a Brighton stitch.

"They're an unlikely pair," Celeste murmured to Harry, motioning toward Vicar and Mrs. Pitt. He nodded, hands clasped behind his back. She narrowed her eyes, genuinely curious how the courtship between the two had progressed. "I wonder about their first meeting. Did she find him captivating? Compelling? Did he find her delightful?"

Harry shrugged. "Some stars orbit in pairs, united by their mutual gravitation. Perhaps it's the same with people."

Only Harry would find something cosmically beautiful about a pair as unromantic as Vicar and Mrs. Pitt, but she had to admit, Mrs. Pitt did seem content with her role in life. A becoming flush stained her cheeks and her angular lines were even a bit softened. Celeste could hardly be blamed if she were the tiniest bit envious.

"I was just telling my Freddie yesterday," Mrs. Pitt said, "how excited the village is for your telescope project, Lord Ashford."

What was this? Celeste edged closer to the

conversation, noting the steep pitch of her father's brows.

"Indeed," Mrs. Pitt continued, "I suggested to Mary Stone, who agreed and mentioned it to Lydia Blackerby, that we should conclude the harvest festival with"—she paused dramatically—"a village viewing!"

Mrs. Pitt leaned back and clapped her hands once at this revelation. A beat of silence passed, so she clarified: "Imagine! An outing for all the villagers, to view the heavens through your new device!"

Celeste forced a smile to her face, although it felt a bit shaky. Harry's brows were knit together, and her father's head was down as he stared at his boots. Her mother, the ever-gracious hostess, nodded politely then suggested an alfresco supper after the viewing. She wouldn't even be here in four months!

"I knew we could count on you, Lady Ashford," Mrs. Pitt said, to which Lily's response was a hesitant smile of her own.

Her father's hand tightened on the head of his cane as she spoke, and Celeste wondered what they were to do now.

CHAPTER NINE

THE NEXT MORNING DAWNED CLEAR and bright, but recent rains had left the path to the top of the Hill muddy in places. Harry joined the rest of the guests to venture out to Ashford's telescope.

Despite being the one to suggest the outing, Miss Pepper arrived last in the drawing room, dressed in a fetching straw bonnet with pink ribbons and a matching pink spencer. Delicate embroidered slippers peeped from beneath her hem. Knowing the Hill as he did, Harry suggested she might be more comfortable in boots. She smiled sunnily and assured him her slippers would be sufficient. And, she added, they matched her ensemble.

Celeste and her mother walked arm in arm where the path was wide enough, setting their pace to Ashford's slower gait. Harry followed, his thoughts alternating between the telescope and Celeste. She, having the advantage of many years navigating the

Hill, had donned sensible half-boots.

As she sidestepped a puddle, she lifted her skirts gingerly, and he caught a narrow glimpse of stockinged calf above the edge of her leather half-boot. Thoughts of telescopes and mirrors and equations fell away like chalk shearing off the Dover cliffs.

She turned, and he quickly pulled his eyes up. A guilty flush heated his neck, and she eyed him consideringly. He cleared his throat. "It's been some time since I've been up here."

"Yes, well, the view has changed quite a bit since then, I would imagine."

The view. She referred to the telescope, of course.

The trees thinned as they neared the top, and hints of a wooden structure peeked through the gaps. Their small party rounded the final curve and entered the clearing at the top of the Hill.

Expressions ranged from pride (Ashford) to curiosity (Herr Kraus) to confusion (the Pepper ladies). Celeste's face was expectant as she waited for Harry's reaction.

For his part, Harry was stunned at the magnitude of the structure. Through his discussions with Ashford, he understood the overall design, but he was unprepared for the grand scale of the thing. He rubbed his jaw and turned to the wooden scaffold which would serve as the telescope's mount. It was a skeleton of Amazonian proportion, bones waiting for muscles to be attached.

The massive iron tube lay to the side, tender shoots of grass sprouting along its length. How many smiths had it taken to craft such a piece? And how many men and horses would be required to lift it onto the wooden mount? Celeste was right to be concerned. The task would be Herculean, near insurmountable.

No, Harry reminded himself. Focus on possibilities, not impossibilities.

Ashford explained the mechanics of the structure. A round dais supported the wooden mount, and small wheels allowed the platform to rotate atop a track. Harry inspected the framework and tested the operation of the platform. He envisioned the pulley system that, once installed, would control the angle of the tube. The platform and pulleys would work together to adjust the telescope vertically and horizontally.

A stone outbuilding sat some distance away. It held a chimney furnace for casting the telescope's mirror. The beginnings of a wooden shed stood at the base of the mount and would eventually house the completed mirror. Harry pictured a viewing platform where observers could look down the tube to see the captured image.

He knew large-scale telescopes had been built

K. Lyn Smith

before. He'd seen pictures and read reports of their successes (and failures), but he'd never seen a telescope of this size in person. Scopes of this magnitude required exceedingly large mirrors, which were simply too blurry to produce images of any scientific significance. But Ashford had a sound theory for improving the mirror and eliminating distortion. His telescope could, in fact, surpass Herschel's. Ashford turned to face him, a grin splitting his face while he awaited Harry's reaction.

"What do you think?"

"It's quite magnificent, my lord." Harry bent to look through the tube. Of course, there was nothing to see but yard upon yard of black iron. But he could imagine the brilliance of the stars and planets that could be seen if the angle and shape of the mirror were ground with precision.

The mirror was the key, and the work required to prepare it, much less install it, was significant. Harry mentally tallied the tasks to be completed and sighed. As the list grew in his mind, weighed against the time remaining before the Round Table, his optimism shrank.

"Is this all?" Mrs. Pepper asked Herr Kraus as she and her daughter gazed at the half-built structure. Celeste's eyebrows lifted fractionally, and Ashford straightened on his cane, face reddening at the slight.

Herr Kraus studied the wide stretch of sky visible

from the Hill in all directions. "*Ach*, Lord Ashford's ambition is truly remarkable."

Harry nodded. "Indeed, the visibility from this point will be astounding. The foundry did remarkable work crafting the tube to your specifications, my lord. Obviously, the scaffold and pulley system still need to be completed, and the mirror, of course . . ."

Ashford sighed and leaned further on his cane. "Yes, the work required for the mirror is extensive."

"But can it be done?" Celeste asked.

Harry rubbed his jaw. "The mirror has to be sized and ground with precision. Then it must be polished, installed and calibrated." He hesitated before adding, "With enough time and manpower, yes, it could be done."

Lord Ashford in top form would be pressed to complete the structure in the four months remaining. But Ashford in his current state . . .

They needed the truth, so Harry added softly, "But I don't see how it can be completed in time for the Round Table. I'm sorry."

Harry studied the massive iron tube and the half-built wooden structure. It occurred to him that he did not suffer Ashford's weakness. He could organize teams to complete the mount. He could attempt, with Ashford's guidance, to prepare and install the mirror.

No, he thought. He could not. He had Plans. Plans

that required his presence in London.

Plans that did not allow him to be diverted, no matter how intrigued he might be.

———

AFTER THE EXCURSION TO THE Hill, Miss Pepper prevailed upon Harry to take a turn with her about the garden. Once she changed her attire, of course.

"This mud has done abhorrent things to my hem and slippers." Her lips formed a small pout while Harry bit the inside of his cheek. He had no wish to spend time alone with Miss Pepper, but he couldn't think of a polite way to refuse her request.

As he waited for her return, Celeste stepped through the conservatory door and stopped when she saw him. Of course, his mind went at once to the night when she'd drawn him into the conservatory and nearly kissed him. Or he'd nearly kissed her, rather. Despite his silent command to his eyes, they went straight to her lips before he regained control.

Miss Pepper appeared then, dressed in a fresh green gown and matching slippers. Her face flushed a becoming shade of debutante pink as she glided toward him. Despite her loveliness, he couldn't muster any enthusiasm for their walk as his mind was preoccupied with Celeste. Er, the telescope.

"Miss Pepper and I were about to take a turn in the garden," he said to Celeste. "Will you join us?"

He tried to sound polite, rather than desperate.

"Oh, I—"

"I'm sure Lady Celeste has other things to do," Miss Pepper said sweetly. "But perhaps you'll join us another time?"

Celeste closed her mouth and nodded. "Of course."

———

HARRY CONTINUED THINKING ON ASHFORD'S telescope as he dressed for supper. Despite Miss Pepper's animated conversation, he hadn't been very attentive on their walk. In fact, he might have offended her with his preoccupation.

And then, her lips had turned down in an expert pout when she learned Harry wouldn't be dining at the vicarage with them, which only confirmed he'd made the correct choice in choosing to remain at the Hall. The prudent choice.

Now, his mind assembled a picture of Ashford's completed telescope. Ashford's plans were clever. They could work, given enough time to see them implemented. And if they were successful, *when* they were successful, the field of astronomy would be transformed. The thought of seeing deeper and farther than anyone had before caused his heart to race.

He lifted his chin to tie his cravat. Why couldn't he solve the challenge of a simple knot as easily as he solved mathematical equations? He fussed a bit more with the linen before his mind abandoned the cravat to his fingers and returned to the telescope.

The problem was quite simple. It was simple algebra, and yet, the challenge called to him on many levels. He listed them in his mind, ticking them off on mental fingers.

Point number one: Harry needed to know if Ashford's theory would work. Admittedly, his need to *know* things, to understand the world, had gotten him in trouble many times before. Despite the improbability of it, *could* they achieve enough altitude to fly from the roof with Ashford's bed linens?

Point number two: He owed much to Ashford. He would go to great lengths to repay the man for his many kindnesses over the years. Harry suspected that Ashford had been behind the mysterious grants that had funded much of his education. Where his own father had been dismissive of Harry's goals and ambition, Ashford had been supportive.

Point number three: Celeste. She looked at him like he could do anything. The expectant hope on her face when they'd viewed Ashford's telescope made him *feel* like he could do anything. Who was he to argue with that?

He surveyed his knot in the mirror. The cravat mocked him with its wrinkles and distressing lack of symmetry. He pulled the blasted thing off, picked up a fresh one and started over.

So, he had three good arguments *for*. The arguments *against* were equally compelling.

One: Cairo. He should leave soon for London and meet with the Transit Commission. He couldn't lose sight of his goal when he was this close.

Two: Celeste. Could she be a point *for* as well as *against*? It had taken him months to stop thinking about her when he arrived in Berlin, and it seemed her gravitational pull had only strengthened with time. If he remained too long at Redstone Hall, she was bound to draw him deeper into her orbit, and he would have no chance of freeing himself. When he thought of it that way, there was no question. He couldn't stay.

He joined Lord and Lady Ashford in the drawing room and attempted polite conversation, but his mind continued turning and twisting the problem of Ashford's telescope. He kept reminding himself he was leaving soon and would not be solving this particular problem, but his mind stubbornly drifted back to the challenge.

But when Celeste entered the room, his thoughts abandoned the telescope altogether. She was radiant in a gown of rich bronze that set off her cinnamon hair, pale complexion and faint freckles. She looked at him with surprise, and he realized his own

K. Lyn Smith

astonished expression must have given him away. He composed his features and focused on her words as they took a turn about the room.

"Have you thought any more about my father's telescope?" she asked.

"Yes. In fact, I've thought of little else."

She nodded, thinking. "Even if it can't be completed in time for the Round Table, do you think my father and I could see it through together?"

"You're staying?"

"I hadn't planned to. I thought to visit for a few weeks, a month or two at most, and then return to Paris. But he seems so . . . distraught over the project. If I can help him see it completed . . ." She shrugged.

"Then yes, with more time and the right teams of laborers to execute your father's plans, I think you could see it completed."

"How much more time?"

"It's hard to say. Six months? Maybe more."

Jenkins announced supper then, and Celeste took Harry's arm as they entered the dining room. Three footmen lined the wall, two in Ashford's ruby-red livery. Lady's Ashford's wigless footman was a swan among ducklings.

"I thought we were having chilled asparagus soup," Ashford said as he gazed at the fish chowder before him.

"Yes, Father, I spoke with Cook. I believe there's

a shortage of asparagus."

Harry smiled. "That's unfortunate."

"Humph," was Ashford's only reply.

Harry dipped a spoon into his soup, which was steaming and delicious with a tomato base. There was nothing chilled or green about it. Not a puréed vegetable in sight.

Celeste tapped him under the table with her foot and he nearly choked. He recalled the image of her shapely calf on the path to the Hill and felt his neck grow red. She looked at him oddly, and he turned his attention back to his soup.

Conversation danced around then finally settled, inevitably, on the telescope. As a footman placed quail in cream sauce before her, Celeste said, "There's nothing for it, Father. We'll have to inform Mrs. Pitt there won't be a telescope this year. She'll have plenty of time to conceive another event with which to conclude the harvest festival. But perhaps next year . . ."

Ashford sighed and swallowed a sip of his tea. Then, grimacing, he motioned to a footman to pour a glass of wine.

"Ashford, you know you're not to have wine. Don't be thick-headed." Lady Ashford gave the footman a stern look.

The poor man looked between Ashford and his wife, then to Jenkins at the far end of the room. The

K. Lyn Smith

wine carafe hung from his uncertain hand. Jenkins gave a hesitant nod and the footman poured, but before Ashford could lift his glass, Lady Ashford snatched it up. She drained the wine, licking a drop from the corner of her lip, before replacing his empty glass before him.

"Lily!"

Harry stifled a choked laugh and focused on cutting a precise bite of quail. He wasn't sure what the proper etiquette was in circumstances such as these. He chanced a look at Celeste, who suppressed a smile behind her own glass.

The sound of Ashford's deep inhale was loud in the silence. Harry suspected he was counting to ten. Or two hundred.

Harry chewed his quail slowly.

Ashford leaned forward and opened his mouth to speak, then closed it and clenched his teeth. Finally, Celeste stepped into the breach.

"Father, the telescope may not be complete in time for the Round Table, but perhaps the Eleven can offer assistance while they're here."

"The Eleven—" Ashford stopped and inhaled again. Then again. His face turned an alarming shade of red and sweat beaded his forehead. He opened his mouth but said nothing. Harry started. Was he choking? Ashford blew rapid, shallow breaths. No, he wasn't choking. Was this an attack of some sort then?

"Ashford?" Lady Ashford's voice rose in concern. When Ashford clutched his chest, she rose. "Jenkins, send for Dr. Grey. Remy, help me see Lord Ashford to his room."

With effort, Ashford rose and leaned on his cane, his other hand shaking as he massaged his chest. Lady Ashford's footman steadied him as they left the room, and for once, Ashford didn't argue the man's aid. Celeste, face pale, rounded the table and followed them.

"Jenkins," Harry said. "I'll collect Dr. Grey myself."

CHAPTER TEN

J ULIAN APPROACHED HARRY IN THE DRAWING room while Celeste and her mother remained above stairs with Ashford. "He's had an attack of nerves of some sort. I don't think it's his heart, but he bears watching. I've given him a draught to help him sleep, and I'll check on him again tomorrow. He's asking for you, by the way."

Harry nodded and took the wide staircase to Ashford's room. Lady Ashford and Celeste sat in plush chairs flanking the bed. Ashford lay in the center of the massive four-poster, propped on pillows, his face ash grey. Harry crossed his arms.

"My lord, you gave us all quite a scare," he said from the foot of the bed.

"Nerves, Grey says." Ashford snorted. "That doesn't sound like a proper diagnosis. I'd like a real physician," he said to Celeste.

She patted his hand. "Would you prefer Dr.

Smythe? I'm sure he would bleed you, and you'd be right as rain in no time."

Ashford grimaced and pulled his hand away then looked at Harry. "If anything happens to me," he began.

"Father!"

"Edmund, nothing is going to happen to you."

"Eventually, something happens to all of us," he told the ladies acerbically. "If anything happens to me," he continued, "I want you to have my notes, Harry. My journals, my instruments, they're all yours."

"My lord, I agree with the ladies. Nothing is going to happen to you."

"You'll take over the Round Table, of course."

"My lord? I haven't attended the Round Table these last two years. Surely someone else has assumed my seat by now."

The Round Table always numbered eleven, representing the eleven named planets. Members came and went, but when one left, usually through death or infirmity, there was always someone else eager to join Ashford's elite group.

Ashford wrinkled his forehead in confusion. "Harry, your seat is still yours. I never replaced you. It's yours . . . as long as you want it, that is."

Harry swallowed. Why couldn't *this* man have been his father? Then he realized, in many ways, he had been.

His eyes burned, and he blinked. All of his carefully constructed arguments against staying, all of his reasons for leaving crumbled like wet sand. Words left his mouth without his permission.

"My lord, you know I hope to join one of the Transit expeditions. I'll need to travel to London in a few weeks to meet with Lord Porter, but I'd like to work on your telescope while I'm here. With your guidance, of course."

He looked up and saw Celeste beaming at him from across the bed, and his mouth kept going.

"I'm not sure how much progress we can make in that time, but we have to try."

———

CELESTE WATCHED AS A GRIN split her father's face then fell away as reason reasserted itself.

"Harry, my boy, that's admirable, but I'm afraid you're right. It can't be done. Not in time for the Round Table, at any rate. There's simply too much to do."

Harry's brows came together, and he rubbed his jaw. "It would be foolish not to try, my lord. Your plans are sound."

"But all the laborers left when I fell ill. You'd have to reassemble and organize them and direct their work."

"The hops are planted, so we should find plenty of men willing to work before the harvest. And the

110

Romany frequent the road between here and Maidstone. They're always seeking extra work," Harry insisted.

"Surely we won't complete the work before you leave for London."

"I can delay my departure a week or two, perhaps. And I can return once I've met with Porter. The Commission won't make their final selections until September anyway."

Her father smiled, thinking.

"But Edmund," Lady Ashford said, "You can't engage in such a taxing project now. What if the strain causes another attack? I'm sure Dr. Grey won't approve."

"How can I be overtaxed with Harry here at the helm? I have complete faith in him."

"If you're determined to persist with this foolishness, I will only allow it if you agree to Remy's assistance."

"The footman?" Her father's eyes widened, and he pulled himself up on his pillows. "Absolutely not. What use do I have for that French upstart?"

"It's the only way, Edmund."

Silence. Her father looked at Harry, who shrugged and looked back. Celeste waited for her father to argue the point—her mother had little sway in his affairs, after all—but to her surprise, he acquiesced.

"Fine. But he'll take direction from Harry. I'll not be bothered with the man."

Celeste watched the proceedings with interest, noting the push and pull between her father and Harry, punctuated by Lily's admonishments for Edmund and negotiations on behalf of Remy.

In the end, they agreed Harry would lead the work on the telescope under her father's guidance if her father didn't allow himself to become overworked. Remy would assist under Harry's direction, requiring little to no interaction with Edmund, but only in tasks Harry felt him capable of performing safely and effectively.

Although her father had initially argued against Harry's proposal, he wore a smile as he settled against the pillows, his eyes beginning to droop from Julian's sleeping draught. It was almost as if he had . . . *expected* Harry to argue and was pleased with the outcome. Celeste narrowed her eyes and thought back to events in her childhood. Had she been similarly managed? The man was quite brilliant.

Brilliance aside, the look in her father's eye was a mixture of hope and pride. Hope that their plan could succeed, despite the near certainty that it would not. And pride in . . . Harry? Most certainly. Celeste knew, as Ashford's only child, she should be jealous. Her father treated Harry like the son he'd never had. But she only felt warm and fizzy inside.

And Harry. He was the most driven man she knew. Perhaps even more than her father, which was saying something. Against all odds, Harry would fight to complete the telescope. He'd given her father *hope*. What a special gift. If Celeste were the swooning sort, she would have been slumped in her chair.

———

WHEN CELESTE ARRIVED AT BREAKFAST the next morning, her father was spreading jam on a scone. He'd been foregoing breakfast of late, so this was a pleasing turn of events. His color was also much improved, although his hand shook as he held the knife.

Harry sat to his right, and they were deep in conversation. A moment passed before they noticed her and scrambled to stand. She waved them back to their seats and went to the sideboard. Dishes and platters lined the polished mahogany, and she lifted their silver covers to gauge the morning's offering.

Their voices flowed around her as she piled her plate with eggs, bacon and a scone. She hesitated then added a second scone before seating herself across from Harry. His eyebrows lifted as he took in her plate, and she blushed when she saw it from his perspective. Breakfast had always been her favorite meal.

She studied the men as they discussed the telescope. Her father's face was more animated than she'd seen it since arriving at Redstone Hall. He explained a rather dull aspect of his theory, and Harry's grey eyes narrowed intently while he listened. Then his hands came alive, gesturing as he responded to a question from her father.

His long fingers drew her attention. A small scar marked the back of one hand, and she smiled at a memory. He'd earned the scar one summer defending her from an attack of Viking invaders. Well, one Viking invader named Julian Grey. Or the Grey King, as they were required to address him. She forced her thoughts from Harry's hands and back to their discussion.

Her father had used his convalescence to perfect his design. Now he unrolled a thick sheaf of papers written in his bold script. He and Harry bent their heads together over one of the drawings. Celeste thought she could dance on the table in her shift, and they wouldn't notice.

Her mother entered and eyed them critically. Celeste shrugged at her questioning glance. The men rose and tried to act as though they hadn't been discussing science at the breakfast table, but the evidence spread on the wooden surface betrayed them.

"Edmund, this isn't the place to discuss ... contraptions."

"Apologies, Lady Ashford," Harry said.

Celeste watched in amusement as they tried to make polite conversation with her mother. But after a few inane comments about the weather, Lily took pity on them.

"For all that's holy, Ashford. Go show Mr. Corbyn your observatory or something. Leave me in peace." Her tone was sharp, but she smiled into her cup as she sipped her chocolate.

"Of course!" Her father rubbed his hands together. "I'll show you the laboratory, too, my boy. We can review my notes in further detail there."

Her mother scowled at Edmund's reference to the laboratory but remained silent as they left the room. She looked at Celeste for a moment then said, "Go. Make sure your father doesn't overexcite himself."

Celeste smiled and kissed her mother's cheek. "I think it's too late for that, but I'll see what I can do."

She followed them, curious to see her father's observatory through Harry's eyes.

The observatory was accessible through a narrow transit room that angled off one corner of the main house. Inside the rounded observatory, Greek columns supported the second-story domed ceiling. The room still had the distinctive smell of new paint and timber, and a pier, centered in the room, held a large telescope. Two counterweights hung off a small shutter in the dome.

"Pull on that shorter weight, Harry," her father said. Harry did, and the shutter opened with a metal-on-metal groan to reveal blue sky beyond the dome.

The room was magnificent, elegant in its simplicity. Celeste had seen it briefly after returning to Redstone Hall, but that had been in the evening, in the shadows of darkness.

Now, clerestory windows bounced sunshine off the white walls. She turned in a circle, struck anew by the room's symmetry. Soft, classical curves juxtaposed against the harder edges of scientific purpose.

The light was pure and white, untainted by blue or red or yellow furnishings. The duality of art and science in this simple space inspired a sense of balance. If she were to design an artist's studio, it would look like this. Well, perhaps without the giant telescope in the center.

As a child, she'd never understood her father's fascination with his instruments, logs and texts. But now she looked at him anew in this restful space, wrapped in white light. Perhaps he felt the same wonder for his astronomy that she did for painting.

―――

HARRY HAD BEEN OUTMANEUVERED. He knew it, but he accepted it. The more Ashford had argued *against* Harry working on his telescope, the more Harry had argued *for* it. Ashford's tactics were brilliant, if transparent.

If he were honest with himself, it hadn't required much maneuvering on Ashford's part. He'd already decided in his heart, if not his head, to stay and assist him.

Now he observed his mentor and knew he was doing the right thing. Although Ashford still moved slowly, his step was lighter and his eyes brighter than they'd been the day before. His color, which had been a startling ash grey the previous night, was much improved.

The older man's ideas for improvements to the mirror were simple but ingenious. Like Herschel, he proposed eliminating a secondary mirror. Instead, he would angle a single mirror in such a way to minimize the loss of light and reduce the distortion.

But unlike Herschel, Ashford proposed changes to the angle and shape of the mirror's face to further improve the image's clarity. He'd tested his theory on a smaller scale with promising results. Given enough time to build it properly, Ashford's telescope could make images viewed through the long tube much clearer than any previously seen.

But Harry still had misgivings that the task could be completed in time for the Round Table. Even with Harry to lead the work—and Lady Ashford's footman, it would seem—the task was monumental. While he thought their efforts might help Ashford's low spirits, he hoped the end result didn't further depress him.

Now he listened as Ashford led him through the observatory. When Harry had last visited Redstone Hall, the observatory wing had been under construction, but now, it rivaled the observatories he'd used in Berlin and Cambridge.

Ashford took them next to his laboratory.

"But you must not refer to it as 'the laboratory,'" Celeste warned. "At least not in my mother's hearing. This has always been, and always will be, the blue drawing room."

While the room's walls and draperies were indeed blue, Harry didn't see anything resembling a drawing room, but he agreed as he didn't wish to anger Lady Ashford.

Ashford grumbled as he led them through the doorway. "That woman has more than enough drawing rooms in this house. I only need the one laboratory."

Harry stopped when they crossed the threshold. The chaos of the room reminded him of Herr Kraus and his bouncing energy. It was an abrupt change from the soothing observatory, and the room's disorder made Harry itch.

He turned in a circle to take in the space while

Ashford went to retrieve his notes. He stopped when he saw the interior wall, covered in gilt-framed paintings.

They reflected the room's chaos, with their haphazard placement and discordant subjects. Small and large paintings nestled together in every open space. Landscapes cozied up to portraits and an odd collection of . . . exotic birds.

He looked at Celeste watching him, and he knew. "These are all yours?" he asked.

"I'm afraid so."

He moved closer and studied the wall. "They're . . . passable."

Her eyes widened. "They're not *that* bad. And I was much younger when I painted them, so allowances must be made. This one" — she indicated a portrait of her father peering through a telescope — "was an experiment in light and shadow. And this one—"

He twisted his lips in a smile, and she stopped speaking. "Celeste, they're magnificent."

"Oh, Harry, they're horrific." She wrinkled her nose and her blue-green eyes sparkled.

His eyebrows rose. "I'm not an expert on art, so I can't speak to the technical aspects, but these reach out on a deeper level." He rubbed his jaw and continued. "I can *feel* what you were feeling, and surely that must be the mark of a skilled artist."

"What do you feel?" she asked, crossing her arms.

He pointed to the portrait of her father. "Ashford has a question in his eyes here, but I can also feel *your* curiosity, wondering what has captured his interest."

"And this one . . ." He paused before a simple painting of the pond between Redstone Hall and Fernwood. Thick fingers of mist hung over the water and grassy bank. A wave of melancholy swept him, almost overwhelming in its intensity. "You must have been sad when you painted this."

She hesitated, brows tipped in a V, before replying, "That was the summer of my fifteenth year. It was the first time you and Julian didn't return to Fernwood, and I was forced to amuse myself. I was quite cross with the both of you."

"Ah, sad and *cross*," he amended.

She smiled, the merest tilting of her lips, and he took a small step back. He cleared his throat and said, "You're very talented."

She turned from him with a sniff. "You needn't sound surprised. But thank you anyway."

He chuckled as she left the room on a whisper of vanilla.

"Here we are." Ashford returned with his notes then cleared a workspace for Harry, transferring papers and journals from one table to another with a heavy thump. The towering piles listed and teetered.

Harry cringed and tempered the urge to square

up the stacks behind Ashford. He turned the button in his pocket instead then took a seat in the chair Ashford indicated. Harry placed his journal in the center of the desk, lining it parallel with the edge, and tried to ignore the leaning piles behind him.

"My lord Ashford." Remy stood in the laboratory entry, back straight in his navy livery, hair perfectly arranged.

Ashford looked up at the interruption, saw the Frenchman and frowned.

"Dr. Grey is here to see you, my lord."

Ashford's eyes shifted from side to side. Harry suspected he was crafting an excuse to avoid Julian's examination, but in the end, he stomped out of the room, his cane punctuating each step.

"Remy," Harry said. "I understand you're to assist us."

"Yes, sir. So Lady Ashford has informed me."

"What experience do you have leading men?"

"I was *un capitaine* in General Napoleon's army, sir. An engineer." His French accent was unmistakable, but his English precise and well-spoken.

Harry stared at the man for two heartbeats then crossed his arms and leaned back. He swallowed and twisted his lips. "An engineer."

"Yes."

"Can I ask how you came to be a footman in Lady

Ashford's employ? It seems you're overqualified for the job."

"There's nowhere I'd rather be." An answer that wasn't an answer. Still, Harry couldn't afford to be particular.

"Well, it happens I'm in need of an engineer. You're hired."

CHAPTER ELEVEN

CELESTE'S FATHER HAD CLEARED A SPACE for Harry to work, and their desks were a study in contrast. Her father's chaos against Harry's order. Harry's inkwell and papers sat at right angles, mocking her father's haphazard piles of journals, instruments and spilled ink. She suspected the men's desks reflected their thoughts: Harry's, neat and orderly. Her father's, chaotic. Both bordering on obsessive in their own way.

Harry and Remy had spent hours the previous day outlining their "battle plan." They'd listed and ordered the tasks that needed to be performed, marking which required more supplies or men or both. She'd offered to help, so two footmen had brought in a small writing desk for her use.

Now she arranged paper and ink to prepare a list of the supplies Harry had requested. Before she could begin, though, her eyes went to the wall of paintings.

She'd long accepted that she was different—felt differently—than others. So when Harry had studied her painting of the pond and felt her sadness, she'd been astounded. There was nothing sad about the painting. It was a pleasant scene of mist and water and grass. Calm and soothing, with soft curves and lapping water. But dabs of blue and indigo—sadness and loneliness—punctuated the scene, and he'd felt it.

Did he truly see her so clearly? She frowned and forced her attention back to her list. *Focus. Supplies.*

Ship-grade pulleys from Dover.

Timber from the mill in Maidstone.

Bolts, screws and chain from the Marshfield smithy.

Rope. Lots of rope.

She placed the completed list on Harry's desk, trying to ignore the pull of the paintings on the wall before her. It was no use.

She relented, found a low set of library steps and dragged them to the wall. She examined the canvases one by one, crouching for the lower frames and climbing the steps to see the higher ones. She was a detached observer, nothing more. She studied each as if it had been painted by someone else. Indeed, they had been, as she was not the same person she'd been years before.

Energy shimmered on the canvases. The lines were youthful and bold. Her younger self hadn't cared if the colors were "right" or if the lines were the correct weight. Instead, she'd focused on the essence of the subject and the attendant emotions. There was no hesitation in the strokes. These paintings were . . . alive. She hadn't captured that level of emotion in quite some time. Her heart beat a steady pulse in her throat, and her breathing quickened.

There was the painting of her father again, his eyes staring through a lens at something only he could see. Yellow wonder.

She smiled at the next one: Julian skipping rocks on the pond. Harry stood to the side, arms crossed as he glared at Julian's triumphant features. A competition then, and Julian had come out the winner. Orange. Merriment.

There was a self-portrait of herself as a girl, sitting atop Bellamy Hill with her father as they gazed at the stars. She and her father were small in scale compared to the expanse above them. The vastness felt blue-green like a robin's egg. Comforting and peaceful.

She leaned in to study the miniatures tucked in the gaps between the larger paintings. She had delighted in crafting stories with the tiny strokes. Relished the challenge of teasing out emotion with little dabs of color on the tiny canvases.

Finally, she studied a larger painting of her mother. Color saturated the canvas. The vague features of her mother's face hinted at vitality tempered by quiet desperation. The colors were too chaotic, the emotions too confusing. Happy, sad, lost, angry . . . all swirled together in a disorganized palette. Celeste couldn't separate her own emotions from those of her mother. Where did her own sadness end and her mother's begin?

Watercolors and oils, large and small, each painting had a story to tell. Her father's wall did not boast the elegant, posed portraits of an accomplished painter. It reflected an unrestrained heart experiencing a full range of emotions. The Academy in Paris would not accept any of these paintings, but they tugged and twisted her senses, nonetheless.

Unsettled, she left the laboratory and returned to her room. Restless energy continued to skip along her spine. She stared at her trunk in the corner, laden with paints and canvases and brushes, unopened since her arrival.

For every canvas her father had hung in his laboratory, there was another stored somewhere. She thought about the observatory, with its pure white light and clerestory windows. Before she could change her mind, she hurried to the bell pull and rang for a servant. When one of the chamber maids arrived, she said, "Tillie, where are the rest of my paintings?"

"Why, they're in crates in the attic, my lady. In the

east wing." At Celeste's silence, Tillie said, "Would you like to have them brought down?"

Celeste thought for a moment, debated. She wasn't sure how long she would be at Redstone Hall, but she felt an urgency to paint that she'd not felt in a long while. And her father's white-walled observatory would make the perfect studio.

Oh, her father would not be pleased to have his observatory invaded, but she might as well enjoy the inspiration while she could. "Yes, Tillie. Please have them brought to my father's observatory. And my trunk as well."

The maid raised her eyebrows but bobbed a curtsy and left.

———

CELESTE HAD NEVER BEEN MUCH of one for mornings, but she was a Johnny jump-about compared to the Pepper ladies. They wouldn't emerge from their rooms until well after luncheon.

Accordingly, birds chattered in the trees two days later when she climbed the Hill to observe the telescope's progress. She raised a hand to shield her eyes against the sun. Why did she always forget her bonnet? Her mother, of course, looked bright and fresh beneath a wide straw brim and green silk ribbon.

Harry and Remy had engaged teams of laborers; their first task was to complete the wooden mount for the telescope's metal tube. Carpenters swarmed like ants, hoisting beams and driving bolts to secure the frame. The sightless iron tube both taunted and encouraged from its place on the ground.

A movement at the edge of the clearing caught Celeste's eye. Robbie, the gamekeeper's son, crouched beneath a tree, nearly hidden behind the low branches. He split his attention between the construction on the Hill and his younger sister beside him. A team of men hefted a large beam to the top of the towering mount, and she smiled at the boy's wide-eyed awe.

Her father and Harry stood shoulder to shoulder on the other side of the hilltop, surveying the work. Harry wore a dark green coat over tan breeches and dark boots. He was hatless, and he needed a comb. He'd obviously run his fingers through his hair a time or three. He consulted his journal—she rarely saw him without it—and pointed out a section of the structure where a change was needed.

Remy provided an enjoyable diversion in practical shirtsleeves and well-fitting buff breeches. He assisted a group of men on a far section of the dais. As he bent to lift a piece of heavy timber, Celeste and her mother both sighed at the mesmerizing sight.

Celeste caught her father scowling in their direction. She cleared the vague look from her face and nudged her mother. Lily started and fanned herself. "This sun is much too warm. I'm returning to the comfort of the morning room. Will you join me?"

"In a moment. I'd like to watch the progress a little longer."

But before her mother could leave, a footman crested the top of the path with three gentlemen. Celeste recognized Lord Knowles, a long-standing member of the Eleven, but she didn't recognize the other two men.

Knowles was one of those unfortunate souls possessed of a large form, but a small mind. He favored purple waistcoats and wore his thin blond hair à la Brutus, brushed forward and waxed into submission around his florid face. His *au courant* style was better suited to a man with less girth and more hair.

Knowles fancied himself an astronomer, and although he lacked the mind of a scientist, he spouted his theories with vigor. As he rarely took the time to support his speculation with logic and evidence, few paid him any heed.

The second gentleman was of the same height as Knowles, but half the girth. He, too, had drab blond hair, but he wore a much more subdued ensemble. A brown coat with simple silver buttons atop tan breeches. The simplicity of his attire only exaggerated Knowles' flamboyance.

The third visitor was much shorter, thinner and darker than the first two, with small, ferret-like features. He paused to inspect the wooden structure while Knowles and the other gentleman approached her father and Harry.

As Celeste and her mother crossed to them, Knowles' loud voice carried across the hilltop.

"I'm visiting m'sister in Maidstone," he said. "M'nephew here is interested in your telescope, and we thought to see how it's coming along." Celeste winced as Knowles clapped her father's shoulder. Edmund glared at him and leaned on his cane.

Knowles turned then and his eyes widened when he recognized her mother. "Lady Ashford. Lady Celeste. What a pleasure. May I present my nephew, Mr. Anders?" Introductions were made, then Knowles turned to Harry.

"Corbyn. Didn't expect to find you here."

Harry crossed his arms. "I'm passing through on my way to London."

Knowles sucked his teeth. "Quite right, quite right." Then with a nod toward the half-finished telescope, he asked her father, "Do you still mean to finish in time for the Round Table? It appears there's quite a bit of work yet."

"It will be finished," her father bit out.

His face reddened, whether from the question, the sun, or overexertion, Celeste wasn't sure. Knowles' presence had caught the attention of several of the workers, and Remy frowned in their direction before setting a beam into place.

His ferret-like companion concluded his examination of the telescope and approached them as Knowles continued. "My friend Timmons here has also taken an interest in your project."

As if on cue, the small man pulled a notebook and pencil from his coat pocket.

"He's had the brilliant notion to chronicle the unveiling. He writes for the *Times*, you know."

He was *that* Timmons? Celeste recognized the name, if not the man. George Timmons wrote scathing accounts of scientific failures. His livelihood was guaranteed by foolish men who believed they could conquer the mysteries of the unknown. Her father's telescope, it seemed, was next in his sights.

Timmons pursed and twisted his lips as he flipped to a clean page. He gave a ferret-ish lick to the end of his pencil and turned to her father. "How did you conceive such an ambitious project? And how do you intend to improve on Herschel's instrument, my lord?"

Celeste watched various emotions chase across her father's face. His mouth opened then closed. He glared again at Knowles and his face reddened further. Celeste worried he might be on the verge of another attack. She reached a hand to him, but he turned and trudged back to the dais, his cane tip twisting the ground with each step.

She watched him go with a catch in her chest. For a scientist, there was nothing worse than to have others doubt one's work. If the Eleven arrived and there was no telescope for them to see, that would be bad enough.

But for a journalist to tell the world that Edmund St. James, Earl of Ashford, had not, in fact, devised a wondrous new telescope . . . Well, that could not be borne.

"Lord Knowles," her mother said. "Can I prevail upon you to escort me down the hill? I fear the sun has become too much for me today." Knowles couldn't refuse her mother's request, and he and his nephew offered their arms to lead her down the hill.

"Mr. Timmons," Harry said, watching her father over the shorter man's shoulder. "I'm sure you can appreciate the magnitude of the endeavor. Let me tell you what we plan."

Celeste sighed helplessly. Her father's telescope had acquired a life of its own. It was a god-like character in a Greek play, directing the actions of mere men. Was there anyone who wasn't anticipating the climax of this particular drama?

———

CELESTE SAT AT HER WRITING desk in the laboratory and tried—for the third time—to draft a letter to Alexandre. With all the activity around her father's telescope, she'd not given his proposal proper consideration. He deserved an answer, but her letter was hard to write when she herself didn't know what that answer was. The blank page stared back at her, unhelpful.

Could she see herself married to him? Sharing a life, building a family? If she were honest, no. She couldn't envision any of those things. But marriages were built on far less, and she and Alexandre enjoyed similar tastes in art. They had the same passion and ambition for painting. Could that be enough?

She drew a deep breath and inhaled Harry's subtle amber and oak scent. That was not helping.

He sat at his desk a few feet from her own, head down, eyes focused on his notebook. She wondered what he desired in a wife. Was he seeking a lady with a shared passion for astronomy? Someone with whom he could discuss mathematical equations? Then she thought of the very un-scientific Miss Pepper and dismissed the question. Clearly, Harry's romantic ambitions were not so lofty then.

She dipped her pen then cursed softly when she noted the inkwell was dry. Harry looked up and smiled, and she blushed to know he'd heard her.

"I think your father keeps ink in his desk." He motioned to Edmund's side of the room.

Celeste stood and rolled her shoulders then walked to her father's desk. She opened one drawer after another before she found a fresh bottle in the bottom of the desk, atop a pile of papers. As she lifted the bottle, she caught the salutation on the page below it. She knew she shouldn't look, but "My dearest Lily" caught her attention.

What was this?

She looked up from her crouching position, but Harry's attention was fixed on his work. She peeled back the top page in the drawer to see the one beneath it.

"My darling," it began. And the page after that, "My love." It was wrong to breach her father's privacy, but she couldn't help herself. She went back to the first page and skimmed the words from her position near the floor. Words like "please" and "sorry" and "incomplete" leapt from the page, and her heart pounded.

She turned the top page over, noting her mother's Paris address, but no franking. The letters had never been sent. Obviously, or they wouldn't be here, in her father's desk.

She thumbed through the pages and checked the dates. At least one a week at the bottom of the stack, stretching to one per month, then the last one, dated one year ago. She closed the drawer and gripped the ink bottle.

"Did you find it?" Harry asked.

She swallowed and nodded.

CHAPTER TWELVE

A S THE SUN BEGAN ITS slow descent behind the trees, Remy trailed the last of the workers from the Hill. His assistance had been a godsend. Harry found him intelligent and easy to work with. Not for the first time, he wondered at the man's story. Why he served in Lady Ashford's household when he was clearly qualified for much more.

Despite his comfort with the man's abilities, though, the thought of leaving to meet with Lord Porter, even for a week or two, made Harry uneasy. He wanted to complete as much as possible before he left for London.

He'd pushed himself each day long after everyone had left. Now he sat midway up on the wooden structure and let the silence settle around him. He was evaluating how much sunlight remained when he spied Celeste coming up the hill, lumbering beneath the weight of a basket. He climbed down and met her, taking the basket.

"What's this?"

"I brought sustenance. I'm guessing it's been some time since you ate, and you missed supper last night. I didn't want you to miss it again."

He thought back over the last two days and realized she was right. He'd finished late yesterday, so he'd taken a tray in his room. And he hadn't eaten anything today since breaking his fast.

She pulled a blanket from the basket and pressed it into his hands. He thought about the work that needed doing, all the reasons why he shouldn't stop to eat, until he spied the eagerness in her eyes. Eagerness to do this kindness for *him*.

This. This was why he shouldn't have stayed. Celeste and her orbit had a way of pulling him from his goals. He swallowed and allowed himself to be pulled. It was only food, and he needed to eat. A short break wouldn't hurt, would it?

"Take a break, Harry," she said, reading his mind.

He spread the blanket on the grass while she pulled food from the basket. Cold chicken, strawberries, pork pies, lemon tarts, scones with a jar of clotted cream. With each item, his eyebrows rose a little more. He looked around. "Are others joining us?"

She chuckled. "No, I think Cook just became a

little overzealous. She has a soft spot for you, you know. Heaven knows why," she teased.

He narrowed his eyes at her. "Yes, because every time lemon tarts disappeared, you told her *I* took them."

"You knew about that?"

"You weren't exactly subtle about it. I think you even had lemon tart on your cheek when you told that Banbury tale one time."

She chuckled. "Hmm. You knew I blamed you, and yet you didn't tattle on me. How noble of you, Harry."

Her words both warmed him and made him uncomfortable. An innkeeper's son was far from noble, no matter how much he might wish her to see him thus. He moved further away, as if inches of blanket might remind him of the distance between their stations.

Next, she pulled out a bottle of lemonade, which she handed to him. Then a bottle of wine. For her, he presumed. Of course, she'd recalled his aversion to spirits.

"You've given my father new hope, a sense that all is not lost with his telescope," she said. "Thank you for doing this, Harry. I know you have other plans, and you didn't have to agree to this, but . . . thank you."

Harry studied the telescope in the waning light.

He sighed as they began to sample the fare spread before them.

"I have to be honest, Celeste. I'm still not sure this is going to work. There's a tremendous amount of work to be done in a short amount of time. But your father would do no less for me. I have to try."

She nodded, chewing. "Why do you think he's so adamant about completing this before the Round Table? Surely the Eleven realize what a monumental task he's set. They wouldn't think any less of him if it's not complete. Although now I guess there's Mr. Timmons to consider."

Harry shrugged. "I couldn't say. His anxiety does seem excessive, but a scientist's credibility is all he has. If that's diminished, no one will take his theories seriously."

She patted the back of his hand and a sizzle traveled up his arm. She'd always had an easy familiarity about her.

"Harry, I've known you for years. If anyone can make this happen, you can. But if it's not meant to be, it's not. Things will right themselves in the end. Maybe not the way we expect or wish, but all will be well. You'll see." She smiled brightly.

"You're that certain?"

"Yes, Harry. I'm an optimist."

"And I'm a *realist*."

"You?" she scoffed. "Harry, you're a dreamer.

You're as much a realist as I'm a . . . a flying pig."

"A flying pig?" He eyed her critically. "No, you most definitely are not a flying pig."

She threw a strawberry at him. He'd forgotten how easy it was to be with her. It was as if the last years had not separated them. Would it always be this way?

He imagined a time would come when she would marry, and then she would laugh with someone else. They would no longer enjoy this ease, this affinity. He felt a moment of sadness for the inevitable loss of his friend.

She interrupted his thoughts. "Just because you've never seen a pig fly doesn't mean they can't."

"Ah. The *appeal to ignorance* trick. I recall my philosophy lessons. But you're not an optimist, Celeste. You're delusional."

She laughed and waved a hand at the telescope. "I have faith that you'll put wings on this particular pig."

———

CELESTE FELT HEAT WASH OVER her every time Harry looked at her. It was ridiculous, truly. He was just . . . Harry. But awareness flowed through her like warm honey, flooding her chest and fingertips and toes.

She had thought to bring him something in appreciation for the work he was doing. The man needed to eat, after all. And they'd often picnicked on Bellamy Hill with Julian.

But she hadn't realized a picnic with just the two of them would feel so . . . intimate.

Harry uncorked the wine and poured her a glass before opening the lemonade. An errant lock of dark hair lay across his forehead, tempting her fingers to brush it back. She took a sip then watched him tip his own glass back.

He'd shed his coat, and the white linen of his shirtsleeves glowed against the skin of his throat. Dark hairs dusted the backs of his hands and his forearms below his rolled sleeves. She marveled at the differences between his hard male form and her softer self.

His hands would make a perfect figure study. They were generous hands, calloused, with wide palms and long fingers. Marked only by the small scar on the back of his left hand.

They were hands that were always in motion. Tapping, drumming, rolling a coin or a stone or a chess piece. They were strong and capable and masculine. She allowed herself to wonder what they would feel like against her cheek, and her heart kicked against her ribs. Oh, this would not do.

He would leave soon, and she . . . Well, she would return to Paris. There was no time, no room in their lives, for hands and . . .

She forced her breathing to slow and turned her head toward the telescope's tube lying on the ground.

"How will you manage the tube?" She stood and marched over to the mouth of the hollow metal. Harry stood more slowly and followed her.

She leaned in to stare down the empty blackness before realizing the view he must have from behind her. She jerked herself upright, and that rush of heat flooded her again.

Heavens! She bit her lip, but she couldn't help her smile as Harry approached, dragging his eyes up to hers.

———

HARRY WATCHED AS CELESTE ROSE from the blanket then walked to the tube, a feminine swish to her hips. He swallowed and took a breath. She was going to kill him. He stood slowly and followed. When she bent to peer down the dark opening of the tube, he pressed a hand to his jaw.

She turned back and smiled at him expectantly. She had asked a question . . . oh, yes. The tube.

He explained the mechanics of it, and the plan he and Remy had devised to maneuver the heavy iron into place. She kept smiling while he talked. Surely, she wasn't interested in his dull explanation, was she?

"I'm sure it will be magnificent when it's finished," she said.

She stood too close. Close enough to kiss. Would she taste like strawberries? Wine? Starlight?

Their encounter from three years before had

replayed itself in his mind many times since then, a melody he couldn't get out of his head. And he'd not even kissed her. What sort of a muddle would his mind be in if their lips had actually touched?

He thought again of kissing her now, but he didn't think a single kiss would be enough. He took a breath, stepped away and looked out over the valley. The night sky unfolded before them, dark velvet growing rich with diamonds.

"This was always a prime spot for star-gazing," he said.

Celeste tugged his hand, and they sat on the wooden dais facing the valley. Her fingers wrapped around his, her thumb stroking the tender spot between his thumb and forefinger. He didn't think she realized she did it, and he was loath to remove his hand.

"Father and I used to watch the stars together," she said, "especially on clear nights like this one." She smiled, remembering, her shoulder bumping his. "One night—I must have been eight or nine—he told me if I counted seven stars for seven nights, the first person I saw on the eighth day would be my true love."

His mouth twisted with humor. "But what if the first person you saw was your grandfather? Or the kitchen maid?"

She chuckled. "I wasn't concerned about such

practical matters. I had a *Plan*, you see. I would make sure the first person I saw was Julian."

Harry felt a twinge of something . . . jealousy? For a boy of ten? He pulled his hand away.

Celeste grimaced. "I was quite infatuated at the time. Julian didn't want to have anything to do with me, though. At any rate, it was weeks before the nights were clear enough for star counting."

"What happened on the eighth day?"

She sighed dramatically. "I stayed awake all night and crept out before my governess woke. I went to Fernwood, certain it was just a matter of time before Julian and I would marry. But Julian was not the first person I saw." She grinned, keeping him in suspense. "It was you."

"Me? How disappointing!" He couldn't help the smile that stretched to his eyes, and his jealousy evaporated.

"It was the first holiday you spent with Julian. You were both coming 'round the copse near the gatehouse, heading toward the pond, but you were in the lead. It was your face I saw first."

Harry crossed his arms over his chest and cocked his head. "And how did you feel about that unfortunate turn of events?"

"Well, at first I was angry—at you, at Julian. At myself for not looking away soon enough." She grimaced. "But like any eight-year-old, I was very resilient. If Julian wasn't my true love, perhaps you would do."

Harry snorted at the bruise inflicted on his pride, and Celeste continued, "Do you remember how much I followed you and Julian that summer?"

"Yes, you were everywhere. Julian joked that you were like a bad rash. When we went fishing, you were there with a bucket of worms. When we played highwayman, you volunteered to be the coachman. Although I think you would have rather been the brigand." He smiled, remembering. "We had to sneak out at an unholy hour to swim so you wouldn't follow us there, too. We didn't think you ever slept."

"Yes, you were horrid to me at times. Eventually, I decided neither of you could be my true love. You were both just a couple of smelly boys. And," she added, "my father was the same person who told me dragons caused sunsets by breathing on the sky. So, you understand why I might have been skeptical of the star counting thing."

Harry grinned at her, and his breath caught when she grinned back. One kiss, he thought. What harm could one kiss do?

"There you are!" They jumped at the sound of Miss Pepper's voice. They turned to see her approaching, accompanied by her mother and Herr Kraus. How had they not heard them coming?

Miss Pepper eyed the remains of their picnic

spread on the blanket. "When neither of you joined us for supper, we came to be sure all is well. But I see we worried for nothing!" She laughed, a bubbly sound that should have been pleasant, but grated on Harry's ears.

He moved further from Celeste and pressed back a feeling of guilt. They had no reason to feel guilty, did they? He thought of Celeste's rounded form as she'd peered into the telescope tube, and a flush bloomed across his cheeks. He began naming constellations in his mind to erase the image.

"Lady Celeste, how kind you are to think of the poor souls working up here," Mrs. Pepper added. Harry gritted his teeth at the reminder that he was one of the poor working souls.

Celeste chuckled and moved to gather the picnic things. "It was nothing so noble as that, I assure you, Mrs. Pepper. I merely wished to enjoy the company of my friend."

She knew how scandalous that sounded, didn't she? Daughters of earls did not have gentlemen friends, much less innkeepers' sons.

Indeed, Mrs. Pepper pressed a hand to her throat and stuttered a protest. Celeste shot him a secret smile before tucking their blanket back in the basket.

CHAPTER THIRTEEN

TWO DAYS LATER, HARRY WAS cautiously optimistic about their flying pig. Perhaps optimistic was not the right word. He was less pessimistic.

Work was underway on the pulleys that would allow them to adjust the angle of the tube, and he and Lord Ashford had returned to the laboratory to work out details for the mirror. With each step, each success, he grew more eager to see it succeed. He needed to travel to London to meet with Lord Porter, but he kept thinking, *Soon. One more day . . .*

Celeste joined them in the laboratory, and Ashford looked up, eyes narrowing at her entrance.

"M'dear," he began in a disapproving tone. "My observatory is not an artist's studio."

Ah. Harry had wondered when *that* reckoning would occur. For several days, he'd noticed Celeste venturing into the observatory. When he'd peeked in to investigate, he'd been surprised to see her canvases propped against the white walls. Ashford, it seemed, had just discovered her incursion.

Harry gathered his notebook to make a strategic exit, but Celeste stilled him with a look.

"I know, Father, but the light in there is perfect for painting. And it's not permanent. Once *Maman* and I return to Paris, you'll have your observatory back like we were never here."

Ashford was silent for a beat, then he exhaled, puffing his cheeks. "This is extortion, isn't it?"

"Is it?" she asked.

"Well, if you think I'll be reduced to bribing my own family to stay—"

"Of course not," she said with a pat on his shoulder. Ashford harrumphed then bent over a pile on his desk, searching for something in his notes. He might grumble about Celeste usurping the observatory, but Harry suspected he would give a great deal more than that to have his family home again. Celeste smiled and took the seat across from Harry.

Some time later, she was recording figures in her small, neat hand while Harry called out measurements. They were engrossed in the work, heads angled together, when Remy entered.

"Lady Celeste, Monsieur Marchand is here to see you," he announced.

Surprise flashed across her face before she smiled. "Alexandre? He's here?" She set her notebook aside and moved around the desk.

Dismay shadowed her face as she looked at her ink-stained fingers and wrinkled gown. She touched a hand to her hair, which had come undone on one side, a stray curl teasing the side of her neck.

"Why don't we take a break?" Harry asked.

"Yes, I think that's a good idea." As she started to leave the room, she paused. "Father, Harry, please join us for tea." And then she was gone. Her quick desertion was . . . unflattering.

"What was that about? Who is this Marchand?" Ashford asked.

"I don't know," Harry responded.

"My lord," Remy said. "The word in my lady's household is that Marchand has requested Lady Celeste's hand in marriage."

A burning started in the pit of Harry's stomach and spread to his fingertips.

"My daughter is betrothed? Why wasn't I told?"

Remy cleared his throat. "She's not yet given Monsieur Marchand her answer, my lord."

"Well, I suppose we should go have our tea and rescue my daughter. See what's what with this Marchand fellow."

Harry thought about the surprised but pleased expression on her face. Her obvious worry over the state of her hair. He didn't think she wanted rescuing, and that fact depressed him.

———

CELESTE RACED UP THE BACK stairs, calling for Odette. Why was Alexandre here?

She'd still not responded to his proposal. Marriage was not a decision to be made lightly, after all. Her own parents were a cautionary tale in that regard. The last thing she wanted was to find herself trapped in a marriage where she was bored or unloved.

She thought of Harry and knew she would never feel *bored* with him. But unloved? That, she thought, was a real possibility. He was too much like her father. His love—his true passion—was for science and the heavens. How could a mere human compete with that?

She gritted her teeth then forced herself to relax. This was not an either/or question. Harry was not one of the choices. She owed it to Alexandre to weigh his proposal on its own merits.

Back in her room, Odette helped her change her gown and fix her hair. With a cluck of her tongue, she re-pinned the ridiculous, disobedient curl on her neck. "It's very romantic, if you don't mind me saying so, Lady Celeste."

"Romantic?"

"Monsieur Marchand traveling all this way to see

you. I think he must hold the true *amour* in his heart."

Did he? Did Alexandre feel a grand passion for her that drove him across the Channel? She tested the theory in her mind then discarded it. No. He'd never hinted at such strong feelings. Was she nothing more than a prize to be acquired then, like a coveted painting? No, that didn't feel right either and was uncharitable toward a man who'd only been kind to her.

She scrubbed her hands to remove as much ink as she could. It was no use. Where were her dratted gloves? Odette handed them to her and buttoned the small closure for her.

When she entered the drawing room, she found Alexandre seated near her mother with one leg crossed over the other. He was elegant and long-limbed; other ladies would find him swoon worthy. Heart-melting. But she felt . . . nothing. Maybe these things came with time. Look how long she'd known Harry before her heart had started seizing in his presence. But she didn't have years and years to wait to feel something for Alexandre.

He stood and smiled. "Lady Celeste, you're a sight for my poor eyes." He approached and took her gloved hands in his. As he leaned over them to press a kiss to her knuckles, she inhaled. His cologne was a pleasant, citrusy scent, but there was no hint of amber or oak. That was disappointing.

"Alexandre, what a pleasure. I wasn't aware you were planning a trip to England." She motioned for him to resume his seat as she perched on the adjacent sofa. The Pepper ladies had already arrived in the drawing room and hovered on the edge of a delicate settee. Her mother called for tea, and they exchanged pleasantries about the weather while they waited for the tray to arrive.

Her mother looked up and smiled. "Ashford, Mr. Corbyn, do join us."

The tap of her father's cane was whisper-soft against the plush carpet as he entered. Harry stood framed in the doorway, and her heart did its skipping thing.

The ends of his hair were damp, and he'd changed his worn jacket for a less shabby one of midnight blue. He looked like his mind was still back in the laboratory, though. Like he wanted to be anywhere but there. He entered the room and introductions were made. The gentlemen studied one another before taking their seats.

Finally, the tea things arrived. As her mother poured and passed around slices of cake, Celeste studied Harry and Alexandre. She acknowledged that both men were handsome, striking even, albeit in different ways.

Alexandre was smooth, polished edges. A refined figure cast of molten gold and burnished to a blinding sheen.

Harry was his opposite. Slashing brows, a hint of evening whiskers and hair like rich Parisian coffee. His beauty begged to be touched, while Alexandre's reminded her of fine Sèvres porcelain—beautiful but never something her nurse would have allowed her to play with.

Harry's hands were calloused and mobile, Alexandre's relaxed and elegantly folded. Restrained. Harry was rough industry to Alexandre's polished artistry, dark to Alexandre's light. How could she be attracted to two men of such disparate looks and temperament?

No, she amended. She found Alexandre *attractive*, but she was not *attracted to* him in the same way she was attracted to Harry. Harry's soul pulled at hers. Even while his single-minded passion for astronomy, so much like her father's, repelled her.

He smiled at her now, a slow tilting of the lips that was for her alone, and her insides went squishy. Why couldn't Harry be the man waiting for a response to his proposal? Then she recalled his plans. His dreams. He would leave soon. There was her answer.

After the pleasantries were out of the way, her father began his interrogation. She scoffed at the word, but there was no other way to describe the polite but probing questions he lobbed at Alexandre.

Questions about his background, his prospects, his family.

She ought to be embarrassed, but she felt amusement instead. In the last three years, she'd not had a father to question her suitors, so she settled on the sofa and enjoyed the experience. Until her father furrowed his brow and sharpened his attack.

"Mr. Corbyn and I have been debating the merits of solar spectroscopy to measure the properties of the sun. What are your thoughts on the matter?" Celeste knew they had been debating no such thing. She took pity on Alexandre and prepared to redirect the conversation, but Alexandre surprised them all.

"I read of Herr Fraunhofer's spectroscope and his experiments on light," he said. "His theories hold promise for further study of our universe."

There was a pause as everyone took this in. Then Celeste laughed at Alexandre's deft handling of her father, who merely responded, "Quite right, Marchand, quite right."

———

HERR FRAUNHOFER, INDEED. HARRY SETTLED in his chair opposite Marchand and took the other man's measure. *This* was who Celeste was to marry? *Might* marry, he corrected. The man was much too . . . perfect, with his gilded hair and brilliant smile. His eyes were even . . . topaz? Who had eyes of such a ridiculous shade of brown? There. They were merely

---

brown. Harry suppressed a snort. Celeste would be bored with such flawless perfection within a fortnight.

Ashford—like any good father—subjected the man to a thorough inquiry, which Harry enjoyed. Until Marchand said something clever, and Celeste laughed. Was she *blushing*? He felt the button in his pocket and turned it between his thumb and fingers.

Celeste's hands, which had been ink-stained while they worked, were now covered in silk gloves. He recalled the warmth of her fingers as she'd held his hand during their impromptu picnic. Knew satisfaction that Marchand had not had the pleasure of her bare fingers in his hand today. When he realized the direction of his thoughts, he wondered when he had become so ridiculous.

Lady Ashford inquired of Marchand's travel arrangements and learned he'd taken a room at The Black Swan in Marshfield. "Oh, but you must stay with us," she said. "We won't hear otherwise."

Harry and Ashford stared at her. Harry was quite sure "otherwise" would be acceptable to him, but Marchand agreed, and a footman was sent to collect his things.

Miss Pepper exclaimed, "How wonderful! Now our numbers will be even!" Truly? *That* was her concern?

When the river of Ashford's questions began to

run dry, Marchand turned to Harry. "Have you been to the *Musée du Louvre*, Mr. Corbyn?"

"No, I'm afraid I've not had the pleasure."

"Oh, but you must go. It's beyond transcendent. Lady Celeste has enjoyed the *Raft of Medusa* exhibition. Gericault's portraits and figure studies are also quite riveting. His choice of subjects is nothing short of fearless."

He didn't know what the Raft of Medusa was, but it sounded dreadful. Far from *transcendent*. Portraits, though, he did understand.

"Lady Celeste has always enjoyed portraiture," he said. "Even as a young girl, she would beg us to sit for her." He turned to Celeste. "Do you remember the summer you begged Julian and I to sit for you? You must have painted twenty portraits of us, when we only wanted to fish and swim."

Celeste laughed, remembering with him. "I think you drew the line at posing in Roman costume."

Marchand pressed his lips together, and Harry suppressed a childish smirk.

Celeste sat forward and changed the topic. "Mr. Corbyn has spent time in Berlin, where he's been measuring the distance to the stars. Isn't that fascinating?"

"Indeed?" Marchand's eyebrow lifted. "Surely that's not possible. How does one go about such a futile task?"

Harry may not have known anything about the Louvre, but he knew his way around stellar parallax.

———

VICAR AND MRS. PITT, WITH their unique sixth sense of visitors, arrived close on Marchand's heels. They were shown into the drawing room where Lady Ashford plied them with cakes and tea.

In short order, Mrs. Pitt inquired about the telescope project, reminding them how much Marshfield was anticipating their first up-close view of the heavens.

Ashford mumbled an excuse and left the room, and Harry wondered how soon he, too, could leave without seeming impolite.

"The gentlemen have made remarkable progress," Celeste said. "The mounting structure is almost complete, and work has already begun on the pulleys."

Mrs. Pitt's mouth twisted as if she'd taken a spoonful of chilled asparagus soup. "Surely, Lady Celeste, you aren't spending time at the site with the laborers. There's so much . . . industry . . . involved."

"Well, yes. How else am I to assist?" Celeste reached for another cake and placed it on her plate.

"But certainly there are more . . . ladylike . . . endeavors to occupy your time," Mrs. Pepper said. "Why, just this afternoon, I received some lovely fashion plates from London." Then, nudging her daughter, she added, "It's important for a young lady to remain *au courant*, don't you agree, Monsieur Marchand?"

He smiled agreeably at Miss Pepper and her mother, saying, "I'm sure you ladies could never be anything but."

After further inanities regarding fashion, the conversation turned back to more interesting topics. "I should like to see this telescope," Marchand said.

"Of course," Celeste offered. "I shall take you there. It's quite magnificent. Mr. Corbyn and Remy have been working night and day. It's going to be remarkable when it's complete. I assure you, you've not seen anything like it before."

Marchand stared at Harry, and Harry stared back. Finally, Marchand turned back to Celeste to ask, "Who is Remy?"

"Remy is our footman. You may recall him from Paris."

"Your footman?" Mrs. Pepper asked with a squeak. No one spoke for a moment. "You're working with the footman?" She directed this to Harry, a hint of accusation in her tone.

Harry nodded and forced his hands to still. "He knows what he's about," he said into the silence. "The man's brilliant."

Mrs. Pepper looked skeptical but said nothing.

Conversation turned with alacrity to Marchand's

painting. Mrs. Pitt and Miss Pepper exclaimed in breathless, fluttery tones when he indicated he would submit some of his latest work to the Paris Salon.

"Lady Celeste is considering the Salon as well," Marchand said. "She's quite talented."

"Oh, but you can't mean to *exhibit* your work, Lady Celeste! Isn't that considered terribly *fast*?" Mrs. Pitt asked in hushed tones.

"There's nothing improper about a lady exhibiting at the Salon," Celeste said. She began to reach for another cake then pulled her hand back.

"But aren't there ladies' exhibits in which you could take part instead?"

"Of course." Her voice rose slightly, and Harry sat back. "But why would I want to limit myself to an exhibition for ladies, by ladies? Separating ladies from the general Salon only diminishes the importance of their work. Art is art. It should be recognized as such, regardless of who the artist is."

The Pitts and the Peppers blinked owlishly. Marchand studied his nails, while Lady Ashford passed her daughter another biscuit. Harry grinned.

CHAPTER FOURTEEN

HARRY STARED AT HIS REFLECTION above the washstand, frustrated that he'd let Marchand's talk of the *Musée du Louvre* affect him. In a childish display, he'd countered with a detailed explanation of stellar parallax. He released a tight breath, annoyed with himself.

Marchand, with his perfect golden hair and perfect manners, was a perfect match for Celeste. Perfect. The word drummed through his mind.

The man had all the right answers to Ashford's inquisition. Hints of a fortune, a promising artistic future, good family stock. The comparison between them was stark. Illuminating, for anyone still unaware of Harry's low background and rough manners.

As he returned to the laboratory, he passed Lady Ashford coming from the other direction.

"Have you seen my daughter, Mr. Corbyn?"

"No, Lady Ashford, but I'm on my way to the laboratory"—her eyes narrowed, and he corrected himself. "My apologies, the blue drawing room. Perhaps I'll find her there."

"If you do see her, please ask her to join me in the morning room."

"Of course." He nodded and made to continue, but she stopped him with a hand on his arm.

"Monsieur Marchand must be eager to secure Celeste's hand to travel all this way, *non*?"

He watched her, trying to gauge her intent, but her expression remained serene. "As any man would be, Lady Ashford." He bowed and left, feeling her eyes on his back.

He neared the laboratory but paused on hearing voices in the observatory. He stepped through the transit room to investigate, recognizing Celeste's soft laughter before he reached the observatory's archway.

She stood before her easel, light from the clerestory windows limning her form. Marchand stood close behind her, much too close to his way of thinking. As the Frenchman lifted a finger to point out something on the canvas, his shoulder brushed Celeste's. Quite deliberately.

Where was her chaperone? Surely, they shouldn't be here alone? Harry cleared his throat as he crossed the threshold. Celeste jumped from Marchand's side, and a guilty flush stained her cheeks.

"Lady Celeste," Harry said, forcing his jaw to relax. "Your mother requests you join her in the morning room."

"Of course. Alexandre, please excuse me."

Marchand bowed over her hand and kissed the air above it. "I'd love to see the gardens when you've a moment."

She nodded and turned to leave. Harry held his arm for her, and she placed her fingers—ungloved, he noticed—on his sleeve. He forced the tension from his arm.

As they walked, Harry made a decision. He'd allowed himself to become distracted, but he needed to regain his focus on Cairo.

"I'll be leaving for London at week's end," he said. When she was silent, he continued. "Lord Porter will be there for the Parliamentary session, and I must meet with him about my application."

"Will you—how long will you be gone?" she asked.

"A week, maybe more. But I'll return in time to begin work on the mirror."

She nodded. He studied her profile and resisted the urge to brush the curl from her neck. He reminded himself instead of Cairo and the Flying Pig. Of his desire to help Ashford. He forced his thoughts from Celeste and her perfect, gilded Frenchman.

———

GUILTY HEAT WARMED CELESTE'S CHEEKS, and she willed it down. She had nothing for which she should feel guilty, she reminded herself. Yes, perhaps she'd let Alexandre stand a little too close. But how was she to decide whether to marry him if she couldn't determine if there was any fizz?

And then she wondered if she wasn't giving the poor man false hopes. After the months of their acquaintance, wouldn't she know if he was the one for her?

And Harry. They didn't have an understanding between them, so she didn't owe him any loyalty. Yet she felt as if, in showing Alexandre her paintings, she'd somehow betrayed Harry.

He dropped his arm outside Ashford's laboratory, gave her a short bow, and left without a word. He was leaving for London. She knew he would need to go sooner or later, but she'd hoped it would be later. Her stomach sank a little more at the thought.

She found her mother at a small writing desk in the ladies' morning room. The bow window cast a cheerful beam of sunlight across the carpet, but Celeste's memories of watching her mother's back from the same window washed over her in blue waves. She swallowed her nausea.

"*Maman*, Harry said you wished to see me?"

"Celeste, dearest. It's kind of Marchand to visit,

non? You must be pleased." Her mother rose and joined her on the velvet settee.

Pleased? Confused was a more accurate adjective. With her parents' disastrous marriage, she didn't feel her mother was the right person to offer advice, but she asked anyway. "How will I know?"

Her mother didn't misunderstand her. She breathed a wistful sigh. "If I knew the answer to that, I wouldn't be living in France while your father remains here."

"Did you ever think to return? When you left all those years ago, did you think you would come home?"

Celeste thought she'd avoid the question, as she had so many before. Then, slowly, she said, "At first, I did. I thought I would go away for a few weeks, a month maybe, before your father came to his senses."

"What did he do that was so terrible?"

"It wasn't so much what he did, as what he didn't do." At Celeste's look of confusion, she sighed then continued. "I was young, *ma pauvre*. We both were. I was madly in love with your father. He was everything I thought I wanted in a husband—kind, generous. Dashing," she added with a smile. "But he was in love with his work. You know me, dearest. I do like to be spoiled and indulged. And your father, he is not the indulging type. I didn't feel there was room in our marriage for your father's other love."

She took Celeste's hands in her own. "But my biggest regret, dearest, is the time I spent away from you. I knew you were well cared for, and I feared my unhappiness would affect you as well, so I stayed away. But I thought of you every day, every night, and I wondered how you were growing into a young lady."

Celeste forced a breath in, then out. This was the most forthcoming her mother had ever been, despite Celeste's attempts to understand her parents. "I needed you, *Maman*."

"I know. I can't change the past, but I'm sorry." Her mother sniffed back a tear, while Celeste reached for a handkerchief and blew her nose.

The contrast was not lost on her: her mother, with her dainty, elegant, single tear. Celeste with a red nose and puffy eyes, blowing into a handkerchief. "How do you do that?" she asked with a watery chuckle.

"Practice, dearest." Her mother turned to face her more fully. "I'll never be able to make it up to you, but I shall try. Starting now. With Marchand here, we must maintain propriety. I'll stay until you're ready to return to Paris. I've never been a chaperone, but how hard can it be? And besides," she added with a Gallic shrug, "I think the morning room must be re-done. The upholstery in here is positively outdated."

Celeste smiled. Her mother thought of propriety *now*? Harry had been here for weeks. His appeal was by far the greater threat to her virtue. And yet her mother took no issue with them spending hours alone together. Not that Celeste would be pointing that out.

They had a pig to fly, after all.

————

WITH EFFORT, HARRY FORCED HIS attention back to the page before him. Tomorrow, he'd leave for London. He'd already written out his latest order of supplies and was now reviewing his notes to gauge what needed to be done next.

Celeste and Marchand invaded his thoughts every ten seconds or so, making the task a Herculean one. Or Sisyphean. It didn't help that Celeste sat a scant five feet from him, scratching out a list for her father.

He welcomed distraction in the form of Remy, who joined him to review their plans for the next two weeks. Harry only intended to remain in London a week, perhaps ten days, but one could never be too careful. He wanted to be sure they didn't miss any of the pivotal points in their schedule; otherwise, their chances of completing the Flying Pig on time were next to nothing.

To be truthful, Harry thought they were next to nothing anyway, but he refused to dwell on that.

"Be sure to check the angle of the uppermost pulleys," he reminded Remy, pacing as they spoke.

"Of course."

"And don't forget that our order of copper is due to arrive soon."

"Yes, Mr. Corbyn." Remy gave him a twisted smile, making a notation in his journal before leaving. Harry had complete faith in Remy's abilities—he did. But the time spent in London would be time away from the telescope, and he didn't want to let Ashford down.

He reminded himself of his purpose in traveling to London. Cairo and his goal of joining the Transit expedition were within reach. He forced himself to relax. Pictured himself in the desert, surrounded by instruments and fellow astronomers. Sand blowing, camels groaning, the silhouette of that tiny planet crossing the edge of the sun. Achieving all that he was seeking and defying his father's low expectations.

He hoped that by picturing his success, he would feel the same excitement as when he'd first set out to join the expedition, but his goals felt further and further away, and Ashford's telescope called to him.

And then he thought of leaving Celeste, and his insides quickened then tightened. What was this? Panic?

It was ridiculous. He'd been alone his entire life.

These weeks at Redstone Hall were only a visit. A short interlude in his solitary life. He would be alone again, so this anxiety was pointless. He'd grown used to her company, to her laughter and teasing. That was all. He would grow used to not having her company again.

He thought of the last time he'd left Redstone Hall. It had taken some time before he stopped thinking about her every day. Something told him this time would be worse.

He drummed his fingers against the side of his leg before forcing them to still. He turned papers and notebooks aside, methodically aligning the edges, searching for his pencil. It was just here . . . He felt the back of his neck heating as his anxiety ratcheted up.

Finally, he looked toward Celeste. Her head was down as she studied the page before her, her hand near her ear, twirling . . . his pencil.

"Celeste."

She looked up and smiled. Her nonchalance only irritated him further. She had his pencil and didn't even realize it.

"I believe you have my pencil."

"Oh. I'm sorry." She looked at the pencil between her fingers. "I must have picked it up by mistake."

"You *always* take my pencil." He cleared his throat. "This is my desk. That is your desk. Keep your pencil there and leave mine here." He enunciated slowly so she couldn't misunderstand him.

Her brows rose and her eyes widened. He knew he was being an ass, but he couldn't help himself. He kept his things orderly for a reason. Why couldn't she see that? Why did she insist on disrupting his carefully constructed harmony?

She rose and walked to his desk, the pencil dangling from her fingers, watching him warily. "Your pencil, sir." She held it out to him with both hands, and he took it with a short, jerky movement.

"In future, please try not to disrupt my things." *Stop talking*, he told himself.

She scowled at him as he placed the pencil parallel to the top edge of his notebook. "Well, *in future*, please try not to be an ass." Since she was only saying what he himself had been thinking, he could hardly argue.

"Fine," he said.

"Fine. And while we're talking about common courtesy . . ." Her eyes flashed—more blue than green—and she motioned to the inkwell on his desk. "Why can't you refill the inkwell? If you're the last one to use it before it runs dry, it's only polite to refill it for the next person."

"It's at *my* desk. It wouldn't be a problem if you didn't sit at my desk."

"I don't sit at your desk."

"Yes. You do. You leave your paintbrushes here

all the time. I have to move them to find my papers."

"You're impossible!"

His jaw tightened and he looked pointedly at a paintbrush on the edge of his desk. She grabbed it and spun to leave but stopped short when she saw Remy in the doorway, a sanguine expression on his face. How could he be so cheerful when Harry felt so . . . uncheerful?

Celeste stomped past his engineer, muttering loud enough for Harry to hear, "He's all yours. Good luck." Remy pressed his lips together and Harry had the impression he was trying not to laugh. It only irritated him further.

"*Merde*. You're in a mess of it now," Remy whispered.

Harry sighed. He'd spent his formative years with aristocratic boys, so he knew how to swear in French. Fluently. *Merde*, indeed.

———

"MR. CORBYN." HARRY LOOKED PAST Remy to one of Ashford's ruby-coated footmen. "Lord Porter is here to see you. He's in the library with Lord Ashford." The footman eyed Remy with suspicion.

Porter was here? Harry was moments from going to London to seek him out, and the man was here? He nodded at the footman and stepped past Remy.

The library was a masculine space, decorated in richly hued paintings and textiles in amber and green. It was larger than the first floor of his father's inn and smelled of leather and history. Ashford and Porter stood before the fireplace beneath a massive gilt-framed mirror. Harry greeted the men with a bow.

"Corbyn, it's good to see you again. I hope Berlin was to your liking." Porter's voice was crisp like dry leaves.

After what Harry hoped was a suitable amount of polite conversation, he asked what was uppermost in his mind. "What brings you to Kent, my lord?"

"I'm on my way to Dover, and I heard you were visiting Ashford." Harry counted himself fortunate he'd not yet left for London. He'd only have passed Porter going the other direction.

"You wished to speak with me?" he asked. He glanced at Ashford for insight into Porter's presence, but Ashford appeared as curious as Harry.

"I do. As you probably know, the Commission is nearing their final selections for the Transit of Venus expeditions, including the lead position for Cairo."

Harry nodded. He couldn't tell from the expression on Porter's face if this would bode well for him or not.

"I know you've applied for the position, and to be honest, you're my first choice."

Harry sensed a "but." He wasn't wrong.

"But there are those who hold considerable

influence over the other members. I'm afraid the Commissioners have set their sights on another to lead Cairo."

The air left Harry's lungs on a painful exhale.

"Who?" Ashford demanded.

Porter sighed. "Knowles. He's calling in favors, it would seem."

Harry's jaw clenched. Knowles, who didn't even believe the earth revolved around the sun, would lead an expedition to watch another planet do that very thing. Knowles, who believed the sun was *inhabited*.

Had Porter come all this way to tell him this? Was this the end of his Cairo plans? He had worked too long, too hard, for this. That had to count for something, didn't it? But he knew—history had taught him—that hard work and intellect were not enough in a world that valued rank and power and position. The field of astronomy was still very much a gentleman's pursuit. Until it was recognized as a formal discipline of its own, he—and every untitled scientist dependent on educational grants—would encounter similar obstacles.

His stomach turned, and his father's face appeared in his mind. William Corbyn had never approved of Harry's aspirations. He'd warned that reaching higher than one's station would only lead to a prideful fall. Harry imagined his father would be pleased—gleeful, even—to see his lessons were finally proving out.

Then he looked at Ashford, whose own face was blanched beneath beads of sweat. "My lord?" he said in alarm. "Perhaps we should sit."

Ashford leaned on his cane and took a seat, drawing a deep breath as he perched on the edge of a wide armchair.

"It can't be over," Ashford said. "They don't make their final selections for another two months, do they?"

"No," Porter said, "it's not over, but it doesn't look good. I came hoping to strategize with Mr. Corbyn on his application. Cairo is an important part of the overall expedition. It's central to the other sites, so it's critical that the right team is selected. Knowles will only jeopardize the entire endeavor."

"The expedition depends on all the sites taking accurate measurements," Harry explained to Ashford, "but Cairo is central to collecting all of that information."

He turned back to Porter. "I appreciate your confidence, but what do you think can be done?"

"I'm not sure, but Ashford was telling me about the telescope project you're leading."

"I'm not leading it. I'm merely directing the work to Ashford's specifications."

"There's no 'merely' about it, Harry. This project

wouldn't be anywhere without your leadership."

"Thank you, my lord," Harry said. "But what does the telescope have to do with Cairo?" he asked Porter.

"I'm intrigued by Ashford's project, and the work you're doing. The other Commissioners will be as well. It has the potential to transform the field of astronomy, to make history. If it's successful, it could go a long way to swaying their opinion during the final selection, Knowles' favors notwithstanding."

"Well, then," Ashford said. His face had regained some of its normal color, and Harry relaxed a little. "Let us show you history in the making."

And so, they did.

They led Porter to the Hill where work was proceeding well. Remy, for all Ashford's mistrust of the man, was a remarkably astute engineer. Over the last weeks, he and Harry had amassed a small army to complete the work. Harry surveyed their progress with pride before recalling his father's grave predictions.

He wiped the smile from his face and walked Porter through the workings of the telescope, and their strategies for resolving the mirror's optical issues. Porter nodded and asked questions, marveling at all that had been completed in a short amount of time.

When they showed him the small stone

outbuilding where the mirror would be cast, Porter stroked his side whiskers thoughtfully. "A mirror of this size will take quite a bit of time to craft. Herschel spent months perfecting his, and he's never been satisfied with the optical quality. Do you think it will be ready in time?"

Harry's heart kicked up a pace, as it always did when he calculated the work remaining against the time they had left. He had strong doubts, but Ashford spoke up before he could temper Porter's enthusiasm.

"It will be ready."

CHAPTER FIFTEEN

HARRY WATCHED PORTER'S CARRIAGE PULL away, then he left the house. He walked through the formal gardens to the woods beyond, turning over this latest problem. Cairo was not a sure thing. He'd known that, and Lord Porter's report only confirmed it.

He needed an alternate plan.

Halfway between Redstone Hall and Fernwood, the cool shadow of trees gave way to a grassy, sunlit clearing with a small pond. He stood at the edge of the shallow water and watched sunlight glimmer and dance on the surface. The pond had changed little since he and Julian had fished here. Or since he and Celeste had ventured across on makeshift ships. Without the distraction of the construction on the Hill, the cool, quiet air allowed his mind to clear.

He had options if Cairo didn't work out. There were always options.

One: He could return to the Royal Academy in Berlin. Although his project with Herr Kraus had come to an end, more experiments would soon be underway. Perhaps he could join a team there.

Two: He could write his former professor at Cambridge. The man had hinted several times that Harry should consider joining the faculty as a research fellow or lecturer. Either would suffice, he supposed, so long as he could pursue his own research interests.

And Cambridge, he consoled himself, was not as far from Redstone Hall as Cairo. He could visit Lord Ashford and the Flying Pig if he so desired. What was he thinking? Cambridge was a poor substitute for Cairo.

Three: Britain would send numerous expeditions for the transit of Venus. If there wasn't a role for him in Cairo, perhaps he could go to . . . the Sandwich Islands, or New Zealand. Or frigid and windswept Christmas Harbour. He didn't fancy joining an expedition on the edges of the project, although he realized that all the sites would be instrumental to the overall goal.

Four: Other nations were sending expeditions as well. He could join the Germans, or the Americans. Although it was likely their teams had already been—or soon would be—selected as well.

Five . . . He scrubbed a hand over his face.

Nothing more came to him. So, he had four options, it would seem. None of which appealed so much as his preferred choice of joining the Cairo expedition.

And yet, he was surprised by how calm he felt. Yes, Porter had delivered disappointing news about Knowles and his influence on the Commission members. And yes, there was now even more at stake for the successful completion of the Flying Pig. But while their chances of success were slim, it wasn't insurmountable. And there was no need to travel to London at present. That was . . . agreeable.

He sighed. He really should apologize to Celeste.

—

CELESTE LEFT THE LABORATORY IN a rich temper. It had been some time since she'd felt so much . . . irritation. No, not irritation . . . anger. A blood-red wash coated her vision. She forced her mind to calm, her colors to right themselves, then she replayed her disagreement with Harry in her mind.

He was clearly upset about something, and he'd chosen to exorcise his frustrations on her. His pencil, indeed! And her paintbrushes . . . She tossed the brush on the small writing table in her bedchamber, ignoring the annoying whisper of conscience that suggested he might have been correct about that. She did leave her painting things about. Sometimes.

But he didn't have to be so rude. It wasn't like Harry. He was one of the kindest, gentlest men she knew. And she'd accused him of leaving the inkwell dry. A trivial thing, to be sure, but she could no more control the words flying from her mouth than she could . . . stop him from going to London.

And truly, wasn't that what angered her the most? That he was leaving, and she couldn't stop him? It didn't matter that this trip was only for a week or two. Soon he would leave for good.

She sighed. She should apologize.

After checking his usual places within the house, she changed into boots and left through the conservatory. She marched up the path toward the Hill, yanking her skirt from the brambles that clawed her hem.

She reached the fork in the path and paused. To the left lay the way to Fernwood and the pond. Straight ahead, the Hill and the telescope.

Instinct compelled her toward the pond, and she turned left. The woods were thicker here, the air cooler. Mud sucked at her boots until she reached the soft, grassy edge of the trees that rimmed the pond. As the canopy of branches opened onto blue sky, she shielded her eyes. She'd forgotten her bonnet again.

She was not surprised to see Harry at the edge of the bank. She was growing used to his pull, so it was no wonder she'd been drawn here. His shoulders were rounded, hands in his pockets. Tension rolled from his body like ripples on the pond.

He glanced at her from the corner of his eye, but he didn't turn. Gazing out over the pond, she curled her hand around his arm and pulled until his hand left his pocket. Her hand crept into his larger one, and she wound her fingers through his. His shoulders sagged, and he squeezed her hand. They stood like that for some time before he spoke.

"I apologize," he said softly. "For earlier. I was unforgivably rude."

"No, Harry. You were right. I should not disrupt your things. I'm sorry."

After another few moments, he said, "I'm not leaving for London. I may not be going to Cairo after all."

She knew a moment of relief before the full import of his words registered. She looked at him, but his gaze was still directed toward the water. "What do you mean?"

"Lord Porter paid a visit. He believes the Commission is leaning toward Lord Knowles to lead the Cairo expedition."

"Knowles? But that's—I'm no scientist, but even I know he's a poor choice!" She winced and brought her voice down to a more properly modulated tone. "Harry, I'm so sorry. They'll be fools not to accept you! If they want the most knowledgeable pig-flyer to lead their expedition, they'll select you. I have confidence." He smiled, as she'd intended. "I know this is what you've been working so hard for. Is there truly no chance then?"

He turned toward her. "Lord Porter thinks your father's telescope will impress the Commission. If we complete it, that is. So, it's still possible, but I need to consider other options. I've been thinking I could apply for one of the other expeditions. Britain is sending teams to the Sandwich Islands and Christmas Harbour. But it's likely they've already narrowed down their selections for those as well."

"Christmas Harbour sounds . . . pleasant." She smiled at him.

"Don't let the name fool you. It's on a frigid island near the southern pole. There are penguins."

Her eyes widened. That sounded less pleasant. "What's so important about this expedition?" she asked.

Harry's eyes met hers, and her own burned at the intensity she saw there. "A transit of Venus only happens every century or so when Venus passes over the face of the sun. By measuring that crossing, at different points around the earth, we hope to calculate the size of our solar system. It's an opportunity we won't see again in our lifetime."

"But how? I don't understand."

He looked at her for a moment, then he moved behind her. She watched him over her shoulder. He lifted her right arm and folded her hand into a fist.

"Extend your thumb."

Her hand tingled where he held it, but she extended her thumb. His warm amber and oak scent wrapped around her, and she suppressed a shiver.

"Now, close one eye and mark where your thumb is in relation to the opposite bank," he said, his voice low and rumbly in her ear. She felt silly, standing there with one eye closed, but she did as he asked. "Now, keep your thumb there, but switch eyes. Do you see how your thumb appears to move?"

She tried it. "Yes, but what does it mean?"

"Your eyes represent two of the expedition points, say, Cairo and the Sandwich Islands. We know the distance between the two. If we measure how much your thumb moves, we can use geometry to calculate the distance from your eyes to your thumb, so to speak."

"You can calculate the distance to the sun."

"Exactly." He smiled and his approval warmed her insides. "And one day perhaps, the size of our universe."

She held her thumb in front of her, Harry at her back, and switched eyes again. Mathematics had never been her favorite subject, but she thought she could stand there all day if he were behind her, whispering in her ear. He cleared his throat and stepped away, and she remembered to breathe.

"What will you do if you don't go to Cairo?"

"I'm not sure." After a beat, he continued. "My consolation is that I now have more time to put wings on our pig." He angled his head toward the Hill.

She pasted a smile on her face, although her soul wept for him. He wore a brave face, but she read stark disappointment in his eyes, in the curve of his shoulders. He was watching his dream shatter, like fine china on stone, and the reverberation echoed off her heart.

———

CELESTE AND HARRY LEFT THE pond and joined the others on the Hill to survey the afternoon's progress. Remy perched midway up the scaffolding, assisting two men secure a heavy beam. In a few days, they'd be ready to maneuver the iron tube into place.

Just then, Marchand's golden head topped the rise, followed by Lady Ashford's. Celeste stepped away, putting distance between her and Harry. Harry watched with resignation as Marchand approached.

"So, this is what all the excitement is about," Marchand said. "It's quite . . . impressive." He gazed at the lofty structure, shielding his eyes against the sun.

"Let me show you how it works," Celeste said. She led Marchand toward the base and began pointing out the pulleys and where the viewing platform would be. Harry felt Lady Ashford's gaze on him as he watched Celeste and Marchand.

"You and my daughter have been acquainted for quite some time, Mr. Corbyn."

It was a statement more than a question, but he felt compelled to answer. "Yes."

Her gaze was direct on him, and he resisted the urge to look away. "What do you think will make her happy?" she asked.

"I'm not sure I understand, Lady Ashford."

"I think you must know her like no one else does. More even than I or Ashford. I find myself curious to know what kind of life will satisfy her."

He frowned, considering his words. "Lady Celeste isn't so very hard to know. She wants what we all want."

Lady Ashford's delicate brows raised in question, and he continued. "We like to believe there's a purpose to our lives, a significance despite the vastness all around us. She wants nothing more than for someone to see her, to witness her life and know that she's significant."

Lady Ashford gazed at him, measuring. Finally, she nodded once and turned back to the telescope. "You, sir, have the mind of a scientist but, I think, the heart of a poet." And with that, she left him standing alone.

———

THE HOUR HAD GROWN LATE by the time Harry descended the Hill. He found Lord Ashford tinkering with a sextant in the transit room, his cane leaning against the wall. He held a rag in one hand as he polished the brass, squinting at a perceived scratch.

Harry wondered at Ashford's life. He had his observatory and instruments, and the freedom to pursue his interests. But until recently, he'd lived in this large estate alone, with no family. Was his passion for astronomy enough to satisfy him?

Would he also be alone in twenty years? He'd never given it much thought. He'd assumed he would continue on as he always had been, but such a solitary existence now seemed . . . empty.

Ashford looked up at Harry's entrance and smiled. He continued polishing as they discussed Remy's progress with the wooden mount. When Harry began outlining their plans to install the tube, Ashford set the sextant down and interrupted him.

"Knowles is a mutton-headed clodpate. He's a complete chowderhead."

Harry couldn't disagree, so he nodded, lips twisted in a rueful smile. And then, because Ashford expected more, he added, "A witless loobie."

Ashford clapped him on the shoulder and grinned. "Bacon-brained scoundrel."

"Dunderhead."

"Lubbardly lout."

"Blunderbuss."

After they exhausted their repertoire of insults, some less refined than others, Harry felt marginally better about the whole affair. Not happy by any stretch, but some of the edge of his earlier frustration had worn off.

He still didn't know what his next step would be, or if he could actually secure the Cairo position. But Ashford's stout defense was a vindication of sorts, and Harry's affection for this man grew even more.

He thought again of his father. William Corbyn had been a simple man with a strong liking for gin, and none for books. If the life of an innkeeper was good enough for him, it was bloody well good enough for his son, and he reminded Harry of the sentiment often. *Reaching higher than one's station only leads to a prideful fall.*

But Harry's uncle Albert, his mother's only brother, had argued for Harry's education on behalf of his late sister. And so, against his father's objections, Harry had found himself alone on a stage bound for Eton. He'd been nine years old.

He recalled his first visit home, when he'd still been young enough to be hopeful. He'd bounced with excitement to tell his father of his good marks. He was also eager to make his older sister Eleanor jealous with stories of his adventures.

But his sister had married by then and had a babe of her own. She'd rolled her eyes at Harry's excitement, and his father had grumbled that book learning wouldn't see their inn through a slow winter.

William Corbyn ignored Harry's every attempt to tell him about his months away. When the next holiday came, Harry accepted Julian's invitation to travel to Fernwood. He'd been awed — and envious — when Sir John asked Julian about his term. It wasn't a stretch to understand why, when Lord Ashford had taken an interest in young Harry, he'd been intrigued by the man.

Ashford wrote to him often while he was away at school, inquiring after his studies and praising him when no one else did. Indeed, Ashford's were often the only letters Harry received. Uncle Albert was an irregular correspondent at best, despite his regular tuition payments.

When Albert died in Harry's fifteenth year, Harry had mourned his uncle as well as his education. With no funds for tuition, he'd been certain his father's prophesy would come to pass, but then the unexpected had happened.

"My lord," Harry said suddenly, handing Ashford his rag. "When my uncle died, I thought my schooling was at an end. As you probably know, I didn't have the funds for tuition."

Ashford resumed his polishing, eyes focused on his sextant and its nonexistent scratch.

Harry crossed his arms. "But the dean said there was a grant that covered my expenses. For the rest of that term, and the next after that. And the next." He paused and looked at Ashford before he continued. "Did you—do you know anything about that?"

"Me? Why would I know anything about that, my boy?"

Harry hadn't expected Ashford to confess, but it would have been nice to express his gratitude.

The older man stopped his polishing and placed a hand on Harry's shoulder. "I'm sorry your father wasn't there for you, Harry. Everyone needs someone to see their potential, to encourage it."

Harry nodded and swallowed against the lump in his throat. "Well, for what it's worth, that grant made all the difference."

"Duly noted, my boy."

CHAPTER SIXTEEN

THE DAY THEY PLANNED TO install the iron tube promised to be clear and hot. The solstice had come and gone some weeks back, and summer was upon them.

Harry had organized teams of horses, and men to drive them, while Remy had drawn up plans for lifting and levering the mammoth tube into place on the track that bisected the platform.

Despite the early hour, Celeste was not about to miss the excitement. When she crested the Hill, the gamekeeper's children crouched in the trees ringing the broad, flat hilltop. Robbie and Jenny swiveled their heads from side to side as men raced around the wooden structure, attaching ropes, and calling commands to one another. Lilliputians to the telescope's Gulliver.

Robbie took his sister's hand when Celeste approached them. She smiled and encouraged them to come forward to see better.

"Is it true? Will the stars be closer when we look through the tube?" Robbie asked.

"Yes, that's the hope. The tube will provide a view of more stars than we can see with our eyes alone."

Robbie's eyes grew round. "How many stars? A hundred?"

Celeste plucked a blade of grass and held it up to the sunlight. "Do you see this blade of grass?"

They nodded.

"Now imagine how many blades of grass there are across all the fields before us." She indicated the valley below the Hill. "And think about how many blades of grass grow from Marshfield to Ansley."

Robbie's brow wrinkled as his eyebrows drew together.

"That's how many stars are in the sky. There are so many we can't begin to imagine the size of the heavens. Although Mr. Corbyn there is going to try."

Harry had approached, and they gazed at him in suspicion. He gazed back, pencil poised over his notebook.

"I bet you can't count that high," Robbie challenged.

Harry smiled. "It will be a monumental challenge, to be sure." He started to return to his notebook, then he added, "But everything in the universe, everything we see and everything we don't see, is knowable. If we look hard enough and shine a bright enough torch, we can see the answers."

Robbie crossed his arms, still skeptical. But Jenny, who was not too old for fairy tales, gazed at Harry as if he himself had hung the stars. Celeste knew the feeling well.

———

REMY HURRIED TOWARD HARRY, NOTEBOOK tapping against his leg. "The men are all set, sir."

Harry surveyed the scene before him. The tube had been rolled into place behind the platform's bisecting track. They'd secured eight of the sturdiest draft horses in the county, and four teams were hitched, ready to pull the tube forward. A small army of men stood with ropes to help guide the tube as the horses pulled.

Quite the audience had turned out for the day's event. Celeste held the children's hands a safe distance from the tube. Lord Ashford leaned on his cane, hat shielding his eyes from the sun, while Lady Ashford stood at his side. Even Marchand and Miss Pepper had come to watch, the latter dressed becomingly in a fussy bonnet and dainty slippers. (She still refused to wear sensible boots.) Miss Pepper's manner was flirtatious, although Marchand's face gave away nothing of his own thoughts.

All was ready. "We're set," he told Remy.

They assumed their positions at the front of the tube, pulled on heavy leather gloves and lifted their ropes. At Remy's signal, the horses pulled, and the tube began its slow progress along the track.

Harry's attention swiveled from the horses to the men, to the tube and back to be sure all was well. One misstep was all it would take for the tube to slip off the ropes and crush a foot, a leg, or a man.

The sun was higher now and heated the ground beneath their feet. The birds, normally vocal in the nearby trees, had gone silent. Only the sounds of straining men and horses and metal sliding against wood and ropes could be heard. Inch by inch, the metal advanced over the wooden rails until, at last, Remy called a halt.

He checked the placement of the tube then nodded at Harry. The men shouted, relaxing their hold on the ropes. Harry knew they didn't fully comprehend the significance of the day's work or what this step would mean for the future of astronomy. They were honest men, earning a day's wage. But for Harry, the promise of knowledge — wrapped in a simple metal tube resting on a bare wooden track — was seductive. He looked up and caught Celeste's eye and grinned.

Over the course of the afternoon, they installed a system of pulleys and winches that would allow them to adjust the angle of the telescope. Harry's hands burned from hours of threading coarse hemp through the pulleys, and sweat slicked his face.

He knew Celeste had come and gone, and come again, bringing servants with baskets of food and ale for the laborers. She called up to him as he and Remy installed the final pulley at the top of the structure.

"Your lady awaits," Remy said.

Harry squinted, concentrating on his task, and grunted in reply. "She's not my lady." There, the bolt slipped into place.

"Perhaps you should tell that to Miss Pepper. She seems a mite . . . perturbed."

Harry looked down to where Miss Pepper stood with her mother. When had the Pepper ladies returned? Soft muslin draped her petite frame. He couldn't see her features beneath the broad brim of her bonnet, but her posture was rigid. She didn't look pleased to be back on the Hill.

As he watched, Celeste handed them baskets and motioned to the laborers. He could hear an outraged sniff from his position forty feet above, and he chuckled.

"Watch that one," Remy said before beginning the climb down.

———

CELESTE FIXED A SMILE ON her face when she saw Miss Pepper crest the hill with her mother, wearing a fresh dress and another pretty bonnet on her curls.

"Heavens, Lady Celeste," Mrs. Pepper said. "Whatever are you doing here again? You must be bored to tears." Celeste could have said as much to Miss Pepper, for her manner was not that of a lady intrigued. The younger lady surveyed the dirt and industry of the hilltop with a blank expression, hands clasped tightly before her.

"On the contrary," Celeste assured Mrs. Pepper. "It's rewarding to see how much has been accomplished in such a short time, and the gentlemen will be ready to test the pulleys shortly." She handed a mug of ale to Roberts, the blacksmith's son.

Celeste didn't have much in common with the Peppers, but since they were particular friends of Harry's, she tried to be hospitable. She studied Miss Pepper and searched her mind for something to say.

"Your bonnet is charming, Miss Pepper. I especially like the little bird perched on the brim."

Miss Pepper's face brightened. "Isn't it the most darling thing?" Her forehead creased as she reached a hand to assure herself the little wren was safely in its nest.

Mrs. Pepper gave her daughter an arch look and murmured, "Wrinkles, my dear."

Miss Pepper quickly smoothed her forehead, resuming her placid expression as her mother turned to Celeste.

"It must be . . . freeing . . . to not concern yourself

overmuch with freckles." Mrs. Pepper nodded at Celeste's bonnet-less hair then motioned to her daughter's own milky complexion. "I fear one minute in the sun would render my Anna a freckle-faced country miss."

Miss Pepper had the grace to look embarrassed at *that* conversational lob. Celeste pressed her lips together to avoid responding. Instead, she lifted the baskets at her feet and handed one to each of the Pepper ladies. "I wonder if you would assist me distribute luncheon to the men?"

Miss Pepper's eyes widened while her mother's brows dipped in consternation. When Mrs. Pepper realized Celeste was serious, she sniffed loudly before accepting her basket.

Later, Celeste turned to find Harry at her elbow, poking about in the remaining basket next to her. She handed him an apple and some warm bread. Heat radiated from him and sweat dampened his dark hair. He'd shed his jacket, and his linen shirt clung to his chest and arms. He was wholly too appealing. Until she got a whiff of him. He'd been working in the sun all day, and his normal, comforting scent of amber and oak was . . . Well.

She realized with a start that he waited for her to release a cloth-wrapped wedge of cheese, and she let it go.

"It seems everyone is interested in the day's

progress." Harry motioned with his bread to where Alexandre had returned to the Hill. They watched as the Pepper ladies intercepted him, and Alexandre relieved them of their baskets. Miss Pepper's giggle reached them, a tinkling sound that chimed like silver bells as she placed a hand on Alexandre's forearm.

Celeste cocked her head to the side as the pair laughed together. They were ... flirting. Hmm. Celeste probed her emotions. Like pushing her tongue against a sore tooth, she waited to feel something. Certainly, watching one's suitor flirt with another lady *should have* made her jealous.

Angry, perhaps.

Dismayed, at the very least.

But she felt ... curiously ... nothing. The air around her was colorless. But if the suitor who flirted so shamelessly with another had been a different man ... one with dark hair and smoky grey eyes ... The thought didn't bear thinking.

———

HARRY CRUNCHED HIS APPLE AS he watched Celeste watching Marchand. He was surprised to see the man trifling with Miss Pepper, but he'd learned the lady was nothing if not a persistent flirt.

He remained silent, waiting for Celeste's reaction, but it never came. If she considered marrying the man, surely she'd not approve of his open flirtation, would she? Celeste wasn't the sort of lady who would sit by while her husband dallied with another. He knew such marriages were common among the aristocracy, but if *he* were married to Celeste and behaved in such a way, she would take his head off. He was certain of it. The thought caused him to smile even as he edged away from her.

"Harry, you need a bath." She wrinkled her nose.

"I don't doubt it. But first, let's check our pig's wings." He saluted her with his cheese then went to find Ashford.

"I think we're ready, my lord," Harry told him. Ashford nodded and leaned on his cane as Roberts and Remy began turning large metal cranks.

Inch by inch, the ropes advanced through the pulleys. The mouth of the tube lifted slowly, and Harry released a breath. When the iron pointed proudly to a spot just above the horizon, Ashford beamed and stood straighter. They were one step closer.

CHAPTER SEVENTEEN

CELESTE PULLED BACK FROM THE miniature she'd been painting and admitted that her skill had improved. This landscape was far better than the tiny floral motifs of her earlier years. She set her magnifying glass aside as a gust of wind rattled the clerestory windows, swirling leaves beyond the observatory.

She rubbed the stiffness from her neck, surprised to see that daylight was fading. She'd have to hurry to dress for supper. She left the observatory through the transit room and crossed to the laboratory.

Her father sat at his desk, head bent toward his notebook, an intent look on his face. Harry's inkwell and papers were aligned on his desk as usual, but his chair was empty.

"Father, I'm surprised to see Harry left you to it. Did you convince him to have a break?"

"What's that? Oh, no, he went to check on the

progress on the Hill. I thought he would be back by now, though," he said absently.

"With this weather, surely work has stopped for the day." The impending storm was visible through the terrace doors. Trees beyond the garden wall bent and swayed, and the fronds of a willow danced.

As the supper hour approached and Harry still had not returned, Celeste grew concerned. Wind continued to buffet the house, and the rain would begin soon. When Odette arrived to help her dress for supper, she made a decision. "Odette, bring my cloak please."

"Lady Celeste, you can't mean to go out in this weather!"

"It's not far to the Hill. I'll be back before I'm missed."

She grabbed an oil lantern from the kitchens then exited through the gardens. Wind whipped her cloak about her ankles and icy needles pricked her skin with the first sharp drops of rain.

The acrid scent of the impending storm was heavy in the air, and she hurried her steps. The sight that met her at the top of the Hill left her speechless. The telescope's wooden mount stood in eerie silhouette against the fading twilight, but what caught her attention was the viewing platform. Or what was left of it. The men had completed it just that day, but now it lay in splinters at the base of the structure, a heavy tree limb near the remains.

And several feet from that . . . a prone figure. Harry! She gasped, her hand to her throat, and rushed toward him. Dread crystallized in her blood at the sight of his still form.

"Harry! Harry, wake up!" She prodded him and checked for injuries. He groaned, and she felt blood on the back of his head.

The rain came in earnest then. Frigid sheets that slashed across her vision and doused the summer heat. Steam rose from the ground around them.

"Harry, can you hear me?"

His silvery eyes fluttered and tried to focus on her face.

"Harry, a storm's coming. Can you walk?"

"Celeste?" His gaze was unfocused.

"I'm here. But I need you to walk. Can you stand?" He squinted and narrowed his eyes until he brought her face into focus, then he struggled to his feet. A pained look crossed his face when he put weight on his foot. She braced him with her shoulder while the wind and rain whipped around them.

She lifted the lantern in one hand, grateful for its illumination, then guided Harry around the ruined bits of wood to make their slow descent down the darkening hill. It was clear his head and ankle pained him.

Soon, voices reached them from the path below.

Remy appeared with another lantern and several men. Her father and Marchand brought up the rear. Bless Odette. Celeste relinquished Harry into their hands, admonishing them to have a care for his head.

———

HARRY'S HEAD POUNDED AS RAIN streamed down his face, and his ankle throbbed. Someone—Remy, he thought—supported him on one side. He tried to clear his mind, wipe the haze from his clouded thoughts and recall what had happened, but his mind was muddled, stuffed with wool.

He'd left the house as the weather turned, intent on checking the day's progress. With only weeks until the unveiling, time was short, even accounting for his aborted trip to London.

He'd carefully checked the pulleys and the newly installed tube, given the charge in the air and the increasing moans of the wind. His memories from there were murky until Celeste had arrived. He recalled her worried frown as she'd stared down at him, hair dripping into his face.

He turned from his plodding descent to confirm he'd not imagined her.

Marchand held an arm to guide her down the path. She was soaked through, cinnamon curls pressed to her cheek, her sodden wool cloak poor protection from the sideways rain. She caught his eye and smiled then urged him on with a wave of her hand.

Later, he sat before a warm fire in his room as a servant dried his hair and wrapped him in a thick wool blanket. He was uncomfortable with the attention, not used to servants tending him, but Ashford sat nearby and wouldn't permit him to do anything until Julian checked him out.

"My boy," Ashford began, swallowed, and started again. "When Celeste said she found you unconscious, my heart nearly stopped. This project is not worth your health."

"The telescope—"

"Will live to see another day, I assure you. It looks like the wind took some trees near the top of the Hill, and a hefty branch struck the viewing platform. It's nothing that can't be repaired. You, on the other hand . . ."

"But my lord—"

"Dr. Grey should be here soon. In the meantime, you should get some rest."

"I don't need a doctor," Harry protested.

"I say you need a doctor, so you need a doctor."

Harry relented, too tired to protest. "Yes, my lord."

"Yes, well . . ." Ashford trailed off then pushed himself to his feet, balancing his hand on his cane. A tap sounded at the door, and Celeste poked her head in.

Ashford motioned her in and moved to leave.

"Keep the door open, m'dear."

Celeste nodded and stepped further into the room. Aware of how pitiful he must appear, wrapped in a blanket, he moved to stand.

"Don't," she said, motioning him back to his chair. "Shouldn't you be in bed?"

"I'm told the good doctor will be here shortly. I'm sure I'll be abed soon enough." He hadn't intended his words to come out so shortly. What was wrong with him?

She pressed her lips in that way he recognized when she was irritated. Well, he had a raging headache, so she could afford to be a little irritated. His ankle throbbed in time with his heartbeat. She crossed the room and knelt by his chair. When she placed her warm hands on his forearm, a shiver traveled up to his shoulder.

"Harry, I confess you had me worried. When I found you on the ground . . ."

He glanced at her out of the corner of his eye. Was she concerned? For him? Yes, that looked like worry in her eyes. He sat up straighter to reassure her, and she tucked the blanket more firmly around him. His reassurance died on his lips. It wouldn't hurt to enjoy her ministrations for a bit, would it?

"How are you feeling? Well, of course, you must be feeling poorly." Tuck, tuck.

"Well, my head—"

"Oh, yes, I think you must have been struck by something." She ran her fingers through his hair, feeling the knot on the back of his head. His scalp tingled at her soft touch. She looked into his eyes, a worried frown wrinkling her brow.

"Julian should be here soon. Perhaps he can give you something for the pain. I'm sure it must hurt something fierce. How's your ankle?"

He flexed his foot where it rested on a cushion. "I think I might have twisted it."

She sat on the ottoman next to his leg, and his foot burned where it connected with her hip. She reached for his poor stockinged foot, and he braced himself for her touch. Then she stopped. "We shouldn't move it more than necessary until Julian has a look."

He released a slow, disappointed exhale.

A tap at the open door brought their gazes around to Julian, standing in the entry with his black doctor's bag. He cleared his throat before stepping into the room.

———

HARRY STOOD CLUMSILY FROM HIS seat by the fire, hair sticking out at odd angles from his head. A soft wool blanket draped his shoulders and trailed to the floor. A pale V of skin showed where the blanket gapped near his throat before his dressing gown began. Celeste's heart raced at the sight, and her palms grew damp before she reminded herself he was *injured*. He did not need her gawking at him, no matter how tantalizing that small patch of undressed skin.

Injured. Her heart had stopped, she was sure of it, the moment she saw him lying on the ground. He'd been so still. She couldn't imagine a world without Harry. Even now, the notion sent nausea flooding through her.

Despite her anxiety and Harry's injuries, one positive thing had come from the night's events. She now knew without a doubt that she couldn't marry Alexandre. She finally had her answer. She might admire him and his artistic skill, and they might have shared interests. But she couldn't see spending a lifetime with him. He didn't make her heart pound.

Harry might go to Cairo, and she would probably return to Paris. It was unlikely that they would have a future together. But the feelings she felt for Harry eclipsed anything she would ever feel for Alexandre, and she refused to settle.

———

JULIAN CLOSED THE DOOR BEHIND Celeste and turned to Harry. "I heard you tried to stop a tree with your head."

"Something like that."

"Let's have a look." He pulled a chair toward the bed and motioned for Harry to have a seat on the edge of the four-poster.

"I didn't ask when you tended Ashford: am I

supposed to call you Dr. Grey now?" Harry asked.

"No." Julian chuckled. "The Grey King will be fine."

If Harry had had any strength left, he would've cuffed his friend on the side of his head. In the end, Julian's diagnosis was a concussion and a twisted ankle. He prescribed bed rest for the former and elevation of the leg for the latter.

"You'll feel some dizziness and nausea for a bit, and your head will hurt like the devil for a few days. Send for me if it doesn't improve soon."

"I can't stay in bed. There's too much to do. And now, with the damage to the telescope . . ." How much damage, and how long it would take to repair it, he didn't know. But he couldn't let Ashford down. He shook his head then winced.

"Harry, you've always been stubborn, but now is not the time. Your head and your ankle need time to heal. Doctor's orders."

"And you've always been high-handed. I see some things don't change."

"Yes, well, I earned the right when I finished my medical training. You can order me about when I'm struggling with a math equation, or I need help finding a star, but not before." He waited while Harry settled on the bed then placed a cushion beneath his leg.

As children, Julian had been the scapegrace,

always laughing and making jokes. Never taking himself or anyone else too seriously. But as a physician, he was thoughtful. Sympathetic, almost. The transformation was ... Transformative. Well. Harry marveled at his command of the English language.

"You've grown up," he said.

"It was inevitable, I suppose. How is Lady Celeste?" Julian closed his medical bag, his back to Harry.

Harry blinked at the turn in the conversation and crossed his arms. He sensed a trap. "She's well."

"She's concerned about you."

"She would be concerned about anyone who took a lump on the head. She's a concerned sort of person."

"Harry." Julian turned back to face him. "I don't dispute that fact. But she is *concerned* about you. Don't tell me you're too thick to notice."

"Julian, don't beat about the bush. If there's something you mean to tell me, then tell me."

Julian placed his hands on his hips and exhaled. "I always thought you and Lady Celeste ... You seem well matched. When we were boys, you were closer to her. I admit I was surprised when the two of you went your separate ways."

Harry considered protesting. He opened his mouth to argue, to lie about his affection for Celeste.

Then he looked at Julian's face and knew that his friend *knew*. Julian would call him out on any prevarication.

He exhaled and nodded once. "I don't know what I'm doing here," he confessed, staring at the counterpane.

At Julian's questioning silence, he continued. "I thought to help Lord Ashford, but Celeste is here"—he motioned to his head—"every moment. And when all's said and done, she'll return to Paris, and I'll . . . leave." He scrubbed his hands over his face, wincing as he moved his head.

"So . . . what?" Julian asked. "That's it? You care for her, but your dreams, or some such rot, don't leave room for love?"

Love? Who said anything about love?

Harry sighed. Who was he kidding? Still, he nodded. "That's about the sum of it."

He looked up to see Julian watching him with a thoughtful expression. His friend sighed then said, "So you have no objection if I court her? Do you think she'd settle for a doctor?"

Harry narrowed his eyes at his friend. Celeste and Julian? Years ago, Ashford had said something about Julian courting her. He hadn't believed it then, and he couldn't fathom it now.

Celeste wasn't one to aim for a title, and she wouldn't care that Julian was a doctor. But he didn't think she and Julian had . . . fizz. Hadn't she herself said as much? Julian watched him, waiting for his answer.

"You may have competition from her French suitor. He's waiting for an answer to his proposal." Harry's lips twisted as he mentioned Marchand.

"Ha! I'm not afraid of a Frenchman. The last I heard, she wasn't betrothed yet, so it seems she's fair game. Lady Celeste is a prize worth fighting for."

"She's hardly a trophy to be won in a curricle race." Harry's pulse sped up.

"Easy, my friend. You mustn't become overexcited. I'll check on you again soon. Better yet, you can be my excuse to forgo my mother's grand supper." Julian grimaced.

"Oh, no. You'll not lay the blame at my door for that. Your mother doesn't like me as it is. You and I will both be there, and you can check my head then."

Julian nodded then collected his bag and hat. "Oh, and don't worry yourself overmuch," he said from the doorway. "I proposed to Celeste two years ago, and she turned me down." He pressed a hand to his chest and sighed. "I'll never be the same. But you know, for a genius, you're rather thick."

Harry threw a pillow at Julian as he closed the door. But the room was large, his artillery was soft, and his aim fell short, leaving his pillow to mock him from the floor.

After Julian's laughter faded, Harry climbed between the sheets. His mind kept taking turns with the dual quandaries of Celeste and the evening's events. He closed his eyes and tried to recall the moments before everything went black.

He'd turned at a sound in the trees—footsteps rustling in the leaves, perhaps. Whether from man or animal, he didn't know. He hadn't been able to make out any shapes, but he had the distinct impression someone else had been there. And then later, as he'd flickered in and out of consciousness, he saw a figure below the observation platform.

It would be a long time before he found sleep.

CHAPTER EIGHTEEN

CELESTE KNEW HARRY WOULD BE anxious without his notebook, so she retrieved it from his desk. Plus, it was another excuse to see him again and assure herself he was well.

His black scrawl filled the pages, dark and messy. Sort of like his hair, she reflected, smiling. As she neared the guest wing, she encountered Miss Pepper. Despite the late hour, Miss Pepper's fair curls bounced above a pert ribbon as if she'd just applied the curling tongs. "Are you going to visit our patient?" Celeste asked.

"Oh, yes. I'm sure he must be bored. I thought to read him some poetry."

Poetry. Yes, that will save him from boredom. Harry deserved someone who understood him. Who saw him and recognized his brilliance and vitality. Someone who was *not* Miss Pepper. Did he truly find her appealing? The thought saddened her.

Miss Pepper glanced at the notebook in Celeste's hand. "Would you like me to take that to him?"

"I was just headed there myself. Is your maid joining you?" Celeste asked. She looked around Miss Pepper, ignoring the inconvenient fact that she herself had recently left Harry's room, *sans* maid.

Miss Pepper cocked her head to the side and studied Celeste, eyes narrowing. "What is your interest in Mr. Corbyn? Do the two of you have an understanding?"

Celeste's eyes widened. "My interest in Mr. Corbyn is nothing more than friendship." Her heart pinched uncomfortably before she added, "We've been acquainted for years, as I'm sure he must have told you."

"I'm afraid Harry"—Celeste ground her teeth at Miss Pepper's familiarity—"never mentioned you. But we've had so many other things to discuss, old acquaintances just didn't come up."

"Do you care for him, then?"

Miss Pepper glanced behind her as if to assure herself they were alone. Then with a shrug, she said, "He's bound for Cairo soon, for an extended period of time. I imagine it's an arrangement that would suit us both."

That was her scheme? She wished for an absent husband?

"But . . . what about love? Don't you wish to fall

in love and marry someone you *want* to spend your life with?"

Miss Pepper smiled without mirth. "Marriage is a necessity, Lady Celeste, but love is a fairy tale. Surely, at your age, you know that."

Celeste clenched her teeth. She didn't think Miss Pepper's idea of marriage was something Harry would enjoy. When he committed, he pledged himself wholeheartedly. Just look at her father's telescope.

Then she remembered Harry might not be going to Cairo. How interesting that Miss Pepper didn't know that yet. Celeste smiled sweetly and handed the other lady his notebook.

"If you would kindly take this to Harry, I'm sure he will appreciate it."

She excused herself then went in search of Odette. Miss Pepper may not desire a chaperone, but Harry would need one.

———

HARRY'S EYES WERE DRIFTING CLOSED—finally—when his senses came alert to the sound of the door opening. A single candle still burned in a sconce on the wall, casting long shadows around the room. He was instantly awake. He held his breath until he realized the form entering his room was female.

"Celeste?"

Too late, he realized the female approaching was

too short to be Celeste. He pulled himself up higher on the pillows, wincing at the pounding in his skull. Miss Pepper's artful blond curls came into view as she stepped out of the shadow and into the faint light. "Miss Pepper?" he asked.

She smiled prettily. "I came to see how you're getting on. I was worried when I heard of your accident." She touched a fingertip to the corner of her eye.

"You needn't worry on my account," he assured her. "I'll be right as rain soon enough. Oh, Miss Pepper, you should leave the door open." She twisted her lips and he thought she would refuse, but she went to the door and cracked it an inch, maybe two.

"I've brought a book of poetry. I thought I could read to help you pass the time." She threw a coy look at him through her lashes, and Harry became alarmed. He didn't have the energy to fend her off with a lengthy explanation of Mr. Newton's *Mathematical Principles of Natural Philosophy*.

"That's . . . thoughtful. What else have you brought?" He motioned to the other book she carried, which looked like one of his journals.

"Oh, Lady Celeste asked me to bring this to you, but you should avoid taxing your mind too much." She placed the journal on a table out of his reach. He looked at it longingly. She settled in a chair near the bed, fanning her skirts and twisting a springy curl about her finger. He was not good at discerning when a lady was practicing her seductive wiles, but he started to panic.

The door opened wider, and a maid entered. He recognized Odette, the pretty French maid who had Remy's eye. She took a chair near the fireplace, with direct line of sight to the bed, and unfolded some mending in her lap.

At their questioning glance, she said primly, "Lady Celeste thought you—Miss Pepper, that is— might desire the *chaperon*."

Harry grinned and settled back against the pillow, relaxed now that his virtue was safe. "Miss Pepper?" He motioned to the slim volume of poetry in her hand.

She smoothed a faint scowl from her face and opened the book. Before she could begin, though, she asked, "When do you expect to continue to London?"

He looked up in surprise. "Didn't your uncle speak with you?"

At her look of confusion, he said, "I won't be returning to London just yet."

"But . . . but what about Cairo? Your expedition?"

"As it turns out, I may not be joining the Cairo expedition." He rolled the edge of the coverlet under his finger. "I believe your uncle plans to continue to London, however."

She nodded once, her eyes measuring him. Did she not believe him?

"You're staying here, then, with Lady Celeste?"

"I'm remaining to help Lord Ashford with his telescope project." With Lady Celeste.

She looked at him, then at the maid, before standing.

"What about the poetry?" he asked, motioning to her book.

"I'm sure you need your sleep after such a harrowing evening." She crossed the room with dainty steps, the poetry volume clasped in both hands.

Once she had gone, the maid stood. She set his journal on the table next to the bed, within reach. "*Bonne nuit*, Mr. Corbyn," she said.

"Thank you, Odette." The door closed, and his lids grew heavy. Images of Celeste's blue-green eyes soothed him to sleep.

————

HARRY ROSE EARLY AND DRESSED, careful of his ankle and his still-throbbing head. He wrapped his stockinged foot in a length of muslin to stabilize it like Julian had shown him, but he skipped his boot. It would never fit over the muslin or the swelling, anyway.

He rubbed an unsteady hand over the dark stubble on his jaw. He didn't mean to survive a thump on the head just to slice his own throat.

Shaving would have to wait for another day.

Next, he sent for Remy. The man's response to his summons was gratifyingly prompt. He was out of his livery and dressed to work in tan breeches, linen shirt and grey overcoat.

"I need your help, Remy, and your discretion," Harry said.

Remy stood straighter and gripped the lapels of his coat. "Of course. How can I assist, sir?"

Harry explained his suspicions that someone had been on the Hill. The other man's brow furrowed as he listened to Harry's tale.

"I need you to check the scene," Harry said. "See if you can find anything that will tell us who may have been there, or what they were doing. There's no reason to suspect anything nefarious, but don't let Ashford or Lady Celeste go up there alone. Don't let *anyone* go up there alone, for that matter."

"You can rely on me. I also performed some intelligence work during the war."

Harry's brows angled down. Why was he not surprised? The man had hidden depths. "Yes, well, let's hope it's not as grave as that."

Remy gave him a jaunty salute as he left, and Harry rolled his eyes.

———

REMY WAS LEAVING HARRY'S ROOM as Celeste approached. "How is the patient?" she asked.

"Well enough," he replied, "although he could use a shave."

"I'm right here," Harry called from inside his room.

"Oh, I see what you mean." She eyed Harry critically then said to Remy, "Please ask Cranston to attend Mr. Corbyn."

"Still here."

"You could do it," Remy whispered.

"What? Shave him?" Her voice squeaked on the question, although the thought was intriguing. Heart-poundingly so as she pictured her hands holding his firm jaw, lathering soap above his sculpted lip . . .

"No, she can't," came from inside the room.

Celeste smiled. "Just send Cranston, please."

"Yes, Lady Celeste." Remy strode off, a glint of determination in his eye as though he were on a covert mission. Truly, his dedication was remarkable.

Celeste entered Harry's room and noted the irritated expression on his face. He did indeed need a shave. His night whiskers were dark on his jaw, and her stomach swooped to her toes. She liked this roughened Harry and wondered what the sharp planes of his whiskered cheeks would feel like beneath her fingers.

She fanned herself and his scowl grew. His

inactivity must be grating on him, but she was here to help.

"Private St. James, at your service, sir. I've brought my notebook. You only need tell me what to do, and it shall be done. Your wish is my command."

His lips twisted in a sardonic smile at her teasing and his eyes crinkled.

"Let me rephrase that," she said, recalling one particular afternoon when that sort of promise had gotten her into trouble. She'd been playing Knights and Dragons with Harry and Julian and, as was her habit, she'd insisted on being a knight. Julian and Harry had argued that as the only female, it was left to her to be the damsel. She'd begged and pleaded and promised to follow their every instruction if they would but knight her.

"Your wish is my command," she'd said.

Julian had looked at Harry with a gleam in his eye before turning back to her. She should have been suspicious. "A good knight must know his history," Julian said.

"*Her* history."

"Yes, of course. *Her* history. To prove your worth, you must prepare a five-page account of the Peloponnesian Wars."

"That's ridiculous. Knights didn't have paper, they had scrolls."

"Then, by all means, a five-*scroll* account."

Harry's skepticism as he watched the exchange had given her pause, but in the end, she'd submitted her 'five-scroll' account. Apparently, it had earned Julian high marks with his history tutor.

Now she sat in the chair next to Harry's, notebook and pencil ready. She studied his face, noted his wrapped foot and frowned. "How are you, truly?"

"My head aches like the dev—like the dickens—but Julian left a draught for the pain."

"It's hard to accustom myself to calling him Dr. Grey."

"I have to agree. I remember some of the silly things he used to say and do, and I'm not sure I trust his judgment."

She chuckled. "Be that as it may, he's the only doctor we have. Unless he insists on bleeding you, I think you have to take your medicine."

He snorted and adjusted his ankle to a more comfortable position. She took notes while he gave direction on their next tasks.

"Remy is aware of what needs to be done," he said. "He'll help you manage it."

"Of course. Remy is very capable."

He looked up at her words and narrowed his eyes.

"What?" she asked.

"What is it about the man that ladies find so . . . compelling?"

"Remy?" Not Harry, too? She understood her

father's irritation; her mother made no secret of her admiration for the handsome footman, after all.

But Harry was so confident, and Remy's bright appearance didn't even compare to Harry's dark hair and liquid-silver eyes. Or to the way her heart quickened its pace whenever he looked at her. Or spoke. Or . . . Oh, yes. He waited for her answer. She tapped her chin and watched him from the corner of her eye.

"Well, he's very handsome." She ticked the point off on her finger. "And strong." She lifted a second finger, noting how Harry's eyes had narrowed further. "Have you ever seen him move a piece of furniture? And his eyes"—she lifted another finger—"have the most incredible—"

"Enough." Harry held up a hand.

"But I haven't even gotten to his hair. It's been positively *kissed* by the sun." She sighed.

Harry glared at her, his eyes hard silver now. Surely it was wrong to enjoy this so much.

"Oh! I heard a kitchen maid tell a chamber maid that he saved a kitten this morning." She blinked innocently.

"A kitten? Indeed." He crossed his arms and angled his head at her. It was a look she'd seen often when she poked and provoked.

"Two kittens, I believe."

Cranston arrived then and began shuffling about

with Harry's shaving things. She set aside her teasing to put her mind back on the telescope and her notes. Despite their progress, she knew Harry still had doubts that they would succeed. And since Lord Porter's visit, their success had become even more important. It might be his only path to Cairo.

He ran a hand through his hair. She heard Cranston's put-upon sigh from across the room, as he no doubt lamented the work ahead of him.

She reached over and squeezed Harry's other hand. "It will be all right. Even if we don't finish in time. It will be enough. You'll see."

He nodded and squeezed back.

CHAPTER NINETEEN

ARRY RUBBED A HAND OVER his smooth jaw. He'd never managed a shave as close as Cranston's. It was disconcerting, letting a man that close to his throat with a sharp blade. But Cranston knew what he was about, it would seem.

He thought of Remy's—*completely inappropriate*—suggestion that Celeste shave him, and he grimaced. While he would have enjoyed feeling her hands on him, he was certain his face would not have come out the better for it. One or both of them would likely have been tense, leading to any number of nicks to his poor cheeks. No, Cranston was the better option.

Now he was restless. Sitting idle was not his natural state. He kept his foot elevated per Julian's instructions, but the enforced inactivity was driving him mad. Especially since he knew—could recite from memory—all the tasks they needed to complete today.

He felt for the button in his pocket. Celeste and Remy would manage, he assured himself. But still, he couldn't quell his anxiety.

So, when Remy returned, he almost kissed the man. Almost. "How do the kittens fare?"

Remy's eyebrows arched toward his hairline. "Sir?"

Harry pressed his lips. Kittens, indeed. He waved a hand in dismissal. "Have you found anything?"

Remy nodded. "The boy, Robbie—" Remy held a hand at his waist.

"The gamekeeper's son?"

"Yes. He was there last week, watching the men place the tube, and again yesterday."

Harry nodded, recalling the boy and his sister with Celeste.

"He dropped a toy soldier in the trees and went back last night to find it."

"In the rain?"

"It was an important soldier," Remy said gravely, nodding. "At any rate, he didn't realize you were there last night, but he saw a man carrying an axe. He became scared and ran."

"So, there *was* someone else there. Did he describe the man?"

"Tall and fair-haired. That's about all he could see in the darkness."

"That could be half the male population of Kent."

"That's not all. One of the ropes on the tube was cut. With an axe, I would wager."

Harry straightened. "The tube—is it—"

"It's fine. Listing, but fine. We've braced it until we can replace the rope."

Harry rubbed the back of his neck and cursed his swollen ankle. He needed to be on the Hill.

"I spoke with the gamekeeper; he seems to be missing an axe, but he didn't see anything. I did, however, find this near his shed."

Harry took the silver button Remy held out to him. The face was ribbed, and a laurel wreath decorated the perimeter. Mud had settled in the shallow crevices of the design.

"This is something," he said, "although I suppose it could belong to anyone." Then a thought occurred to him. He wasn't proud of it, but still . . . "What do you make of Marchand?"

"Lady Celeste's suitor?" Remy rubbed his chin. "There's something off about the man. I can't put my finger on it, but . . ."

"Off, how?"

"He seems too perfect, if you ask me."

This was ironic, coming from the man who saved small kittens before breakfast.

Remy narrowed his eyes at Harry. "Why, do you think it could have been him?"

Harry wanted to say *Yes. Yes, it was him.* But to be

fair, he hadn't seen anyone, and he had no reason to suspect Marchand other than his own pettiness. The man had no motive for damaging the telescope. Although he *was* fair-haired. And tall.

"I don't know," he said. "But keep a close watch just the same. We should update Lord Ashford. We'll need to secure the site more carefully and post a few men to guard it at night. And care should be taken to guard Robbie's safety."

"Do you think he's in danger?"

"I hope not. But we don't know if he was seen."

"It's difficult to know if the attack was directed against you or the telescope. You should also have a care for your own safety."

Harry scratched his jaw. With the rope to the tube cut, he was likely just an unfortunate casualty of an attack on the telescope. He didn't have enemies. He wasn't the sort of man who made enemies. No one cared about an insignificant scientist, so he had trouble placing any credence in Remy's words. But he nodded just the same. "I'll be careful."

———

CELESTE SPENT THE BETTER PART of the morning watching for Alexandre. Now that she knew she couldn't marry him, she was anxious to give him her answer. Letting him continue without an answer would be unkind. Guilt soured her stomach; he'd traveled to England to see her, and now she was about to reject his proposal.

When luncheon came and went without a glimpse of the man, she went searching for him. She finally found him seated in the gardens with a notebook and pencil in hand. He stood at her approach and offered a polite bow.

He really was the perfect man. It was a shame he wasn't perfect for her.

"Lady Celeste, now that the storm has passed, it's a fine day to enjoy the garden. Will you join me to see the roses?" He held out his arm and she placed her hand in the crook of his elbow.

"What are you working on?" she asked, indicating his notebook.

He smiled sheepishly. "I was composing a poem. I'm afraid it's not very good."

Before he could read it to her, she hurried to speak. "Alexandre, you asked me a very important question in Paris."

He stopped walking and turned to her. "Yes."

"You've traveled a long way, and I truly appreciate your company. Indeed, I'm very fond of you."

"You need say no more," he said with a small smile. Then, "Have you considered submitting your latest paintings to the Salon?" he asked.

She blinked. "What do you mean?"

"The ones you shared in your father's

observatory. They're quite good, and I think there's a chance one of them might be accepted, perhaps with a bit of refinement here and there."

She stared at him, uncertain. "Do you think so? What sort of refinement?"

"I would be happy to work with you on them. At the very least, we can polish your application to the Academy. Tell me you'll think on it. Your work is too powerful to go unnoticed."

She was uncertain what to say. Did he understand she couldn't marry him? "I want to be clear, Alexandre. I—I can't marry you. I appreciate the honor of your proposal, but I'm sorry."

He placed his hand over hers on his sleeve. "I understand, but that doesn't mean we can't work together to see your paintings exhibited in the spring. And perhaps in time, you'll change your mind."

She shook her head and opened her mouth, but he stopped her with a look. "Tell me you'll think on it. I'll return to Paris after the harvest festival. You and your mother may join me if you desire."

She nodded, unsure what question she was answering.

———

HERR KRAUS STOPPED BY HARRY'S room that morning to take his leave. "The ladies are intent on London," he explained.

The speed with which Miss Pepper had decided

to depart was a bit lowering, although Harry had to admit to some relief that he wouldn't need Odette's chaperonage again.

"Join me when your work here is complete," Kraus continued. "If you don't go to Cairo, that is, although I have every expectation the Commission will make the right choice."

His confidence was a balm, even as Harry thought it might be premature.

After Kraus left, he enjoyed a dull lunch with only himself for company. He gazed about his room, searching for something to occupy his mind or his hands. It was no use.

He requested an extra cane from the attic and limped to the laboratory. Although nausea crested over him whenever he stood, the relief he felt to be *moving* was worth it.

A fresh box of pencils lay straight and precise in the center of his desk. He smiled. Celeste's desk was vacant, but Ashford sat before a table of instruments, cleaning rag in hand.

"Have you seen Lady Celeste, my lord?"

Ashford looked up. "Ah, you just missed her. I believe she went in search of Marchand."

Harry blew out a heavy breath then hobbled to his desk and sat. *Your every wish is my command.* Truly? Then why was she—he cut off his thinking before he could be ungracious.

He pushed himself up again and left through the terrace doors. He would check the progress on the Hill himself.

The air was heavy and humid after last night's storms, but the sky was clear. He stepped off the terrace, intent on the path to the Hill. Movement to his right caught his eye, and he saw them. Celeste faced Marchand, one hand resting on his sleeve.

Harry's stomach clenched, and he forced himself to look at the man objectively. Had he been the one to hit him over the head last night? As much as he wanted to, he couldn't reconcile his attacker with the polished man standing amid the roses, much less imagine a motive for such an attack.

Marchand placed a hand on top of Celeste's then. Harry tore his gaze away and stomped to the gate. His cane crunched the gravel and pain stabbed his ankle with each step.

————

HARRY TRIED TO STAY ANGRY with Celeste over the next days, but he was unsuccessful. She had but to look at him, smile and tease him through her lashes, and his poor mood fell away like an oversized coat.

He couldn't begrudge her happiness.

It was unreasonable, and unfair, to expect her to remain unmarried. Marchand was part of her life in Paris. He would be there when she returned. If she wished for Marchand, he would try to be happy for her. He admitted that trying and doing were two different things . . . but still.

He renewed his focus on the telescope with vigor, and he and Remy began the painstaking work on the mirror. The first step required them to cast a large metal disc that they would then grind and polish to a reflective sheen.

Over the next week, Roberts, the blacksmith's son, advised them. Using an age-old process, they fashioned a four-foot mold of sand, clay, and horse dung of all things. Roberts explained how the dung would allow steam to escape during the casting.

Next, they melted a bronze alloy in the chimney furnace. The heat in the small stone outbuilding was staggering, the work wretched. His father would dance to see his son's fancy education ground beneath the heel of such humble labor. But each night, he climbed between his sheets with a bone-weary sense of satisfaction.

He saw little of Celeste. He rose with the sun and crept back through the servants' entrance after dark, sweaty and rank from the day's work. But on the third day, once the molten metal had been poured into the mold and left to cool, they broke early. The sun was a flat disc behind thin clouds, brushing the tops of the trees. When Remy continued on the path to Redstone Hall, Harry broke off toward the pond.

The cool water lapped against the bank, beckoning. He removed his boots and shirt and waded in, feeling the mud beneath his toes. He bent and splashed his face then ran wet hands through his hair. He relished the cool water on his scalp after the heat of the furnace.

There were less than five weeks until the Round Table. Until Timmons arrived to write his story. Despite the progress they'd made this week on the mirror, there was still much to do. He refused to delude himself. There was still every chance they wouldn't complete the telescope in time. And then what?

Ashford would be embarrassed. And Harry . . . well, he wouldn't go to Cairo. Or the Sandwich Islands or Christmas Harbour, for that matter. He would probably go to Cambridge.

He'd received an encouraging reply from his former professor. There was a position waiting for him when he was ready. And he was surprised to find the idea wasn't completely . . . repellent.

———

CELESTE MISSED HARRY. SHE'D SEEN little of him the past days. How much worse would it be when he left for good? She pushed that thought aside for another time. He hadn't left yet.

When she saw Remy return through the garden gate, alone, she left the conservatory to meet him on the path. Before she could ask, he said, "Mr. Corbyn is at the pond."

She closed her mouth. Was she that obvious? But she simply nodded before continuing through the gate.

When she emerged from the trees near the pond, she stopped short. Harry's boots and shirt lay on the bank in a tidy pile. She lifted her eyes slowly to see he stood in the shallow water at the pond's edge, and her breath caught.

He'd rolled his trousers and his bare calves were firm above the waterline, his dark hair wet. He was trim, sleek and solid. The muscles and tendons of his back and shoulders shifted beneath smooth skin. Her artist's mind, which recognized a perfect figure study, gave way to her female mind and her stomach dipped.

Years ago, she'd come upon Harry and Julian swimming. They'd been mere boys then, and she'd hid in the trees, a hand clapped over her mouth to muffle a giggle.

That Harry had thin arms and legs, sticks really, that were much too long on his body. Try as she might, she couldn't reconcile the firm, arresting man before her with the spindly-legged, narrow-chested boy.

With a start, she realized she was spying again. Breathe. She was not a ten-year-old girl anymore.

He went still, as if he sensed her gaze on him. The muscles in his back shifted before he began to turn. She didn't wait to see his face but fled through the trees.

————

HARRY SENSED EYES ON HIM, and his thoughts immediately went to the night he'd been attacked. Had their villain returned? He began to turn, and quick steps sounded through the trees. He peered into the shadows and spied . . . cinnamon hair. Not a tall, fair-haired villain, then.

He smiled and looked down at his wet feet and chest. His smile grew to think of Celeste spying on him. He wasn't generally a vain man. He didn't refine too much on his appearance, but a tiny part of him was pleased she'd seen him. Let her think of her perfect Frenchman now.

Then his eyes narrowed, and he placed his hands on his hips. He squinted at his clothing on the bank, watching for movement, then sighed with relief when his shirt appeared to be snake-free.

————

CELESTE RACED DOWN THE PATH, cheeks burning, the image of Harry's wet shoulders firmly engraved on her eyelids. She was an artist. She could appreciate the human form objectively. She'd have to, if she expected to be taken seriously, but part of her understood why women were banned from the life study classes at the Academy. Which was ridiculous, truly.

She was certain she could study and analyze any figure. Apply the right amount of distance to remain impassive and impersonal while depicting bone and muscle and sinew. Any figure but that one.

There was no way she could remain passive while gazing on Harry's form.

As she reached the bottom of the path and approached the garden, she spied Remy in the shadows of a tree near the gate. An ember glowed then faded as he inhaled on a cheroot. He saw her, a knowing smirk on his face as he blew a stream of blue smoke.

He knew. He knew what she'd find when she went to the pond. The wretch!

She narrowed her eyes at him and stomped past. His chuckle followed her, flaming her face anew.

CHAPTER TWENTY

ESPITE HIS EVERY DESIRE TO the contrary, Harry knew he could not miss Lady Grey's supper. The event was the pinnacle of her annual house party, but he dreaded polite conversation. He would rather calculate parabolic equations for the Flying Pig's mirror, but this was Julian's mother, so he resigned himself.

They were to gather in the drawing room before leaving for Fernwood. The clock told him he had ten more minutes. He was struggling with his cravat when Cranston poked his head in.

"Lord Ashford sent me to inquire if you need assistance." He took in Harry's crumpled linen and rumpled hair and sighed. "Of course you do."

Harry relinquished control of the cloth—truly, he'd had none anyway. He tipped his chin up while Cranston unwound the offensive linen. The valet wrapped a new length about his neck and tied it in a perfect Mathematical. How did he do that? Harry turned his head to the left and right and nodded. The man was a genius.

Cranston then attacked his hair with a comb. "What did you use," he asked, "the gardener's rake?"

Harry didn't think his hair looked that bad, but apparently it wasn't up to snuff. He let Cranston have his way, turning the button in his pocket while Cranston worked. When he finished, Harry's hair was perfectly coiffed, each lock in its place. It made him itch.

Once the man left, his fingers twitched as he resisted the urge to run them through his hair. It was a losing battle. He ran one hand through, ruffling the side. There, he thought on an exhale.

When he entered the drawing room, Ashford was checking his timepiece. He glanced up and his brows lifted. "I sent Cranston to assist. Did he not find you?"

Harry pressed his lips together. "He did, but there's no help for it, I'm afraid." He motioned to his hair.

"Ah. I miss the days of wigs."

"Indeed."

Lady Ashford joined them next. She was handsome in a gown of red silk, or satin or some such. Harry watched Ashford take in his wife's appearance. The man started to smile, before pushing his features into a frown. Lady Ashford frowned back.

Harry wasn't sure what had occurred to divide them so, but he hoped to never experience that level of discord. Both seemed unhappy with the state of affairs, but neither seemed able, or willing, to address it.

"Dearest, you look splendid!" Lady Ashford pressed her hands together as Celeste entered. Harry's breath caught in his throat.

Celeste wore a rich emerald gown that made her eyes more green than blue. It looked soft to the touch—velvet, he assumed. He imagined smoothing his hands along her ribs, along the pile of the fabric, feeling its smooth texture. The bodice was . . . small. Surely Ashford would object to that? He waited . . . But no, Ashford remained silent on the subject of his daughter's bodice.

She wore her cinnamon hair in an elaborate knot, dotted with tiny shimmering diamonds and pearls. More glowed at her ears and throat, like stars riding a moonbeam to earth.

When he looked up, Marchand had joined them. The Frenchman bent over Celeste's hand with compliments on his lips. She looked at Harry over Marchand's shoulder, an odd look on her face. Wondering at his silence, no doubt.

Ashford had determined the carriage seating.

Harry would ride with Marchand, and Celeste with her parents. Harry wondered if it was too late to send his regrets. Thankfully, the distance to Fernwood was short.

Remy was dressed again in his navy livery. He held the carriage door for Harry and Marchand.

"After you." Marchand motioned to the door.

"No, I insist," Harry said. He felt Remy roll his eyes behind them.

Marchand finally entered and Harry followed. His fingers tapped a rhythm on his thigh as the carriage began rolling.

He studied Marchand in the dim light. His hair, of course, was perfectly styled. His cravat, perfectly creased. The man's fingers rested calmly on his leg. Harry forced his own to still. Marchand's buttons were silver, but they appeared to be a crest of some sort, not a laurel wreath. He sighed.

"You're well acquainted with Sir John and Lady Grey?" Marchand asked.

"Yes, I attended Eton with their son, Julian. Dr. Grey."

"Ah."

"How did you come to know Lady Ashford?" Harry asked. Apparently, they were to make small talk during the short trip to Fernwood.

"I don't recall, to be honest. I've had her acquaintance for some time." Well, that was suspicious. Lady Ashford was quite memorable. Not forgettable in the least.

He looked out the window at the darkness, and his mind drifted to the Flying Pig and the tasks scheduled for the morrow. What were Celeste and her parents talking about now?

"How long have you known Lady Celeste?" Marchand's words interrupted his thoughts.

Harry turned from the window to face Marchand. He may have acknowledged that Celeste might marry the man, but that didn't mean he had to like it.

No, he didn't like it at all. In fact, Marchand was not the man for her. He was all wrong. He wished her all the happiness she deserved, but she'd simply have to find someone else.

"I've known her since we were children, when I spent holidays at Fernwood."

"So, she's like a sister then?"

"In that I desire her happiness? I suppose so." In other ways . . . No. He crossed his arms and looked into Marchand's eyes. Willed him to see the truth. Marchand's gaze narrowed, then he nodded. Yes, he understood.

When they arrived at Fernwood, Harry waited while Marchand stepped down. The Fernwood servant who assisted them from the carriage didn't have half the panache of Remy. The man wore a white periwig and black livery. He was quite forgettable, in fact.

Celeste and her parents were already circulating with Lady Grey's guests in the drawing room. Lady Grey introduced Harry and Marchand to two dozen guests, and Harry struggled to remember names.

"Lord Blackwood, may I introduce Monsieur Marchand? He's a member of the Royal Academy in Paris and has taken an interest in our little hamlet. Perhaps we'll be the subject of one of his next masterpieces." She laughed and fluttered a hand at Marchand before recalling Harry. "Oh, and Mr. Harry Corbyn, of course."

And so it went. When he finally reached Celeste's side, he breathed a sigh of relief and whispered, "You look lovely."

She smiled, her face glowing, and his heart kicked his ribs. It was worth a carriage ride with Marchand.

Julian approached then with a scowl. "Mother, Harry's recovering from an injury. He shouldn't be circulating the drawing room."

Celeste's face fell. "Of course!" she said. "Harry, you should have a seat. Your poor ankle." She fussed over him until he was seated, his cane propped next to him. Was all this fuss necessary? Then Marchand scowled from across the room, and he relaxed.

But when Celeste left his side to greet one of Lady Grey's guests, he realized the limitations of his invalid state. Marchand joined her and smirked at Harry from his place at Celeste's side.

Julian took the seat next to him and stretched his legs. "Do you think an announcement is coming soon?"

Harry started at the words. "What do you mean?"

"Marchand's been here for some time now. Have they reached an understanding, do you think?"

Harry looked at Celeste again, wondering. *Had* she given the man her answer? Wouldn't she tell him if she'd accepted Marchand's proposal? But no, why would she?

———

CELESTE'S HEAD POUNDED, A DRUMMING tattoo that stabbed behind her eyes. Her parents had bickered during the—thankfully short—ride to Fernwood. They'd alternated between her mother's disdain for the state of Edmund's laboratory (truly, would some order be such a terrible thing?) to her father's frustration with the upholsterer's bills (there was nothing wrong with the draperies in the morning room). She'd given up mediating and had descended the carriage steps with relief.

At Fernwood, Alexandre attached himself to her side. He might as well have made a declaration. His slow smiles and gentle touches at her elbow were giving Lady Grey's guests the wrong impression. She caught more than one speculative glance directed their way. Had he forgotten their conversation in the garden so soon?

"Are we to expect an announcement soon, Lady Celeste?" Lady Grey inquired when Alexandre turned to address another guest.

"No, Lady Grey. Monsieur Marchand is a friend from Paris, nothing more."

Lady Grey patted her arm. "Well, it doesn't hurt to keep the gentleman waiting, but I wouldn't make him wait too long." She leaned in to whisper. "If you wish to make an announcement tonight, I'm sure we can do it up right."

"Oh, no, that won't be necessary," Celeste assured her. She wished for nothing more than a soft pillow and a cool tisane.

Harry looked especially handsome tonight. His cravat was crisp, although he'd clearly run a hand through his hair. Whenever he looked at her, the warmth of his silver gaze caused a shiver to chase down her spine.

When she'd dressed for the evening, she wondered if he would appreciate her gown. His silence had disappointed her, until they arrived at Fernwood. *You look lovely.* How could three simple words outshine the elegant, flowery compliments from other gentlemen?

She forced her thoughts back to the present. Mrs. Pitt was recounting the latest efforts of the Ladies' Alliance for Compassionate Benevolence. "You must say you'll join us, Lady Ashford. With so many men returned from the war, many of them broken, it's our duty to see them restored to a serviceable place in the world."

To Celeste's surprise, her mother agreed. "You're quite right, Mrs. Pitt," Lily said. "Only they and the Lord know the horrors they've suffered." Celeste listened as her mother asked questions about the alliance and offered suggestions.

It was not that her mother was uncharitable, but she was French. Half French, at least. Expecting her to sympathize with soldiers of the opposing army seemed . . . optimistic. But then, Celeste reminded herself that her mother may be half French, but she was also half English, even if she found her English half easy to forget.

Finally, supper was announced. Lady Grey made sure her guests entered by rank and honor. Celeste and her parents. Lady Grey's cousin, Viscount Blackwood. Alexandre. It was some time later before Harry entered, escorting a young lady. Miss Kate Montgomery, if she recalled, who was visiting from London with her parents.

Centuries of Greys surveyed the dining room from wood-paneled walls. Elaborate floral arrangements in chased-silver urns decorated the table, and fourteen place settings lined each side. Gleaming crystal and polished silver sparkled in the candlelight. Lady Grey had outdone herself this year.

Celeste looked down the expanse of linen to where Harry spoke with Miss Montgomery. She was a pretty brunette, charming, with a ready laugh and an entertaining sense of humor.

As Celeste recalled her virtues, Miss Montgomery dimpled at something Harry said. He responded with a smile of his own, and the throbbing in Celeste's head picked up tempo.

———

A WEEK LATER, THE HOUSEHOLD gathered in the drawing room after supper. The night was warm and humid after days of late summer storms, and everyone seemed on edge.

Alexandre was overly solicitous despite Celeste's rejection of his proposal. Or perhaps because of it. His renewed efforts threatened her patience. Couldn't he see that an extra touch on her elbow or a flowery compliment wouldn't change her mind?

Harry's fingers tapped an anxious tattoo while he watched Alexandre with . . . suspicion? Animosity? It had been a month since Harry's injury. He'd abandoned the cane, although she detected a slight limp at times.

He'd been pushing himself on the telescope. She narrowed her eyes as she studied his. Tiny lines fanned out beside his grey eyes. His errant lock drooped over his forehead, and he shoved it back into place.

Remy, dressed again in his navy livery, was hovering more than usual. Which meant her father was glaring more than usual. Truly, her father should be more appreciative of all that Remy had done to build his telescope. Only her mother seemed unaware of—or unconcerned with—the underlying tension.

"Why don't I play for us?" she asked, motioning toward the pianoforte. That was met with equal expressions of horror, although Harry tried to temper his. Even Remy winced. "Oh, very well," she muttered, but she was smiling. Her mother was incorrigible.

"Perhaps Lady Celeste should decide the evening's entertainment, since it's her birthday," Alexandre said. Celeste stared at him for a heartbeat and mentally calculated. Yes. Yes, it *was* her birthday. Was that why he was being so nice then? How was it that no one else, including her, realized the date? Everyone was silent for a moment, then voices erupted around her.

"*Ma pauvre!* How did we forget?"

"M'dear, my apologies!"

"We must celebrate! Remy, please ask Cook to send up something special from the kitchens."

Harry was silent, watching her. She assured everyone it was no matter. Heavens! She too had forgotten the date. Remy returned with a tray of lemon tarts and champagne.

"To Lady Celeste!" Alexandre toasted.

"Hear, hear!" her father replied.

Celeste watched Harry as he nibbled a lemon tart, his glass untouched. The air in the room was tight, and she opened the terrace doors to the breeze. As she did, she caught the barely-there glimmer of a shooting star arcing over the horizon.

"Did you see that?" she asked the room. "A shooting star!"

Her father and Alexandre rose to watch over her shoulder.

"It's not technically a star," her father informed them. He then explained the science behind meteors.

"Ashford, you take all the romance out of it."

"Nonsense," he grumbled. "What could be more romantic than the truth?"

"We should all make a wish," Celeste said.

"The ancient Greeks believed a shooting star was the sign of a falling soul."

"*Maman*, that's depressing."

"I didn't say that's what it means. I was merely sharing what the Greeks believed."

Alexandre said, "Some say a shooting star signals an imminent marriage." He looked at Celeste meaningfully.

Harry shook his head and spoke up. "No, I'm

certain that's *not* what it signifies. It's the universe telling us something wonderful is about to happen." Celeste looked at him, surprised by his fanciful superstition. He cleared his throat and shrugged. "But of course, the universe doesn't truly speak to us."

"Of course, it does," she said. "Everyone knows when you cast a wish on a falling star your dreams will come true. It's as simple as that."

———

HOW HAD HE FORGOTTEN HER birthday? Especially as she'd always made a point to remind him and Julian of it each August. And each year, she'd reminded them that, according to her father, three celestial bodies had been in perfect, sublime alignment the night of her birth: Venus, Jupiter and a waxing crescent moon.

He watched her take a second lemon tart and his heart clenched. This was what Celeste feared: invisibility, with no one to remark her life. To bear witness.

His head pounded in time with his heartbeat, and his ankle throbbed anew. He didn't believe the stars could grant wishes, any more than he believed the universe was speaking to them. But he wanted to believe, if only to convince himself that Celeste would realize her dreams.

No more shooting stars appeared, and after their

impromptu celebration ended, he pushed himself to his feet and strode down the dimly lit hall toward the laboratory.

"Harry." Celeste called to him, and he waited. She looked up when she reached him, concern etched on her face. "Are you well? Does your ankle still pain you?"

"No, not overly much." Her eyes pierced him, reflecting the candlelight, and he felt the familiar tug of her drawing him nearer. He straightened. "I'm sorry I didn't remember your birthday."

"Pish," she whispered with a flutter of her hand. "How can I expect others to recall it, when even I didn't remember?"

He started to tell her that she deserved to have her birth, her existence, celebrated, but he didn't get the chance.

"Lady Celeste?" Marchand called from the doorway of the drawing room.

She looked back at Marchand before whispering, "Good night, Harry."

And then she was gone.

CHAPTER TWENTY-ONE

THE FALLING STAR'S FLEETING BEAUTY lit an answering flame inside Celeste. After leaving Alexandre and her parents, she went to the observatory and painted well into the small hours. She'd need to find her bed soon, though, if she were to be of any use to Harry and her father. She stretched and relished the lengthening of her tired muscles.

Several miniatures lined the worktable next to her oak-handled magnifying glass. They weren't submission-worthy, but they were an enjoyable break from the weightier subjects of her larger paintings.

She set the latest aside to dry, then she took time to clean her brushes and straighten her paints. The soft smell of linseed oil filled the air as she worked, and candlelight outlined the edges of her larger canvases propped along the curved walls.

As she moved to leave, a soft, winking light

beyond the upper windows snagged her attention. She stepped to the side to see the sky more fully, and more flashes arced across her vision in quick succession. She watched for a moment in wonder, then she raced through the transit room to the laboratory.

She wasn't surprised to find Harry hunched over his notebook, even at this hour. Stubs sputtered in the candelabra next to him, casting a dim pool of light. He wore his spectacles, and she could see a slight smudge on one of the lenses. Night stubble covered his jaw, and the faint scent of amber and oak reached her.

The picture he presented was quite endearing, and her heart skipped. No matter what happened with her father's telescope, she wanted Harry to succeed. He was good and brilliant, and he yearned for knowledge. Burned with the wanting. He deserved to achieve his dreams. If he wanted to go to Cairo, she wanted that for him.

She spoke his name twice, to no avail, before placing a hand on his shoulder. He had long since shed his coat, and his shoulder was warm through the layers of his shirt and waistcoat. He looked up and a moment passed before his gaze sharpened and he focused on her face.

"Celeste? Is all well?"

"Come, Harry. Look." She seized his hand in hers

and pulled. He frowned but came willingly, and they crossed the room, navigating her father's instruments and models in the dim light.

She tugged him toward the windows and a broad vista of falling stars. They radiated from a constant point, and thin phosphorescent streaks trailed each meteor like fine scratches upon the heavens. Dozens upon dozens fell, crossing and tumbling over one another. She watched Harry's face as he took in the sight, their fingers twined together.

"Remarkable," he whispered. "Is this what you wished for last night?"

She chuckled. "No, but it's a good substitute. Is that Perseus?" She indicated the origination point.

"Yes, you can see Cassiopeia there to the right." He indicated the W-shaped constellation with their joined hands.

She pulled him to the door, intent on the terrace, but he tugged her hand. "We'll see better from the roof."

"But your ankle," she protested. He only tugged harder, and she let him lead her to the back staircase and up three flights to the expansive slate parapet.

"You should have brought your journal," she said. "Certainly, you'll want to take notes or measurements."

"Yes, but not yet. Let's just watch." He gazed at the sky above and around them, eyes wide with wonder as he took in the sparkling cascade. "Have you ever seen anything so humbling?" he asked.

Tears burned the backs of her eyes—for his wonder as much as for the silent celestial pageantry that surrounded them. "No," she whispered as the universe folded its arms around them.

If Harry was right—if falling stars were indeed a sign that something wonderful was about to happen . . .

She turned, and her heartbeat quickened when she saw he watched her. His eyes shifted from soft grey to fierce, molten silver and bright energy fizzed through her veins. It was hot and intense, and comforting all at once, because it was Harry.

He stood close, and she inhaled his faint amber and oak scent. Only a few inches separated them. If she tilted her head another inch . . . Surely one kiss wouldn't hurt.

———

FALLING STARS REFLECTED IN CELESTE'S eyes as more cascading flashes bloomed and winked out behind her. He should probably retrieve his journal, as she'd suggested, but coordinates and measurements were a distant notion.

Her lips, however, were close, her hand warm in his. His brain reminded him that he was leaving soon. When the telescope was complete, he would go. She would return to Paris. There was no point in a kiss that would only pull him tighter into her orbit, but he found he didn't care at this particular moment.

He leaned closer and paused. She moved a fraction of an inch, and then he touched his lips to hers. A whisper-soft press of his mouth, testing, feeling. She sighed and he breathed her in.

Her lips were as soft and lush as he'd imagined. He pressed harder and lifted a hand to her cheek, stroking her softness with his thumb. She placed her hands on his chest, burning him through layers of shirt and waistcoat. Drawing him ever closer in a tight spiral. He began to pull away, but her lips followed him.

The stars that fell around them froze behind his eyelids. The kiss stretched on, their breath mingling, the silence of the night heavy and still. Her warm vanilla scent surrounded him, and his heart skipped and stuttered as her fingers threaded through his hair.

Dimly, a noise sounded at the edge of his awareness, but he was lost in the sensation of her hands in his hair, her lips beneath his. He dropped his hands to her waist, and his arms tightened, pressing her closer, until his mind registered the noise as the sound of a door.

He pulled away and pressed his forehead to hers, trying to control the racing of his heart. Her lashes fluttered and she looked at him with bright eyes.

The noise . . . He glanced behind her to see the

rooftop door was closed. Someone had seen them, but he couldn't bring himself to care. She squeezed his hand and pulled him to the slate. They leaned against a chimney and watched the heavens rain starlight.

———

SLEEP DID NOT COME EASILY, and what little Harry did find was restless and broken. He supposed that was what happened when foolish men lost their hearts. He admitted, finally, that his heart belonged to Celeste. He no longer had possession of it. It continued to beat, to pump blood to his extremities, but he'd lost all autonomy over it.

It had been inevitable, a force beyond his control, like the sun rising each morning and grass greening each spring. But he understood the rising sun. He could explain it. He did not understand, could not explain, the force behind his feelings for Celeste. He rather thought the distinction was an important one.

Remy reported that reactions to the night's meteor event were mixed. One of the maids had swooned on seeing the stars fall, exclaiming, "Oh, surely this must be the end!" A sturdy footman had caught her, though, and all was well.

The villagers of Marshfield had been awed and mystified. They disagreed on whether it was better to know the science behind the event, or simply accept it as God's will, and Lord Ashford's telescope gained ever greater significance. Every Marshfielder, young and old, anticipated the end of the harvest festival when they would see into the heavens for themselves. Harry suppressed a groan at the thought.

"Did you enjoy the shower, my boy?" Ashford asked as he tucked into his eggs.

Harry swallowed. "Yes, my lord. It was spectacular."

"Hmm. It was, it was." Ashford looked up then and leveled a speculative look on him, his blue eyes piercing and bright. Harry fought to hold his gaze, but in the end, he turned to Celeste, who was adding another Bath bun to her plate.

She blushed when he caught her eye, and a tiny smile tipped the corner of her mouth. She turned her attention to her chocolate, and he fought to keep a silly grin from his face. His lips burned, as if her own were still pressed to his.

One kiss. That was all it took. Imagine the puddle he would become if he had a lifetime of kisses.

Ashford, as it turned out, had made copious measurements and notes. He had logged coordinates, times and duration of the shower intervals. He was more than happy to share them, he said, in case Harry had missed anything.

———

LATER THAT EVENING, HARRY RUBBED the back of his neck as he picked his way down the path from the

Hill. The spreading darkness slowed his progress, but a thin scrap of moon yielded some welcome illumination.

He passed through the garden gate, intent on the terrace, when he heard a soft whisper beyond the rose bushes. He stepped off the path to investigate but stopped short when he recognized Remy and the maid, Odette, in a passionate embrace.

He retreated silently, but it was too late. Remy glanced up and their eyes met.

"Apologies," Harry murmured.

Remy removed his hands from the maid's backside, and she hurried past Harry, gaze averted. He politely ducked his own head but caught the hint of a pleased smile on her face as Remy adjusted his collar.

"I'm sorry, I heard a noise and . . ." Harry trailed off, as there was really nothing to say. He turned to go.

"No, your timing is fortunate."

Harry stopped, confused. "How's that?"

Remy sighed and ran a hand through his disheveled locks before lighting a cheroot. "She refuses to marry me. But why would she buy the cow when she's getting the milk for free?"

Harry coughed a surprised laugh. But Remy's face was earnest, so he pressed his lips together. "And . . . you're the . . . cow, in this analogy?"

Remy nodded, drawing on the cigar. The end glowed before he exhaled. "I've allowed things to progress too far, and now she has no reason to marry me. Your interruption was timely. I suppose I should . . . I don't know."

"Withhold your favors?"

"Precisely! Although, with Odette, that's easier said than done."

Harry nodded as if he understood.

"I can't control myself around that woman. She drives me to madness."

Harry swallowed, certain he didn't need to hear more. But more was coming, it would seem.

"I can't sleep. I can't eat. I can't think of anything but her. And the telescope, of course," Remy amended. "I'm running out of ways to get her to say yes, but I don't know how much longer we can continue like this."

Harry couldn't believe he was going to ask, but he did. "What is the lady's objection to marrying you?"

"She thinks I'm too far above her, if you can believe it."

"Too far . . . because of your service in the army, you mean?"

Remy glanced at him from the corner of his eye before tapping ash from the cheroot. "Yes. *Mon Dieu*, I've been a bloody *footman* for three years. I don't know how else to show her I'm not above her reach."

"Wait." Harry held up a hand. "You mean to tell me . . . you've served as Lady Ashford's *footman* . . . you gave up a career as an *engineer*, because of a lady?"

"Not just any lady! Odette, man!" He blew a puff of smoke into the air before extinguishing the cheroot with his boot.

"That's—that's . . ."

"I know. It's pathetic."

"It's ingenious. And pathetic. But mostly ingenious. No wonder all the ladies are in love with you." Remy looked at him like he'd gone mad. Harry clapped him on the back. "Soldier on, my friend. If she's worth having, she'll come around."

He could only think how much Celeste would *love* hearing this story. Sadly, he didn't think it was a confidence he could share.

CHAPTER TWENTY-TWO

THREE DAYS UNTIL THE UNVEILING

HARRY DIDN'T KNOW WHAT TO do about his feelings for Celeste. He was at a loss. It was a puzzle to which he was unaccustomed. Whenever he had a problem, he unpacked it piece by piece until he arrived at a solution, but he feared this problem was unsolvable.

Despite his intentions to focus on the telescope, his thoughts kept returning to her. During moments of weakness, when he was tired or his vigilance slipped, he wondered what a life with her might be like. What would it be like to build a home, a family, together?

Was there room in his life for such things?

Would she even welcome the idea? She had all but proposed to him three years ago. But he was not so arrogant he didn't realize he'd been a means to an end. An escape. But that was then. Would she feel the same now? Thoughts of her were driving him mad.

Now that he was, in all truth, not bound for Cairo, he gave more and more thought to Cambridge. It was close, relatively speaking, to Redstone Hall. Would she be miserable as wife to a university lecturer? Could *he* be content with such a life?

Twice, he mentioned his options for the future to her. An experiment of sorts, to gauge her level of interest. Admittedly, they were oblique references, so he was not surprised when the results were inconclusive. She was supportive, but nothing more.

So, he was testing more direct lines of inquiry in his head, discarding ones that were too contrived, or too awkward, or too . . . bloody hell. Yes, he was definitely going mad.

He forced his attention back to the four-foot mirror in front of him—again. Since removing the metal disc from its mold, he'd spent hours grinding the metal with course emery. The goal was a perfect, infinitesimal concave curve. Grind, measure, grind, measure.

The shape needed to be precise to concentrate light into a clear image. There was no room for error. With Remy's input, he'd devised a tool to speed the grinding and control the depth of the curve. It was still laborious, but they couldn't complete the mirror in time without mechanical aid.

He wiped his hands and made a notation in his journal, looking up as Celeste entered the outbuilding where he worked. Brilliant sunlight cast her shape in sharp relief until she closed the door.

She wore an old apron over her dress, ready to work. She had perfected the mixture of emery and water, not too wet, not too dry. Despite his protests — an earl's daughter did not belong in a smelting forge — she'd insisted on helping him.

Harry had suggested to Ashford that perhaps it was inappropriate for his daughter to be *working*, but Ashford merely shook his head. "You've met my daughter, haven't you?" Given his own past experience with Celeste and the word *No*, what could he say to that?

So, she arrived every day. And every day he debated whether a future with her was possible. Whether she would welcome such a future. He wondered again how to approach the subject.

"You've made quite an impression on young Robbie," she said. "He's been asking about you, wondering how many stars you've counted so far."

He smiled. "It seems a long time since we were that young."

She handed him a horsehair brush to clear the metal dust from the section he was working. "You would make a good father, Harry."

At last! Now this, *this* was something he could

work with. He was formulating a reply—something about her future as a mother—when her next statement jerked his thoughts to a standstill.

"Will you tell me about your own father? You never spoke of him when we were children."

He looked up, then back down to the metal disc. He considered ignoring her question, then he remembered who was asking. Celeste and *No* and all that.

"There's not much to tell," he hedged. "You already know he was an innkeeper. Innkeeping was all he ever knew, all he ever aspired to do."

"Did he enjoy it?"

He sighed. This topic wasn't going to be as short-lived as he'd hoped. He turned back to the mirror and continued his grinding. Somehow, talking while he worked seemed easier.

"I don't think so, no. When my mother died, he began drinking, or so I've been told. She died of a fever when I was two, and to be honest, I don't recall what he was like when he was sober."

He told her then about his father's lack of imagination, how William Corbyn had never been able to see a better life for his children than the one he himself led.

"Did you ever return after you finished at Eton?"

He nodded. "I meant to show him that he was wrong, that there was a better life out there." That he could be more than an innkeeper's son, he thought but didn't add.

"What happened?"

He snorted. "Nothing. He'd died three months before, and no one knew where to contact me." His mouth twisted into a rueful smile. "My sister and I aren't the best of correspondents."

"Oh, Harry."

He paused, hands braced on the table where he worked, breath frozen in his lungs. Then he felt her smaller hand curl into his, her warmth spreading through his fingers, up his wrist and arm. He released his breath slowly.

She spoke as she held his hand. "As a child, I thought my father—I thought he was invincible." Her words were tentative, as if she were testing them. He waited for her to continue.

"A god with no faults, no flaws. He could accomplish anything to which he set himself. Every child needs that hero in their life. But then, my mother left, and I blamed *him*. I know how ridiculous that sounds, but I blamed him for not loving her enough. For not being the perfect person I imagined him to be. Overnight, he became a man. Just a man, with lost hopes and failed dreams of his own." She shrugged. "I don't suppose either of our fathers were the heroes we needed them to be, but perhaps they were only meant to be men."

Her words hit him, and he swallowed. He thought of all the years he'd tried to make his father proud, to prove him wrong. To show him there was more out there and he meant to have it . . . But he'd never seen his father as a man, with his own lost dreams.

The chill he didn't know he carried warmed. He felt something inside shift and slide, like crusted snow melting on a rooftop.

———

THEY WORKED IN SILENCE, GRINDING and polishing the metal blank into shape. Their conversation turned in Celeste's mind, the rough surface smoothing and revealing like the mirror they worked. She'd never told anyone the thoughts she'd shared with Harry. She'd never acknowledged them to herself until now. But she realized the truth of them. And she felt . . . lighter . . . for it.

Her father, with his single-minded devotion to his science. Her mother, with her own wants and desires. They were two people whose dreams just . . . didn't align. But that didn't mean their dreams weren't singularly powerful. Uniquely theirs. Equally important.

And of course, she thought of Harry. Of his dreams. She watched him work, bent over the metal disc as she stirred the emery mixture. He worked to help her father achieve his dream. He *literally* had his nose to the grindstone.

Harry deserved to have his own success. And he would, even if he had to make a stop in Cambridge — or Christmas Harbour or the Sandwich Islands — along the way. She knew he would achieve wondrous things. Not for his father. Not for her father. But for himself.

And with dreams that big, there wasn't room in his life for the dreams of another, no matter how much she might wish otherwise. He would leave, then, and she suspected she would never be the same. She thought of their kiss on the rooftop, with the stars raining down on them. It would have to be enough.

Her eyes burned but not from the emery, and she blinked. "I imagine I'll return to Paris once the harvest festival has ended," she said.

Harry stopped grinding and looked up.

"My father is recovering, and Alexandre thinks I should submit to the Salon in April." The possibility both excited and terrified. Even as the thought of leaving England again scratched her heart with its rough edges.

Harry studied her for a heartbeat, then he smiled his slow smile. "They would be fools not to accept you."

She returned his smile. "You know, there's always an assembly at the end of the harvest festival. Mrs. Pitt has been planning it for months, and The

Ladies' Society will unveil their latest needlework. I understand it's a magnificent series depicting Saint Arnulf of Metz.

"Who was . . .?"

"The patron saint of hop-pickers, of course. The very *Catholic* patron saint. Our good vicar is sure to expire on the spot."

"Did you contribute anything to the series?"

"Needlework? Heavens, no. I'm sure poor Saint Arnulf deserves better than my poor stitching." She paused then said, "I will be put out, Harry, if you don't dance with me."

He slowed his grinding then bent and checked the curve of the metal with his palm. Glancing up at her, he said, "I would be honored, of course." The rest of his sentence went unsaid. *If I'm still here.*

Celeste thought she must surely be mad to torture herself this way, but she couldn't stop herself from wondering what it would be like to dance with Harry. To feel his arms around her, his broad palm at her back. And if he thought he would satisfy her with a boring quadrille, he was the one who was mad. She was counting on a waltz.

"Pass my notebook, please." His words brought her out of her musings. As she passed the thin journal, her hand brushed his and their eyes caught. She stopped breathing and looked at his mouth. The memory of the soft-but-hard feel of his lips on hers was vivid and colorful. A white-hot swirl of shimmering gold and silver. Surely this wanting would go away, wouldn't it?

He pulled on the notebook, drawing her closer.

The door to the outbuilding opened, sunlight blinding them both, and Remy's dark outline appeared in the opening. She dropped the notebook and stepped to the side.

———

"THIS HAS TO BE THE most painful courtship in history," Remy said as they left the forge. "More, even, than my own."

"There is no courtship," Harry bit out.

"*Bien sûr*." His words said "of course," but his face said something else entirely.

"Did you need something?" Harry asked.

"The men who were on guard last night"— Harry's attention sharpened—"they heard something in the woods. Footsteps, perhaps. They investigated, but they were hesitant to leave the telescope for too long."

Harry nodded. "They did the right thing. I don't like this." He both dreaded the unveiling and wished for its swift arrival, if only to put an end to the strange goings-on.

He would have his wish soon enough. There were only two nights left. The laborers had completed the mounting structure, and the mirror was all that remained. This afternoon they would install the heavy metal disc, and tonight they would test its clarity against the night sky. If the mirror required adjustment, there was only one more night to test it.

It was cutting things much too close to Harry's way of thinking.

———

Harry pushed back from the worktable and set the spherometer down. "I think that's the best we'll do for now, my lord."

Ashford, sweating in the enclosed forge, bent to survey the curve of the mirror. "It's excellent work, my boy. Let's give it a try."

Remy left to gather men to help maneuver the mirror into place, and Celeste hung her apron on a peg by the door. Harry crossed his arms and watched her move.

She had a smudge of emery on her cheek, and a thick curl had come loose to trail down her neck. His favorite curl. Despite her mussed hair and stained cheek, Harry thought her the most beautiful woman—inside and out—that he'd ever seen.

Two more nights. One way or another, this would all be over in two more nights. And then . . . what?

He looked up. Ashford watched him watching Celeste. Harry cleared his throat and wiped his hands before joining Remy.

———

THE MIRROR DIDN'T WORK. After six men loaded it onto a low cart and hefted it into place, after the sun set and night fell, Harry and Ashford climbed to the telescope's observation platform. They checked the view down the tube to find a blurry image reflected in the mirror. Fuzzy stars merged with more fuzzy stars.

Harry looked at Celeste and Remy standing below and shook his head. Their shoulders fell, and Harry blew out a breath, cheeks puffing.

This was to be expected. Mirrors of this size, to these exacting specifications, took *months* to craft. They'd created this one in weeks. There was only one more night to get it right.

He turned to Ashford and stopped. The older man's face had bleached white and sweat beaded his brow. Not for the first time, Harry wondered about the urgency. Why was it so critical to complete the telescope by the start of the Round Table?

He understood that Timmons would be there, ready to write his account of the event. But what was the worst that would happen if the telescope weren't complete for another day or two beyond that?

"My lord," he began. "I understand the importance of the telescope. But what's the worst that will happen if it's not finished until the *end* of the Round Table?"

Ashford stared at him for a beat, then he looked

at Celeste standing below them. He rubbed a hand over his face and closed his eyes. "Harry, there's more at stake than you know. Please, indulge a foolish man."

Harry watched him for a moment then nodded. "I'll do my best to see it finished, my lord."

"I know you will. Your best is enough. Remember that, Harry, no matter what."

CHAPTER TWENTY-THREE

TWO DAYS UNTIL THE UNVEILING

SIX LABORERS RETURNED TO WRESTLE THE newly adjusted mirror back into the tube, and now there was nothing to do but wait for night to fall. Everyone was gathered in the drawing room after an early supper, and tension simmered while they waited for the sun to set.

Harry was itchy and restless. He invited Celeste to join him in a game of chess, hoping to distract himself. Her moves were bold, but unskilled. She really had no aptitude for the game. No finesse. Her king fell promptly, as expected, and he shook his head as she reset the board.

Before his knight could capture her queen yet again, a young footman entered the drawing room. He stood straight then abandoned his dignity to exclaim, "My lord, there's smoke on the Hill!"

Confused silence hovered for a moment before pandemonium erupted. Everyone pushed through the terrace doors to the path beyond the gardens. A blue cloud rose from the top of the Hill, further dimming the fading sunlight. Harry's blood rushed in his ears, and through it, he heard Lord Ashford call for water buckets.

He jumped. How they would get enough water to the top of the Hill, he didn't know, but they had to try. They couldn't *not* try.

Jenkins and Ashford organized the servants while Harry and Remy raced up the path with shovels. When they neared the top, they found James, one of the grooms assigned to the overnight guard. He lay off the path, a lump on the side of his head. The second guard bent over him, trying to rouse him, and James moaned as they approached.

"Did you see anything?" Harry asked the second guard.

"No, sir. James heard something, and when he didn't return, I came to investigate. I found him here then saw the smoke."

"Send someone for Dr. Grey," Harry instructed.

He left the man in Remy's care and continued into the clearing. One corner of the wooden structure burned, and flames licked the chestnut timbers. Smoke billowed from the skeletal frame in great blooming waves while the iron tube glowed like a giant fireplace poker where the flames rolled over it.

Servants arrived soon after and attacked the flames with whatever was at hand. Buckets of water, blankets, shovels of dirt. Faces were sooty and sweaty by the time they conquered the fire.

Harry surveyed the damage in the waning light. The tube popped and cracked as it cooled, smoke curling off the iron. Charred bits blackened the wooden mount, and the air was bitter with the smell. Several of the timbers would have to be replaced.

Soot clouded the mirror. They would have to remove it once the tube cooled and clean it for tomorrow night's unveiling. Today's refinements would have to be enough.

The pulley system was inoperable, the tube arrested at a forty-degree angle. Assuming the mirror afforded a view of anything, it would be limited to a narrow strip of the heavens just off the horizon.

Ash caught on the breeze and spiraled, tumbling like shooting stars to settle on his shoulders. Even Harry failed to miss the irony of *that*.

Ashford stared, stark disbelief etched on his face, his cane sinking into the soft earth.

"Mr. Corbyn." Harry turned at Remy's low voice and saw a dark torch in his hand, the end covered in pitch. "This was found near the base."

Harry rubbed his burning eyes. Given the

previous attack on the telescope, he wasn't surprised to learn the fire had been deliberate, but he was disheartened. Who could possibly wish harm on Ashford's project?

"Thank you, Remy. There's not much more we can do tonight. It's not safe while our arsonist may still be out there." He peered into the darkness thickening in the trees. "Please see that everyone returns safely."

When the servants had all left the Hill, Ashford began his slow descent and Remy followed. Harry drew a slow breath then another. His plans for Cairo had been tenuous at best before tonight, but they might as well have gone up in smoke with the telescope's mount.

Anger rose in his chest and his breaths came faster. He tugged both hands through his hair then crouched, elbows on his knees. He swallowed and choked the emotion back.

He slowly became aware of a hand on his shoulder. He stood, feeling older than his six and twenty years. Celeste wrapped her arms around him, her front to his back. He looked down and saw her white hands wrapped across his waist. Warm through the fabric of his shirt. He inhaled a stuttering breath then turned in her embrace.

She had soot on her forehead, and her hair had come undone on one side. The sinking sun lit her cinnamon curls from behind, but it was her eyes that caught him — fathomless blue-green pools that pulled him to her. Helpless to resist, even had he wanted to, he plunged his hands into her hair and pressed his lips to hers. She drew a breath — drew *him* — in and returned his kiss.

This kiss was not the hesitant almost-kiss of three years ago, nor was it the beautiful kiss they'd shared on the roof beneath a shower of cascading stars. This kiss was raw and elemental, forged of pain and frustration and the desperate yearning to comfort and be comforted.

She was exotic warm vanilla and wood smoke, twining around him. He pulled her into him, reveling in the feel of her mouth beneath his, the balm of her soul to his.

The kiss went on and on, until, dimly, foreign sound intruded on his awareness. Steps crunching stone on the path. No! The steps neared and then stopped, and a throat cleared. Harry pulled his lips from Celeste's and looked up.

A small bespectacled man stood before them, notebook in one hand and a pencil in the other. Mr. Timmons.

———

CELESTE'S HEART POUNDED A FURIOUS beat. Her lips felt naked, bare, without Harry's covering them. She should return to the Hall, but she couldn't muster her bones and muscles into proper formation to descend the path. Harry's kiss had turned her into a limp and quivering jelly.

When she'd witnessed his anger and frustration, she'd wanted to curl around him and absorb his pain. And when he'd kissed her with such naked emotion, their breaths mingling, she'd wanted to climb into him. To become part of him. Was this love? Lord, she hoped not.

This, whatever *this* was, had to go. She was returning to Paris, to her plans of painting and Salon submissions. And Harry would surely go . . . wherever Harry would go. Wherever his dreams took him next. She'd already convinced herself it was best this way.

While she waited for her breathing to slow, Harry addressed Mr. Timmons' questions about the fire. The writer's pencil bobbed as he scratched in his little notebook. He was openly skeptical of Harry's explanation of an overturned lantern, but even more doubtful that the telescope could be repaired by tomorrow's unveiling.

Harry, though, was more determined than ever to see the project through. Despite the improbability, he assured Mr. Timmons that the telescope would work. She wanted to rail at him and his single-minded obsession, force him to accept that it would not work. To accept that failure was . . . acceptable.

She tried to consider their dilemma rationally. What was the worst that would happen if the telescope couldn't be repaired by tomorrow? They still had a week during which the Eleven would attend her father's Round Table event. A week before the harvest festival concluded and Marshfield came to see the Earl of Ashford's miraculous new device. All was not lost if they had to postpone things a bit.

Yes, Mr. Timmons was here. He would likely write a withering story about the follies of men if the telescope didn't impress him. He had an editor to please and papers to sell, after all. So her father would be embarrassed. And probably Harry too, now that his wagon was hitched to her father's star, so to speak. But embarrassment could be survived.

And yet, her father was adamant, manic almost, that the telescope be completed *tomorrow*.

Harry interrupted her musings and held his arm for her. "Mr. Timmons, it will grow dark soon," he told the man. "You won't enjoy the trek down the Hill without a lamp."

Timmons poked at a charred timber with his pencil then joined them.

Night was settling in by the time they reached the last curve at the bottom of the Hill, the moon providing brief illumination through the clouds. They picked their way, mindful of dips and ruts in the path, until Harry stumbled on something. Celeste came to a jerking stop next to him, and Timmons almost ran into them from behind. Harry held up a hand and bent down, feeling in the dark.

"Harry?"

"It's a man."

"What? Is he—?"

"I don't know. I think he's alive."

The clouds shifted then, and moonlight lit Remy's face. He was pale and deathly still, and Celeste gasped.

"Timmons!" Harry said. "Help me carry him to the house."

Timmons was a full head shorter than Harry, and not nearly as strong. Celeste ran ahead and brought back two burly footmen, who assisted as they carried Remy through the library.

Her father gaped. "What's happened?" he demanded, and Harry explained in short, terse sentences.

Her mother took one look at Remy's still face and her own blanched.

"Send for Odette," she instructed Jenkins, then she followed the footmen as they carried Remy's inert body to the servants' quarters. Julian, who was still tending the guard below stairs, wouldn't have far to travel for his next patient.

Celeste watched her father's eyes narrow before

he too left the room, his cane thumping on the library's marble floor.

———

HARRY STARED ACROSS THE LIBRARY at Marchand, checking again for silver laurel-wreath buttons and signs of guilt. But no, he reminded himself. The man had no reason to injure Remy or set fire to the telescope. In fact, his face was drawn and pale. Shaken, much like Harry's own, he imagined. Not the face of a guilty conscience then.

Julian was grim when he rejoined them. Remy had suffered a sharp blow to the back of his head and had not yet regained consciousness. "With cases like this, it's hard to tell when, or if, the patient will awaken. How long do you think he's been unconscious?"

"We came upon him ten minutes after he left us, fifteen at most," Harry said.

Julian nodded. "Keep him comfortable. I'll return in the morning but let me know if he awakens in the meantime."

When Julian left, the atmosphere in the library was somber. Harry stood at the windows with his arms crossed, disbelieving that Remy, who had been so *awake* hours earlier, now lay still as death. No telescope—no science—was worth this.

Lady Ashford and Celeste sat beside each other on the large velvet sofa. Lady Ashford wiped a tear from her cheek, while Celeste gripped her hands in her lap. Marchand, still pale, excused himself and retired for the evening.

Ashford sat in a leather chair before the fireplace, withdrawn. He stared unseeing into the hearth, gazing at a point in the flames none of them could see. His words, when he spoke, were so soft Harry could barely hear them.

"This has gone too far."

"My lord?"

"What do you mean, Edmund?" Lady Ashford asked.

Celeste looked up. "Father, do you know who attacked Remy? Or why?"

Ashford balanced both hands on the head of his cane and angled his head down, eyes closed. Deep grooves lined both sides of his face. He sighed. "I suspect I do."

————

"FATHER! YOU MUST TELL US. Whoever did this can't be allowed to hurt anyone else."

Ashford considered for a moment, then he looked up with a resolute expression on his face. He stood, levering himself with his cane, his back to the popping firebox. Nodding once, he said, "I've something to confess. I've done something of which I'm . . . not proud."

Harry straightened and prepared to excuse

himself. This sounded like a family conversation that didn't concern him.

"Harry, this concerns you, too."

Harry looked up sharply, and Ashford gave him a weak smile.

"Like it or not, you're part of this family."

Something shifted in Harry's chest, like a bubble rising, and his mouth went dry. To hear this man refer to him as family . . . He moved further into the room, away from the windows, and settled his hands in his pockets.

"What are you talking about, Edmund?" Lady Ashford asked.

"I made an unfortunate—and unconscionable—wager with Lord Knowles." He looked at Celeste, regret and sorrow shadowing his eyes.

"Last autumn, as the Round Table was coming to a close, Knowles and I were discussing—arguing, rather—the latest theories. I might have imbibed a little too much."

Lady Ashford snorted and looked away, and a cold foreboding slithered through Harry, threatening the bubble in his chest. His father had enjoyed gin, and he knew nothing good ever came from too much drink.

Ashford sighed then forged ahead. "Knowles wagered that I couldn't devise a better telescope. One with greater range and more precision. He said there is only so far our science will take us, and some things must always lie beyond our understanding. The man has no imagination, so naturally, I disagreed."

"What—" Lady Ashford inhaled. "What were the stakes?"

"He had already boasted that he would be selected as the lead for the Cairo expedition. I knew our Harry was hoping for the same." He smiled sadly at Harry then continued. "And I knew Harry would be a much better choice than Knowles. But Knowles . . . well, he had favors to call in with the Commission."

Harry nodded; they knew this.

"So, when Knowles said he would withdraw his application if I could, in fact, build a better telescope, it seemed like a good solution."

"But the selection isn't final yet." Celeste added. "Lord Porter thinks Harry may still be in the running, despite Knowles' influence. And despite your interference."

"Porter is well-meaning but overly optimistic. Knowles' grip on the Commission is heavy. Even with Porter and a successful telescope on your side, the Commission won't go against Knowles." He directed this to Harry with an apologetic twist of his lips.

Harry was silent as the bubble in his chest

exploded. There wasn't much to be said. Ashford spoke the truth. The odds of his being selected *were* poor. He'd known as much when he submitted his application. But hearing it laid out so plainly was disheartening. Ashford had known all along, even while Harry shared his naive hopes with him.

"So, Knowles offered Cairo," Lady Ashford said. "What did you wager in return?"

Ashford grimaced. "I offered him Dante."

"Your hunter?" Celeste asked, a small furrow creasing her brow.

Ashford nodded. "He'd been hinting that he'd like to buy him off me to improve his stables, so I thought it a fair wager. But, as it turns out, he wasn't interested in Dante."

"Oh, Edmund. What did you do?" Lady Ashford asked.

"As I said, I had imbibed too much. So, when he suggested Denton Manor as comparable stakes, I . . . agreed." Lady Ashford gasped, her gaze flying between Ashford and Celeste. Celeste's eyebrows reversed course and angled into her hairline.

"Denton Manor? But that—that's part of my dowry."

Ashford added quickly, reassuring her, "I was confident I would win. I'd been working for some time on plans for a new, better design. It was just a matter of completing it by the next Round Table."

"But then you became ill, and the project fell behind," Celeste said, and Ashford's head dropped between his shoulders.

"Did you know?" Celeste directed that question to Harry. He stepped back and turned the button in his pocket as his anger rose. How could she think he knew such a thing?

"Harry didn't know," Ashford continued. "His arrival, though, was a godsend." He faced Harry. "There was no chance of success without you. And the Frenchman, of course," he added as an afterthought. "I thought if the telescope was completed, you could go to Cairo and Celeste could keep Denton Manor."

Emotion—a swirling mixture of disbelief and betrayal—choked Harry. He forced it down to examine later and asked instead, "What does Knowles want with Denton Manor?"

"It abuts his property to the north," Celeste said.

Ashford nodded. "Indeed. He's coveted Denton Manor for some time. It would double his own estate."

"What will you do if you lose this silly wager?" Lady Ashford asked. "How will you make that up to our daughter, Edmund?" Celeste opened her mouth to say something then closed it again. It appeared she, too, was curious.

"I don't know." Ashford shook his head. "I don't

know."

"Well," Lady Ashford said. "It seems you have a telescope to perfect. By tomorrow." She stood and shook her skirts. The silence as she left the room was deafening.

"Knowles." Harry said after a lengthy pause. "You think he's behind the attacks on the telescope then?"

"It makes sense. If it isn't ready by the start of the Round Table, he wins."

"But . . . that's cheating," Celeste said. "Worse, it's criminal."

"I don't think he's overly concerned about that. There were rumors some years back about another wager . . . I think he left the country for a time, but nothing was ever proven."

"And you still placed a bet with him?" Celeste's voice rose as she asked the question. Harry suspected she was holding her anger with a tight rein.

Ashford rubbed a hand over his eyes. "I admit, it wasn't my finest hour. You must know, m'dear, how sorry I am. I never meant to hurt you." He looked at Harry. "Either of you."

Celeste waved his apology away—either unable or unwilling to accept it—and focused instead on how to proceed. "If we can prove Knowles has engaged in dishonorable acts to win the wager, he'll have to forfeit."

"Yes, but we don't have any evidence he was behind the incidents. And we can hardly accuse the man outright without proof."

"The first attack," Harry said, rubbing his jaw. They looked at him as he reached into his pocket. "Remy found this the night of the storm." He showed them the laurel-leaf button.

"It doesn't look outlandish enough to belong to Knowles," Celeste said. "And if it does belong to him, how could we prove it?"

The three of them stared at the button, each lost in their own thoughts.

Harry opened his mouth to speak then closed it again. In the space of Ashford's five-minute confession, he had careened from bright joy, to dark, nauseating defeat.

To hear Ashford call him family had caused his chest to expand, but then to find that his dreams were nothing more than high stakes between two gentlemen . . . His breathing increased, his chest rising and falling as panic threatened.

Then he looked at Celeste, at the face that had become so dear to him in the last months. Her dowry—her very independence—was at risk. He knew she required Denton Manor to maintain her independent lifestyle in Paris. Without its income . . . what? Would she have to leave Paris? Marry Marchand? Would she still be able to apply to the

Academy, to submit her paintings to the Salon? She deserved choices.

Ashford's pig needed to fly.

CHAPTER TWENTY-FOUR

THE DAY OF THE UNVEILING

ELESTE SPENT THE SMALL HOURS of the morning turning in her bed. Her braid unraveled, and the sheets twined about her legs in an uncomfortable twist. Her restless night was no surprise with all that had happened yesterday. The fire. The attack on Remy. Her father's confession. Harry's kiss.

When her father revealed his wager with Knowles, a hot queasiness had flooded her. He'd gambled with Harry's future. Her future.

If he lost, even Alexandre wouldn't marry her. And Harry couldn't afford to marry her, even if he wanted to. Her dowry was the only thing that would make it possible for them to be together.

And if her father won, she would keep her dowry,

but Harry would go to Cairo.

So many questions had tumbled through her mind as her father told his tale. But the one that had escaped her lips, the question that she couldn't call back, was whether Harry had known. Even as she'd voiced the words, she knew the answer.

Harry had no talent for lying or deception. And his one true passion was . . . knowledge. He would have pursued the telescope for nothing more than to satisfy his own curiosity. His urgent quest to know and understand.

But the words were out, and his reaction had sliced her heart. Shock and betrayal had chased across his face before he composed his features. Guilt riddled her. She thought of his kiss, and her desire to curl around him, absorb his pain. Would he accept her comfort today? Could she undo the pain she'd caused?

The sky was beginning to lighten, the sun's edge not yet visible over the horizon, when she rang for a maid. She expected one of the lower maids, so she was surprised when Odette responded. The pretty maid's eyes were bright and red-rimmed, her cheerful disposition subdued.

"Has Remy not awakened yet, then?" Celeste asked softly.

"*Non.*" Odette twisted Celeste's curls into a knot, focused on the simple task she'd performed many times before.

Celeste spun and placed a hand on her arm, stilling her. "Odette, you should attend to him. My mother doesn't expect you to be working now."

"Lady Ashford, she is exceedingly kind, but the work is welcome." Her eyes shone, and a tear hovered on her lashes.

Celeste squeezed her hand. "He will recover," she assured her.

"*Oui*, I'm sure you must be right, Lady Celeste."

The mood in the house was somber. Celeste went to the dining room to take a quick meal before journeying up the Hill. Her mother was already seated, and a ruby-liveried footman poured steaming chocolate into her cup. The spot behind Lily where Remy usually stood was glaringly empty.

Lily issued crisp orders to Jenkins between demure sips. The Eleven would begin arriving soon. Her mother still planned a festive—if optimistic—supper to celebrate the unveiling, and it seemed nothing was going to derail that. Not the villainous attack on Remy, and certainly not her husband's idiocy or a failed telescope. Napoleon might have won the war if Lily St. James had served as his general.

"Have you seen Father yet?" Celeste asked from the sideboard.

"*Non*." Just the one word then. That was telling.

"Harry?"

"He was starting for the Hill when I came down. Julian and Alexandre were with him."

Celeste piled her plate with Bath buns before realizing she couldn't possibly eat them all. She put one back before moving down the sideboard to a silver bowl of cherries and plums.

"When do you expect the Eleven will arrive?" she asked.

"Lord Porter sent a message yesterday. He and Lady Porter should arrive in time for tea. And Lord Knowles is visiting his sister in Maidstone." Her face scrunched in a delicate grimace. "He should arrive for tea as well. I imagine the others won't be far behind."

Celeste sipped her chocolate, wincing as the hot liquid scalded her tongue.

Her mother pulled a deep breath and closed her eyes briefly before speaking. "Your father . . . *c'est un imbécile*. It's indisputable. Irrefutable." Clearly, she felt the point needed emphasizing. "But he did what he did out of affection for your Harry. Even if his methods were *stupide*."

She paused a moment and traced the lace pattern on the tablecloth before continuing. "After you were born, Dr. Smythe said I wouldn't bear another child. I—Your father was devastated. We always expected to have a large family, you see. Is it any wonder he loves that boy as his own?"

Celeste stared at her mother, surprised by her words. She'd always wondered why she'd been an only child.

"Do not be like me," Lily continued. "It's fine to be angry. A little grudge won't hurt. But do not hold onto it for too long. We will find a way to make this work." Her speech concluded, she kissed Celeste's cheek and left to check on Remy.

Celeste blew on her chocolate and turned her mother's words over. They were ... sensible. Surprisingly so, despite Lily's emphasis on her father's questionable intelligence.

When she stepped onto the wide terrace, she found the universe didn't care that her insides were in knots. The day promised to be bright, the sky an unblemished crystal blue. A crisp wind blew down from the Hill, carrying the acrid scent of doused wood smoke. It was the kind of morning that signaled the change of the season, from hot, humid summer to brisk fall. It was the kind of morning she usually loved.

When she reached the crest of the Hill, she found a crowd of Marshfielders. She recognized Mrs. Gilkerson's nephew, and Roberts from the smithy. Several of her father's tenants, and a handful of village lads. Julian was also there, as were Alexandre and Harry. Her father stood on the dais, pointing and shouting directions.

Harry left the others and approached her.

"What's happened?" she asked.

"The villagers heard about the fire, and they've come to assist with repairs. It would seem our endeavors over the last weeks have caught the imagination of Marshfield."

"Truly?" Although why that was surprising, she didn't know. The village had been abuzz with talk of astronomy ever since the meteor shower, much to Olive Pitt's dismay. If Marshfielders were talking about stars and the heavens, they weren't talking about the upcoming harvest festival.

She was pleased to see Alexandre taking part in the repairs. He wasn't aware of her father's wager, but he clearly sensed the urgency at hand.

Harry turned to go, and she placed a hand on his sleeve to hold him. "Harry, I should not have asked if you were aware of my father's wager. I knew before the words were out of my mouth that you were not. You're incapable of lying."

His eyebrows went up at that. "Thank you? I think."

"Sorry." She winced. "What I meant is that I know you, Harry. You're not a deceptive person. I don't know why I said what I did. Please, say you'll forgive me?" She waited expectantly, hopefully, her stomach turning her Bath buns in anxiety.

He pressed her hand where it rested on his arm

and smiled. "Celeste, there is nothing to forgive. You were shocked by your father's admission. What he did was . . . well, that's neither here nor there. We need to focus on how to repair the damage and prevent you from losing Denton Manor."

She nodded, relieved. She didn't deserve his forgiveness, but she would accept it all the same.

Over the next hours, the workers removed the worst of the charred wood and replaced it with new timbers. Harry inspected the pulley system in the light of day and confirmed it couldn't be repaired quickly. They had to hope for a good showing from the scope's current angle.

As suspected, the giant mirror was horribly clouded with soot, but the men were adept by now at the laborious process of removing and reinstalling it. Even cleaned, though, there was no certainty it would yield a clear image.

As several men trundled the heavy disc off to be polished yet again, Alexandre asked the obvious question on everyone's tongue: "What if it doesn't work?"

"It will work," her father replied as he checked the angle of the tube against his sky charts. Regardless of the odds against them, he was still obstinately, desperately optimistic.

Despite their varied backgrounds and experience, the men worked like a well-tuned orchestra. They followed her father's direction until he finally declared an end to the day.

Harry sighed. "That's the best we can hope for, my lord."

Her father was quiet for a moment, then he said, "It's good enough, Harry. Good enough."

Harry's jaw was clamped tight, and if Celeste wasn't mistaken, her father's eyes were shiny. *Imbécile* or not, he was her father, and it hurt her to see him so distressed. She looked up at the sky, where the faint shape of clouds emerged on the otherwise pristine horizon.

The universe, it seemed, had a dreadful sense of humor.

CHAPTER TWENTY-FIVE

ARRY'S ANXIETY WAS TIGHTER THAN his cravat, pressing and squeezing his throat. Remy still had not regained consciousness, and Harry went to check on him once more after returning from the Hill.

Odette and Lady Ashford had been keeping a regular bedside vigil, dribbling water into their patient's mouth from a soaked cloth and taking turns encouraging him to wake.

Despite their efforts, Harry was disheartened to see Remy so still, a bandage around his head, blond eyelashes dark against his sallow cheeks.

As the Eleven began to arrive, Harry joined the others in the drawing room. When Knowles appeared with his nephew and Mr. Timmons, Celeste's demeanor turned frosty. She openly studied his apparel, likely checking him for laurel-wreathed buttons.

There was nothing so tame about the man's attire, though. He sported a grape waistcoat with raspberry stripes and a cravat the color of ripe apricots. Harry thought he looked like a fruit compote. His Brutus hairstyle—rendered inflexible by an excess of pomade—made Harry itch to run a hand through his own hair.

For Harry's part, he checked *everyone's* apparel, but he hoped he was more covert than Celeste.

One attack could be explained by a vagrant or other random encounter, but the fire, combined with the attacks on Harry, James and Remy, suggested a deliberate scheme. A source who was known to them. Likely someone in this room.

He hesitated to make assumptions about Knowles' involvement. While Ashford's wager afforded him motive, there was no proof. Harry didn't want to focus on him to the exclusion of the true culprit.

So, he studied all the guests' buttons and gauged their expressions, but it was no use. There were no missing laurel-wreath buttons. No guilty faces.

The ladies were all turned out in delicate slippers and gowns of velvet and silk, lace and satin. They would remain behind while the gentlemen made the trek up the Hill. A walk in the dark, along an uneven path, was more than they were willing to endure for a chance look at the heavens.

The drawing room was loud, which was typical of Ashford's Round Table events. The Eleven debated theories and hypotheses, shared treatises and the results of experiments. Knowles was in rare form, arguing his latest theory. He'd recently read a report of bat-winged creatures on the moon, and he thought the account had merit.

When conversation turned to the telescope, Ashford described the attacks on both instrument and man. Knowles seemed shocked. He was either innocent of the attacks, or he was very good at deception.

"But I don't understand," Lady Beson said. "Why would anyone want to impede your efforts?"

"That, indeed, is the question, Lady Beson." Ashford eyed each man as he spoke. "Because to do so in such a despicable and dishonorable manner is not the behavior of a gentleman."

"I should think not! Such behavior is so very . . . common. Thank heavens you yourself weren't injured." Murmurs of agreement flowed through the room.

To add to Harry's unease, the clouds that had begun forming that afternoon had not ceased their march across the sky. He feared they would do more to affect tonight's outcome than last night's fire. With nothing to observe, Ashford would have to forfeit. Clearly, he hadn't anticipated that complication when he wagered his daughter's future.

As if his thoughts had summoned her, Celeste appeared at his elbow. She, unlike the other ladies, intended to join the gentlemen on the Hill. To that end, she wore a sensible gown of dove grey muslin. It was unadorned and serviceable, not particularly fetching, as far as gowns went. He rarely noticed ladies' gowns, or the forms within, but with Celeste, he noticed everything.

He glanced down, wondering what shoes she wore beneath her dress. She read his mind and lifted her hem a scant few inches to display a pair of sturdy half-boots. He smiled and offered her his arm as Ashford began shepherding the observers to the terrace.

The Eleven took their time assembling at the top of the Hill. Once there, Lords Porter and Beson held lanterns up to inspect the intricate pulley system. Others peered into the stone outbuilding where the mirror had been built. With pride, Ashford pointed out Harry's grinding tool that had shortened the time needed to craft the mirror.

"Quite impressive, Corbyn," Porter said.

"Thank you, my lord. Remy, our engineer, and I developed it together." He felt like he should say more—something witty and intelligent to remind Porter he was the better choice for Cairo—but his heart wasn't in it. His mind kept straying to Celeste at his side and what she would do if Ashford lost his bet.

Celeste tensed as clouds continued to roll and tumble across the sky. "I don't like the look of the sky," she whispered.

Her warmth heated his side as she leaned toward him, and it was a full moment before he could respond. "Nor do I."

Rustling sounded behind them, and a flash of pale skin betrayed a wide-eyed Robbie, whose gaze was fixed on the telescope. Harry motioned for the boy to stand with them, mindful that dangers still lurked on the Hill. If they were wrong and Knowles wasn't to blame, then they were no closer to identifying the person responsible. And if Knowles was behind the attacks, Harry felt better having Robbie in his sight.

Porter lowered his lantern and motioned to the observation platform. "Ashford, we should begin if we wish to outrun the clouds."

Ashford looked up and nodded. "Yes. Yes, of course." He climbed to the observation platform and straightened his coat while the Eleven clustered below him. "Friends," he began. "Until a mere two hundred years ago, everything we knew about our universe we saw with our naked eye."

Harry looked at Celeste and she shrugged. They'd not expected a speech, but then Harry realized a cluster of clouds had stalled forty degrees off the horizon. The telescope was blind.

Ashford's voice resonated as he settled into his monologue. "Then when Mr. Galileo turned his telescope toward the sky, our world became larger, deeper."

He continued on in this vein for some moments, ignoring his audience's shifting impatience until Knowles shouted, "Move it along, Ashford!"

Ashford glared at him then grumbled, "Yes, quite right." He called for one of the footmen to rotate the telescope, but clouds had fully covered the sky by that point, and Knowles complained.

"Concede, Ashford. I told you this wouldn't work." He turned to Timmons, who scratched a stubby pencil across his notebook. "What will you write in your story now?"

"Knowles," Porter said, "you know science can't be rushed. Didn't St. Augustine say, 'Patience is the companion of wisdom'? Although I'm sure your experience with either virtue is limited."

Other members of the Eleven laughed while Knowles glared. Harry rubbed his chin, too anxious for laughter.

"The sky's clearing!" Beson said, drawing everyone's gaze. The moon lit the edge of the clouds, and a small patch of star-speckled sky emerged low on the horizon.

"Charles!" Ashford motioned again to the footman to turn the crank. As the mount rotated, the Eleven shuffled to follow its path. Finally, the telescope pointed its iron finger at the small opening.

Ashford gazed into the tube while the group below remained silent, as if a noise would jar the stars from the heavens. Harry held his breath, and Robbie's small hand wrinkled the sleeve of his coat.

Ashford pulled his head from the tube and consulted a chart before disappearing again. When he emerged next, he wore a broad grin and motioned for Porter to ascend to the viewing platform.

Harry itched to see what Ashford had seen, but he realized the wisdom of securing Porter's impartial judgment before the clouds could thwart them again. He pressed down his impatience as Celeste's hand tightened on his arm.

"Mr. Timmons!" Ashford called while Porter climbed. "I guarantee you'll want to write about this in your paper." He rubbed a hand over his face, smoothing the marionette lines around his mouth, and relief relaxed his features. He threw a wide smile down at Harry and Celeste.

As Harry watched, the opening in the clouds grew rather than shrank. He held an expectant breath, dizzy with anticipation, his heart thumping in his chest.

Porter studied the sky to gain his bearings before leaning in to view the image reflected in the telescope. "Is that—by all that's holy, that's Rigel! I can see her sister star clearly. Remarkable!"

Porter referred to the double star at Orion's left foot. Its components—two stars orbiting together—had been logged decades before, but they'd never been observed distinctly. Porter descended, shaking his head, and Harry released his breath.

Ashford's Flying Pig was a success.

He stood motionless for a moment, amazed, shock rooting his feet to the ground. Then he ran a shaky hand through his hair and laughed. Even Knowles' scowling face couldn't suppress the grin that stretched his mouth.

Knowles ascended next. His side whiskers quivered, and his thick lips flattened as he checked the view in the telescope.

Everything was going to be all right.

Harry smiled at Celeste, and she beamed back. He checked himself before he embraced her in front of everyone, but only just.

Robbie's excitement was tangible, and he bounced as he watched each man take a turn at the telescope.

Finally, the last of the assembled gentlemen stepped up. Anders, Knowles' nephew placed a boot on the ladder, and moonlight caught his face. Robbie gasped. "Sir," he tugged on Harry's sleeve and pointed at Anders. "It's him!"

"What?" Harry asked.

"That's the man wot broke the telescope."

CHAPTER TWENTY-SIX

HARRY LOOKED AT ROBBIE THEN at Mr. Anders, whose own eyes had grown wide. Timmons' head snapped up and swiveled between them, ears cocked. He raised his pencil and licked the tip.

"Are you sure, Robbie?"

Robbie nodded.

"Knowles? Did you know about this?" Ashford asked from his perch above.

"What are you on about, Ashford?" Knowles looked from Ashford to his nephew and back again.

Ashford's voice carried above the small crowd. "Did you and your nephew have anything to do with the attacks on my telescope? On Mr. Corbyn and the others?"

"What? That's preposterous!" Knowles' gaze shifted from his nephew to Timmons then to the others gathered around.

"Did you start the fire?" Harry asked Anders.

Anders opened his mouth to respond, but Knowles cut him off. "This is preposterous," he repeated. "Don't say anything," he ordered.

Anders ignored his uncle. "I don't know to what you're referring."

"I believe you lost this," Harry said. He held up the silver button.

The man's face was composed until he saw the button, then panic lit his features. He turned to push past the others, but Porter stepped in front of him.

"Mr. Anders, arson and assault are serious crimes. And if the footman dies, you'll hang for murder." Harry watched as Anders' eyes widened in righteous affront before he deflated.

"Porter," Knowles said. "You can't go about accusing innocent gentlemen of heinous crimes on the word of a . . . a miscreant."

"I'm not a mis—mis—miscreant."

"My point," Knowles said, motioning to Robbie. "The boy is uneducated. He's an unreliable witness at best."

Harry tightened his hand on Robbie's shoulder and pulled him closer.

"Knowles," Porter said. "Unless you wish to have this discussion here, I suggest we adjourn to the library for a more private conversation."

Knowles looked at Timmons and the faces of the Eleven before turning on his heel.

A choice between following Porter and taking a turn at the telescope was no choice at all. Harry called out to Ashford, "We have another observer, my lord."

He motioned Robbie forward, and Ashford beamed as Robbie placed a foot on the first rung. Harry climbed the ladder behind him, and together they stepped onto the viewing platform with Ashford.

The telescope was pointed at a tiny, murky drop of the Milky Way's spill, forty degrees off the horizon, near the foot of Orion. But when he and Robbie gazed into the tube, the haze resolved into a glorious multitude of stars. Diamonds of all shapes and sizes glittered and shimmered.

Robbie's hand gripped his sleeve in wonder, reminding Harry why he loved the heavens.

When he pulled his head from the mouth of the scope, he was surprised to see Celeste at his side and Ashford down below. He shifted to the side to make room. Her grin was wide, her eyes as bright as the stars he'd just seen as she leaned in.

———

PORTER'S QUESTIONING OF ANDERS REVEALED that the man was aware of his uncle's wager. As his heir, he had a vested interest in his uncle's holdings, and he'd taken it upon himself to secure a favorable outcome.

He admitted to damaging the telescope with the gamekeeper's axe but was reticent when questioned about the attack on Harry. On his uncle's advice, he refused to answer any of their questions about the fire or the attacks on James and Remy.

Knowles claimed ignorance of the whole affair and promptly returned to his sister's estate in Maidstone. After Anders was remanded to the Marshfield gaol, everyone enjoyed a festive supper full of speculation about the man's motives.

Harry watched Ashford, the man he'd always thought of as a mentor. The man who had been like a father to him. Who, in one ill-advised moment, had gambled with Harry's future. With Celeste's future. Despite the telescope's success, the sharp lines around his mouth were back. His posture was that of a defeated man, not one who had achieved a monumental success. Harry knew Ashford regretted his actions, but he couldn't bring himself to accept and forgive. Not yet.

"Mr. Corbyn." Charles the footman approached him with a smile after supper. "Remy is awake, sir. I thought you'd want to know."

Now this was great news!

Harry nodded and left the noise of celebration to follow the footman. His relief that Remy was awake was a palpable thing. As he neared the man's room,

Odette exited. The pretty maid blushed even as she beamed a broad smile at him.

Remy reclined against the bed's low headboard, a pillow at his back. He had a similar, beaming smile on his face. Harry assumed it was due to Odette's visit rather than his own.

A bandage still circled the man's head, and a large, purpling bruise covered one side of his jaw. Harry motioned to it, saying, "I suppose that will only endear you to the ladies even more. Some chaps have all the luck."

"Luck? Is that what we're calling it?"

Harry's grin slipped and he grew serious. "You're well?"

"I'll live to see another day, or so Dr. Grey tells me."

"That is good news indeed."

Remy's expression turned serious as well, his own grin falling as he looked at Harry. "It was Knowles' nephew. The dull-looking fellow with the blond hair."

"We know. Robbie identified him from the night of the first attack, and he confessed. At least to the first incident."

Harry described the evening's events, and Lord Ashford's bet with Knowles. He left out the details about Denton Manor and Cairo.

Remy seemed skeptical that a frivolous wager

over a telescope could lead to such dramatic events, but he held his tongue. A man of uncommon sense, it would seem.

"Knowles has far-reaching influence, but your identification of Anders can't be ignored. He'll be dealt with," Harry said.

Remy nodded, thinking. "So, the telescope . . . it worked, then? Ashford won the bet?"

Harry drew a breath then nodded. "It worked." He turned the enameled button in his pocket, relieved to only have the one to carry now. There was not room in his pockets for more than one button. It was a ridiculous habit anyway. Probably one he should try to break. He forced his hand to still.

"I hate to have missed it, but . . . you don't seem pleased."

Harry closed his eyes briefly. "I'm tired, I suppose. As you must be. I'll go and allow you to rest." He turned to leave then paused and added, "I'm glad you're well."

Remy grinned a cat-in-the-cream grin. "She said yes."

"Pardon?"

"Odette. She said yes."

Harry took a moment to adjust to the change of topic, then comprehension dawned. He shook the other man's hand. "Congratulations! I was right. You *are* a lucky man!"

"Luck had nothing to do with it."

Harry chuckled. "And a humble one, I see."

———

HARRY WANTED NOTHING MORE THAN to find his bed, but he couldn't say no when Lord Porter invited him to share a brandy in the library.

They settled on two overstuffed chairs before the fireplace, and Porter congratulated him on the telescope's success while Harry studied the amber liquid in his glass.

"When we met some weeks back, I told you I supported you for the Cairo expedition."

"Thank you, my lord. I appreciate your confidence."

"With Knowles' . . . family troubles, shall we say . . . he'll be withdrawing his application. The Commission meets in two days and will find they're short a lead astronomer in Cairo. And with your and Ashford's success tonight . . ."

Harry held his breath.

"You'll need to present yourself before the full Commission, of course, but it's safe to say the position is yours. If you want it, that is."

The blood slowed in Harry's veins before rushing to catch up with his heart. He scrubbed a hand over his face as he stared at his untouched brandy. His sleep-deprived mind could hardly comprehend what he was hearing.

Two days. The Commission would meet in two days. There would be lengthy preparations before the expedition left in eight weeks. He needed to go straight away. Where could he find Celeste? He wanted to tell her. He *needed* to tell her.

He rose to leave, to find her, then he recalled Porter. The man watched him, waiting for his answer. He must think him mad.

"Of course, I'll be there. Thank you, my lord." He bowed and left the room.

He was going to Cairo. He ran a hand through his hair and tugged.

———

CELESTE KNEW THAT NOTHING GOOD came from listening at doors. Tonight's victory, after so many weeks of anxiety, had left Celeste spent, and she couldn't bear another of the Eleven's energetic discussions. She went in search of Harry instead.

The door to the library was cracked, soft light spilling into the hall. She smiled—he must have sought an escape as well. She began to push the door wider when Lord Porter's voice on the other side stopped her.

I supported you for the Cairo expedition.

She should have left or, at the very least, announced herself, but she didn't.

The position is yours. If you want it, that is.

Of course, I'll be there.

Harry was leaving.

Now she stood before her worktable, searching distractedly for her magnifying glass. It was nowhere to be found.

Frustrated, she turned to eye her latest canvases propped along the wall instead. She'd begun separating them into piles based on their suitability for submission. The "no" pile was much larger than the "maybes" while the "yes" stack was nonexistent. She sighed. It was no use trying to organize her canvases. She couldn't concentrate with Harry's words echoing in her mind.

Of course, I'll be there.

The moon had risen beyond the line of clerestory windows. She blew out the candles and rotated the crank to open the dome's shutter. Silvery light poured in from above, glinting off the edges of her father's instruments.

Harry was leaving. Probably soon. She'd known the time would come when he would move on to his next project, so she shouldn't be surprised.

She heard a sound in the archway and turned. His familiar form was silhouetted against the light from the transit room. His hands were in his pockets, shoulders hunched. Restless energy vibrated off him.

He told her about his conversation with Lord Porter, and she tried to react as if she'd not been listening at doors.

"It's not certain, of course," he said. "But Porter believes it's merely a formality at this point." His face was transformed in that moment, his joy riveting. She couldn't pull her gaze away from the bright light in his eyes, the broad grin on his beautiful mouth.

"Harry! That's wonderful!" She meant it, she truly did. He deserved to realize all of his dreams. She stepped up and embraced him, holding him to her. The backs of her eyes stung, and she pressed the tears back as her heart cracked a little more.

He held her tightly for a moment, arms warm around her, then he pushed away. "I must leave tomorrow."

"So soon." It was a statement, not a question.

He turned and paced the room in long strides. "The Commission meets in two days, and there's a lot to prepare before we sail for Cairo."

She folded her hands before her waist, holding herself together. And then, because she needed to know, she asked, "What are you chasing, Harry?"

He stopped and faced her, blinked.

"You chased a dream to Berlin three years ago. You chased my father's dream here. You're chasing a dream to Cairo. What are you looking for, Harry? What do you hope to find?"

He sighed and ran a hand through his hair. Her heart pinched further; she loved when he did that.

"Nothing. Everything." He exhaled. "I can't

explain it. It's less about the finding than the seeking."

Pieces of her shifted and collided inside. There was truth in his words, for him and for herself. They were both seeking something that was just beyond their reach. As endless and exhausting as it sounded, she didn't think either of them could ever stop.

Still, she said, "If you're looking to do something meaningful, to *become* something meaningful, you can stop." She lifted his hand in hers. "Harry, you're there. Don't let your pride be your guide."

He opened his mouth to respond then closed it again. Finally, he said, "Pride is all I have."

She wanted to weep for him. "No, Harry. You have so much more than that. You *are* so much more than that."

He watched her face, listening, but not hearing. "I love—" he began, and the breath froze in her lungs. "I love that you see that in me."

She pulled in a heavy inhale and tried to smile.

The expression on his face was thoughtful, his eyes a brilliant, shimmering silver.

"Perhaps—"

Her breath stopped again as she waited for him to continue.

He looked at her canvases propped against the curved wall and his jaw flexed. "You're preparing to return to Paris?"

What if she said no? Would he stay? She thought he might. At the very least, he'd question his decision to go. Her heart twisted painfully, as if it were being cleaved in two. One half desired his happiness, the other, hers. She wanted to stamp her foot in frustration. Why must she choose, sacrifice one for the other?

She swallowed and chose. "If I leave soon, I can apply again for the Royal Academy."

He nodded, his bottom teeth scraping his lip. Then he lifted a thumb to her cheek and wiped her tears. "I believe I owe you a dance," he whispered.

She sniffed. "You'll miss the assembly. It's not for two more days."

He took her hand and pulled her toward the telescope in the center of the room, beneath the dome and into the moonlight.

"What are you doing?"

"Claiming my dance."

Her brows lifted as she looked at the limited floor space. "But there's a telescope—"

"Then we'll dance around it."

He placed her left hand on his shoulder and gripped her right in his warm palm. Then he slowly moved them in a soft, three-step rhythm. There was no music, only the light of the moon and stars beyond the curved line of the roof to guide them.

His hand was firm on her back, sitting slightly

above the curve of her hip. She smiled to feel it inch lower and settle a little indecently.

Warmth flowed where their hands and arms touched. She recalled their last kiss, and her lips, her fingers, her stomach all tingled. Definitely *fizzy*. The feeling was thrilling, and sad at the same time, because she feared she'd not know it again. Not like this.

She looked into his face and found him watching her. His slow smile melted her insides until she had to look away.

They stopped moving and stood beneath the dome's shutter. Silver moonlight gleamed on the telescope's brass and reflected in his eyes. He inched his head nearer, allowing her a chance to retreat before he touched his lips to hers.

She savored the soft pressure of his mouth before pulling away and accepting the truth. She would always be his, but *he* would always be running, chasing, forever out of her reach. She smiled and placed a hand along the side of his cheek.

"Go, Harry. Do something wonderful." And she knew he would.

CHAPTER TWENTY-SEVEN

OW COULD ONE PERSON FEEL two opposing
emotions at the same time? It shouldn't be
biologically possible. Harry had been
ecstatic to hear Lord Porter's words, to know how
close he was to his goal. But then he'd thought of
leaving Celeste and had almost told Porter thank you,
but no. The urge to abandon his dream and steal off
with Celeste was overwhelming. It terrified him, how
easily he could give up on everything he'd been
working toward.

And her tears, glistening on her cheeks, had
almost done him in. He rubbed his lip and recalled
her beneath the observatory's dome, moonlight
streaming around her.

Her allure was more than the lone cinnamon curl
that caressed her neck (although he adored that). It
was more than her blue-green eyes. When she smiled,
light poured from her onto him, drawing him into an

ever-tightening orbit. There was no scientific rationale, no equation to explain it.

Sharing his news with her had heightened his joy despite his conflicting emotions. That had been unexpected. With no family to care if he succeeded or failed, he was accustomed to keeping his achievements to himself. But Celeste cared. She *wanted* him to succeed. Telling her of Cairo had intensified the flavor of his success.

He'd thought of asking her to go with him. The idea had flashed through his mind, brief and exhilarating.

Then he'd looked at her paintings surrounding them and thought about her life in Paris. Her hopes to study at the Academy. What could he give her in Cairo to compete with that? And he couldn't ask her to wait years for him to return.

So, in the end, he'd settled for one dance. One last memory to see him through the months and years ahead. Maybe, over time, with enough distance, the ache behind his ribs would ease.

———

HARRY ROSE THE NEXT MORNING before the sun breached the horizon. The house was quiet save for whispered footsteps as the servants began their day.

He packed his few belongings and debated what to do until he could take his leave of Ashford and Remy. Despite Ashford's betrayal, he could hardly leave without a word.

He settled on a walk in the garden. Part of his mind hoped to encounter Celeste. The other part dreaded it. They'd said their goodbyes last night, and more words wouldn't help anything. The garden, though, was empty. He wasn't surprised. She was not an early riser.

Gravel crunched behind him, and he turned to see Remy approaching.

"I heard you're leaving, and I wanted to say how much I've enjoyed working with you."

"The feeling is mutual," Harry said. "The telescope couldn't have succeeded without your efforts." He paused then asked, "What will you do now?"

"I've agreed to assist Lord Ashford repair the pulleys on his . . . flying pig."

Harry's brows lifted. He didn't think anyone knew the name he and Celeste had given the telescope, but Remy merely grinned before continuing.

"I'll have a wife to support soon. Odette would like to see London, so I'll seek employment there. Perhaps I can find an engineering firm willing to overlook my French background. If not, we'll return to Paris." He shrugged, unconcerned, and added, "So long as Odette's with me, it matters not where we are."

Harry thought the Frenchman had a tough road

ahead, but the man was nothing if not determined. They were quiet for a moment. He suspected Remy had something else to say, so he waited, tapping his hat against his thigh.

"Lady Celeste," Remy began. "She is not her mother."

Harry's brows inched toward his hairline. "No, of course not."

"Some women prefer to be the center of a man's world, which is all well and good if the man is . . . seeking a center for his world."

Harry nodded, not sure he understood where this was going.

"But some ladies—" He stopped and cursed and Harry chuckled. "I'm making a muddle of this. Suffice to say, you are making a mistake leaving without Lady Celeste. I would be lost without my Odette, and she without me. I think it must be the same for you and Lady Celeste."

Harry rubbed the back of his neck as he studied Remy. Finally, he sighed and said, "I appreciate the sentiment, but the paths of our lives are leading us in different directions."

"So, clear a new path." At Harry's blank look, Remy continued. "This button you carry—"

Harry frowned.

"Lady Celeste puts her heart into her painting, which means you carry her heart with you. It will guide you back." Remy left on that cryptic sentiment, gravel crunching under his boot.

Harry pulled the button from his pocket and stared at the tiny rosebuds. Her miniatures, of course. How had he not seen it before? He studied the fine lines, the elegant curve of each brush stroke. He was deep in his examination and didn't hear more footsteps until Ashford spoke.

"Harry, Lord Porter told me you're off to London soon."

Lady Ashford walked beside her husband, one hand in the crook of his elbow.

He bowed to them both then replied. "Yes, my lord. My lady. He's hopeful the Commission will approve my application to replace Lord Knowles."

"You've done well, son. I can't thank you enough for everything you did to see my telescope completed. Despite my actions—"

"No thanks are necessary, my lord," Harry assured him.

"Nevertheless, I wanted to be sure you know how proud I am. And I hope someday you'll find it in your heart to forgive the foolish actions of an old man."

Harry's eyes widened. Despite his conflicting emotions toward this man, his heart swelled at Ashford's words.

Before he could form a response, though, Lady Ashford leaned forward. "My husband may be proud of you, but I am not. I am disappointed."

And . . . his heart deflated.

"Lily!"

Celeste's diminutive mother crowded him and pointed her finger in a Gallic expression of distaste. Harry resisted the urge to loosen his cravat.

"You know my daughter like no one else, but you are like all men. You see only what *you* want, what *you* need." Harry stepped back, but she had said what she needed to say. She threw her hands up and turned on her heel.

"I will never understand that woman," Ashford said with a sigh.

Harry nodded his agreement as they watched her leave, skirts twitching in irritation.

Ashford turned back to him. "For what it's worth, I see how you look at my daughter." If it was possible, Harry's level of discomfort climbed higher, and he did adjust his cravat then. "If you and Celeste decide to stop dancing and do something about it, I'm supportive. I wish you luck and good fortune, my boy."

And with that, he was gone, and Harry had no idea what, precisely, he'd wished him good fortune with.

———

ODETTE'S CHEERFUL VOICE GRATED ON Celeste's ears, and she pulled a pillow over her head. When she finally dragged herself from bed, the maid helped her dress in a green muslin day dress then took much too long with her hair, twisting and pinning the disobedient locks until Celeste shooed her away.

"Ooh," Odette muttered. "Love, it does make the heart grow peevish."

When Celeste descended the stairs, the house was abuzz with the guests' excited ambitions for the day. The ladies meant to take an excursion to a picturesque bluff while the Eleven planned a rousing debate on some new scientific theory. She didn't recognize the topic—electromagnetic-something-or-other.

Harry, Remy informed her, was in the garden with her father. She debated going to him but decided against it. There was nothing more to say, and her tears were too near the surface.

She went instead to her father's laboratory, seeking comfort in occupation. But with no telescope to complete, she found herself at loose ends. She joined the ladies in the drawing room, but their energy was exhausting. Much as she tried, Celeste couldn't muster any enthusiasm for their excursion.

Eventually, she made her way to the morning room, where her mother's renovations were nearly complete. The cocooning silence was a relief. Bright sunlight streamed through the undraped bow window, and she settled in a chair and tried to read.

Through the door, she heard Jenkins ordering a

horse from the stables, then Harry's distinctive steps echoed on the marble floor. She braced herself for the sound of his leaving. The heavy entry door opened then closed, the sound no less final for being muffled beyond the morning room door.

She turned from the large bow window. She couldn't watch him ride away. If he turned back, she might be tempted to run after him, to beg him to stay and give up his dreams.

So, she couldn't watch him, for fear that he would turn back. And she couldn't watch him, for fear that he wouldn't.

———

HARRY MOUNTED HIS BORROWED HORSE and paused. He tried, but he couldn't resist the urge to turn back once more. The house was still, the windows empty. He settled again in the saddle and urged his horse forward.

He passed the gatehouse and wound along the road away from Redstone Hall. Bellamy Hill rose in the distance, the telescope sagging at forty degrees. Earnest, despite its scars. Their pig had, indeed, grown wings.

He passed three Romany wagons outside Marshfield, itinerant families seeking harvest work. As he entered the small town, Mrs. Pitt's preparations for the week's festivities were apparent. Bunting hung across the main thoroughfare, and flowers sat in every shop window. Fresh paint decorated the doors to the town's assembly room, where he was to have shared a dance with Celeste. Would she still go? Would she dance with Marchand? His stomach clenched at the thought.

Marshfielders hurried about with an air of eager festival-wrought excitement, and Roberts waved from the blacksmith's shop as Harry passed. He nodded and continued, his heart breaking a little more with each clop of the horse's hooves.

How could so much levity be had when he was feeling this poorly?

And how could he feel this poorly when his dream was within reach?

CHAPTER TWENTY-EIGHT

IN THE DAYS FOLLOWING HARRY'S departure, Celeste tried to find a private moment with Alexandre. If she didn't know better, she would say he was avoiding her, but at last, she ran him to ground at the telescope. He studied the structure as it pointed blindly into the starless afternoon sky. Blue smoke streamed from his mouth as he exhaled around a thin cheroot. He turned and straightened at her approach.

"Lady Celeste."

"Alexandre." Before he could snuff the cheroot, she held her hand out to him. "May I?"

His brows lifted and, after a brief hesitation, he handed her the rolled cigar.

She studied it then tentatively inhaled. Not tentatively enough, however. Her lungs burned and she sputtered a cough, eyes watering. "Why, that's absolutely horrid!"

He chuckled. "I can't disagree." He took the cheroot from her and snuffed it beneath his boot.

Together they admired the skeletal outline of the telescope, its ribs supporting new ropes and pulleys. She suspected he was composing a painting in his mind's eye, because she was doing the same.

"Did you enjoy our harvest festival?" she asked.

"It was diverting," he answered. Ah, an answer that wasn't an answer then.

"I've been a poor hostess," she said.

"You've been a bit distracted." He motioned to the telescope, but, she noted, he didn't disagree with her. He was being kind, not pointing out her misery, although she was sure it wasn't a secret. She wasn't that good at lying.

"You asked me to return to Paris with you after the festival concluded," she reminded him.

He nodded and looked at her. "I would ask again if I thought the answer would be favorable. Would it?"

"No," she said softly. "I can't return with you." She wasn't sure what she would do, where she would go, but she did know she wouldn't leave with Alexandre. Paris and its artistic society still tempted, but leaving with Alexandre felt like a betrayal of Harry. Even though Harry was gone and would sail for another continent soon enough.

Alexandre turned back to the telescope and

sighed. "I knew that. I think I always knew your answer would be no."

"I imagine there must be much to do to prepare your submission for the Salon."

"Yes . . . although I'm not sure that's what I'm meant to do next."

She wasn't sure what to say to that, so she remained silent. It was ridiculous, the way they stared at a jumbled mix of wood and iron as if it held all the answers. She turned to him.

"I wish you the best of luck, Alexandre. You've been a good friend to me and to my mother."

He nodded and held his arm to escort her from the Hill.

———

OVER THE NEXT DAYS, CELESTE wandered Redstone Hall with a restlessness she couldn't settle. She walked the laboratory, touching instruments and notebooks until her father thumped his cane and scowled. Harry's chair was empty, his box of pencils centered on the desk. She could picture him with his head down, tugging his hair. Could hear his low, soft laugh. Would his ghost always haunt her like this?

She hated this maudlin feeling, and she tried to shake it off in the garden. But summer's warmth had fled, leaving watery sunlight, paper leaves and bare branches. The garden's bleakness mirrored her own. She sighed and returned to the house.

She hesitated at the threshold of the observatory. Pictured mixing her paints and setting up a new canvas. The routine, which was normally satisfying, caused her stomach to turn. She couldn't paint. Not today. Probably not tomorrow. But someday soon.

Finally, she joined her mother in the morning room. Lily stood in the center while Remy held a painting for her approval. Her mother had been updating the walls with some of Celeste's pieces, and the portrait Remy held showed her father cleaning one of his instruments. His eyes were trained on an imperfection only he could see.

Such realism was frowned on by the Academy and would never be selected for exhibition, but her mother found it "stimulating." Celeste suspected it was simply her way of offering support.

"A bit lower, *mon cher*." Remy lowered the portrait. Her mother nodded in approval, and Charles stepped up to mark the place where it would hang.

Remy would leave for London soon, but he insisted on serving her mother until then. It was an arrangement that suited them both. Celeste knew her mother would miss him when he left. And poor Charles. Although he was attractive enough, he lacked Remy's innate charm. Certainly his cheekiness, although she supposed that was not a trait one typically sought in a footman.

After Remy and Charles left, Lily approached

Celeste. "*Ma pauvre.* You are restless. You miss your Mr. Corbyn."

Celeste sighed and turned to her mother. "How did you bear it, those first years when you and Father were apart?" She thought of her father's letters, collecting dust in the bottom of his desk.

"Not well, I'm afraid. I tied my happiness too much to another. I would not wish such pain on you, dearest. It is better that Mr. Corbyn leaves now, before you form a stronger attachment." Her mother sighed then continued. "I thought he might be different, but *non.* Men like him, they are devoted to their work. They don't make room in their hearts for others' dreams. And you, dearest, deserve to realize your dreams."

Celeste felt an unfamiliar affinity for her mother. She'd missed years of motherly advice, but in that moment, the kaleidoscope of color that swirled around Lily slid and shifted to blue-green. Peace.

Her mother loved her, no matter how unconventional that love was. Whether Celeste agreed with her advice, Lily desired Celeste's happiness above all else.

"Harry's dreams are of principal importance to him," she said. "But I think I love him."

Her mother looked at her with a sorrowful expression. "If you *think* you love him, then you do not." She studied her hands then added, "If you return to Paris, you can apply for the April exhibition."

Celeste thought of Paris, where she was building her skill and reputation as an artist. She had friends there, and her talent was gaining recognition. She still wanted to attend the Academy, and she thought she had promise for the Salon. Even Alexandre had said as much. She owed it to herself to explore that, to see where it led, didn't she?

Then why did the thought of returning to Paris feel . . . flat? Fizz-less?

————

CELESTE CLIMBED THE HILL A week later to where the telescope stood sentinel. The sun was dipping below the horizon, and a chill settled in. She looked out over the sprawl of the manor and its outbuildings, and the harvested valley beyond. The scene was lovely. There was a certain peace to the undulating hills and valleys, the verdant seasons. Even the dry browns of winter.

A rustling sounded in the bushes rimming the hilltop. Small footsteps crunched leaves, and Robbie showed himself. He paused when he saw her then smiled shyly. A curl of dark hair drooped over his forehead, reminding her of Harry. Robbie's younger sister stood behind him.

"Good afternoon, Robbie. Hullo, Jenny."

"My lady." Robbie glanced at the telescope then

shifted his gaze back to her. Jenny hung back, watching her with wide eyes.

"Did you come to see the telescope?" She urged them closer. Robbie nodded, admiring the length and breadth of the tube. He gazed at the observing platform, his expression bright and open, full of awe.

"You mustn't touch it without anyone present, but you may come to the kitchens any time and ask for my father or one of the footmen to accompany you."

Robbie nodded his agreement. "Are the stars so very far away, my lady?"

"Indeed. Further than we can begin to imagine."

"But how do we know?"

She thought for a moment. What would Harry say? "Well, we can't go to the stars, of course. But scientists believe we can use geometry to calculate the distance." At his confusion, she clarified. "Mathematics."

His mouth curled in a mixture of disgust and disbelief. "Maths never did nobody any good, my lady."

She pressed her lips together, thinking. "Here, let me show you. Imagine your thumb is a star." He looked at his thumb, then he looked at her with skepticism. Jenny studied her thumb then put it into her mouth.

Celeste took Robbie's hand gently, held it up and extended his thumb. "Now, close one eye, and place your thumb over the chimney there in the distance." He hadn't mastered winking yet, so she held one hand over his right eye.

"Now, we'll switch eyes. Did you see how much your thumb moved against the background?"

Robbie nodded, frowning.

"By measuring that and the distance between your eyes, a scientist can calculate the distance to the chimney. Or to a star."

"Cor!" Robbie showed Jenny how to do it, and they marveled as their thumbs moved across their fields of vision. They tried this new "trick" on the old chestnut tree behind the Hall and on Fernwood in the distance. Celeste chuckled, absurdly proud to see the wonder on their faces.

As the darkness grew, she pointed out the constellations to them. Jenny thought they were pretty, but Robbie was full of questions, none of which she could answer. Was this what Harry felt, then? The staggering weight of unanswered questions?

She missed him, and wished he were here. He could bring the stars to life for Robbie and Jenny in ways she could not. She didn't know if this *wanting* would ever go away.

————

HER FATHER SURPRISED HER WITH a sheaf of papers that evening as they settled down to a game of chess.

"What's this?"

She unfolded the pages and flattened them. They were legal documents, and her breath caught.

"You can't know how sorry I am for what I almost cost you, m'dear," her father began. "I've placed Denton Manor in a trust. It's secure, safe from drunken wagers." He grimaced. "When you marry, you can decide if you want to transfer it to your husband or leave it in the trust."

She looked at the pages in her hand then at her father's contrite expression. "Thank you," she whispered. She placed one hand over his and squeezed.

As a girl, she'd been disillusioned when she realized her father was only a man, not the hero her younger self wanted him to be. But perhaps he could be both. She realized how unfair she'd been to him. No one could live up to the expectations a child had for a parent. She relaxed and allowed forgiveness to fill her hollows, to crowd out harsher feelings.

As they played, she told him of her encounter with Robbie and Jenny. "Our universe is truly amazing. It's a shame they don't have a way to learn more about it."

"Indeed. Young Robbie reminds me of Harry. Harry has always been insatiable in his learning." He watched her expectantly.

She kept her expression neutral. She couldn't go

through life like this. As a friend of her father's Harry was bound to come up in conversation. It was possible they would see one another again. Would he be married then? Would she? The thought caused yet more uncomfortable tightness in her chest. Enough.

"Father, have you considered giving lessons to the local children? Not as a tutor *per se*, but they don't have any other way to learn of the stars and planets, and you have a unique gift for mentoring young minds." She had a sudden inspiration. She tested it, turning it one way then the other, before saying, "I could stay to assist you."

He studied her for a moment, considering her words. "You may have something there, Celeste. But as much as I would appreciate your company and assistance, you need to find your own way. You have too much to offer the world than to remain here."

She stared back at him. Tears tightened her throat and she nodded.

"I'm not asking you to leave, mind you, but I don't want you to settle for a life here when you're meant for so much more." He looked toward the sofa where her mother studied fashion plates. "You would not be satisfied without finding your own passion."

"I'm not sure what my passion is."

His brows pulled into a V. "Are you not? M'dear, I've watched you these past four and twenty years.

You delight in the *discovery*. You enjoy trying new things. *That* is your passion."

"So, you're saying my passion is for . . . finding my passion?"

"Well, when you put it like that, it does sound ridiculous. But yes."

CHAPTER TWENTY-NINE

THE COMMISSION MET TWO DAYS after Harry returned to London. In light of Knowles' withdrawal, the vote to award Cairo's lead position to Harry was unanimous.

Harry tried to be overjoyed. He truly did. He was grateful to Lord Porter and the other members of the Commission for their confidence in him, but his heart was heavy without Celeste.

He missed talking to her, sharing with her. Watching her move. Watching her breathe. He missed Celeste.

There were a multitude of things to be done before the expedition set sail for Cairo. Harry made lists. Lots of lists. For weeks, he worked well into the night before collapsing on the narrow, too-short bed in his rented room.

There were supplies to be ordered, instruments to be calibrated, personnel to be trained. He'd been assigned a team of fellow observers and assistants. They were agreeable men, dedicated to the project.

Every activity was recorded for the permanent record. Harry's hand ached by the end of each day from the volume of entries. Whenever he tried to read his messy script, he missed Celeste's small, precise lettering.

He logged his team's training. Their gear would ship to Cairo in pieces. It would have to be assembled there and maintained by the team over the next years, so they practiced taking the instruments apart and reassembling them.

He painstakingly noted meetings with the Admiralty, the Royal Observatory and the Commission. Meetings to discuss the status of his team's preparations and the state of their instruments. So many meetings.

He recorded the team's collaboration with other astronomers—whether from university or private observatories.

He negotiated rates for instrument maintenance and repair work and logged it all.

The activity distracted him from, but did not erase, his memories. His lips burned whenever he thought of Celeste and their kisses. How could a few kisses distract a man to the point of madness?

He sighed and lit another candle for the long night ahead. He had several messages still to review from the afternoon post. As he thumbed through his correspondence, his eye snagged on one franked by the Right Honorable Earl of Ashford.

He dropped the others, broke the seal and unfolded the page. His heart picked up speed. Indeed, it was a letter from Ashford with a detailed accounting of events in Kent since Harry's departure. He skimmed the words quickly.

Ashford wrote of the Round Table and Beson's latest theory on polarimetry. Fascinating, but not what he was looking for.

Marchand had departed shortly after Harry. Alone, it would seem. That was good. He'd clearly not been the man for Celeste.

Remy had nearly finished repairing the pulleys and would leave soon for London.

Robbie visited the telescope often and was an apt student.

Ashford also described the festival and Olive Pitt's successful assembly. Marshfielders had turned out on the Hill in high numbers to see the telescope for themselves, and Lady Ashford had outdone herself with a lavish picnic on the grounds of Redstone Hall.

What Ashford didn't write about: Celeste.

There was no mention of her. None. He read the letter again more closely. How could the man write such a complete report and not make any reference to his daughter?

Harry thought back to her letters to him in Berlin. He supposed he couldn't expect her to write now, but that didn't mean he didn't wish it.

———

CELESTE WAS STILL PONDERING HER father's words. If he was right, and her passion was for finding her passion . . . well. That was quite liberating. Perhaps she'd been too rigid in defining her dreams. Paris and the Academy. It was a worthy dream, but there was nothing that said she had to pursue one dream to the exclusion of all others, was there?

She descended the stairs and joined her parents for breakfast. Edmund had piled a plate high with kippers and bacon, while Lily sipped her chocolate. Celeste stopped short at the wall of silence that greeted her. Both of them were tense. Clearly, they'd had a row.

"When do you return to Paris, dearest?" her mother asked when Celeste had taken her seat.

"I . . . I'm not sure. Why do you ask?"

"I should like to return with you."

"You'll come with me? To Paris?" Celeste felt like a simpleton, repeating her mother's words. She thought—hoped—her mother might have settled back into her old life, and she was surprised she'd wish to leave, row or not.

Her father glowered and tucked into his kippers.

"Yes, the morning room is complete. My work here is done." She pursed her lips and sipped her chocolate. Her father lifted his newspaper and unfolded it for an effective shield.

Celeste watched them for a moment, marveling at their stubbornness. Finally, she stood and dropped her spoon with a clatter to her saucer. She marched from the room, arms rigid at her sides.

She entered the laboratory, opened her father's desk and removed the thick stack of letters. Sometimes, she reminded herself, a lady needed to take drastic measures. Hadn't her mother said that very thing? What she was about to do might be immoral. Unethical. But things had gotten out of hand.

She returned to the breakfast room and motioned to Jenkins, who signaled the footmen to leave.

"I don't know what you've argued about this time, but it's clear you've learned *nothing* in the last months," she hissed. Her father lowered his paper, and her mother raised an eyebrow at Celeste's outburst.

"You"—she pointed at her mother. "You think he doesn't care anything for you, so you hurt him in return." Her mother stiffened.

"And you"—she stabbed a finger at her father then dropped the pages onto the table at her father's elbow. "You write letters that you don't even send. She wants you to *fight* for her, and you do nothing."

She braced her hands on the table, drawing deep breaths.

"Letters? What is she talking about, Edmund?" Her mother eyed the pile on the table like she expected it to rise up and strike.

"I'm sorry, Father. I didn't mean to invade your privacy, but I found the letters in your desk." She looked at him, begged him with her eyes to hear her words. "They shouldn't go unread."

And with that, Celeste left, head high despite the shaking of her hands. Jenkins lurked outside the doors, trying to appear like he wasn't listening, but the corner of his mouth turned up as she passed.

She found herself outside the transit room, still shaking. She inhaled a calming breath. Today, she would paint. She stepped over the threshold then into the observatory beyond.

Her paintings were where she'd left them, propped along the curved white walls. She strode to her workspace but stopped when she saw a folded note. Her heart quickened when she saw her name inked across the white paper in Harry's messy, black scrawl. Slowly, she unfolded the note.

Happy birthday, Celeste. Do something wonderful. I know you will. Perhaps you'll think of our flying pig when you use this.

P.S. My apologies for disturbing your things.

He'd left her a gift. When had he—? It must have been after their last encounter, else she would have seen it. A sob choked her as she thought of his note lying here all this time, unread.

His note had been propped against a simple wooden box. She eagerly lifted the lid. Nestled against a piece of linen was . . . her own magnifying glass. The worn oak handle had been replaced with one of metal. The same metal, if she wasn't mistaken, that reflected the heavens at the bottom of her father's telescope.

The new handle was simple, with smooth lines that curved to wrap around the lens. The face of the handle held small, handmade etchings. They were simple, unrefined. A moon and tiny stars. A tear escaped and trailed down her cheek, then another.

She swiped them away and sniffed, recalling Harry's words to her from three years ago. *Find it, Celeste. Whatever* it *is that makes your life meaningful. Find it and hold on.* Her sob broke free and she laughed then cried. Harry was her *it*.

In a moment of blinding clarity, Celeste realized she was not her mother, and Harry was not her father.

Yes, she and Harry had different goals, different dreams, but that didn't mean they were mutually exclusive. They could strive for their dreams together, support one another, together. And their achievements would be more spectacular for having another to share them with. For the first time since Harry had left, she felt excitement bubbling through her, light and fizzy.

———

"MR. CORBYN? MR. CORBYN!" The booming voice rose above the din of the dining room, drawing Harry's mind from where it had wandered.

"Pardon?" He dipped his spoon into his chilled asparagus soup and pressed down a shudder.

"I asked your thoughts on methods for determining star composition."

He dined with a gathering of illustrious gentlemen scientists to discuss forming a society for the advancement of astronomy. But, despite the intriguing conversation, his thoughts returned to Celeste again and again. As they had every hour of every day for the last month.

He wondered if there was enough time and distance to exorcise her from his mind. He didn't think even the continent of Africa would be far enough.

When the supper ended, Harry returned to the small desk in his rented room. His team would sail for Cairo in a month, and there were still any number of details to sort. He resigned himself to a night spent preparing dull financial reports.

He kept precise scientific notes, but he found the

expedition's financial minutiae tedious. And so, as receipts arrived, he'd stuffed them into his portfolio to address later.

Whenever he thought to review them, something else would divert his attention. A meeting with Lord Porter, or an issue with one of the instruments. An interesting bird outside his window. But he couldn't put it off any longer.

He donned his spectacles and pulled a thick stack from the leather case. The numbers swam in front of him, and he sighed. Perhaps he could assign one of the junior members of the team to handle these. He tapped the pages to align them.

Something heavier, concealed within the pile, thudded against the wooden desk. A bit of blue, on the corner of a page there. No, it wasn't a page, but a small bit of . . . enamel . . . caught in his papers. He pulled it from the stack and his breath caught.

It was a miniature in rich shades of indigo and violet.

Negative space created a showering cascade of stars in varying degrees of illumination. They tumbled from a single point in a pre-dawn sky, and a lone figure stood at the bottom of the image. He recognized his own silhouette gazing at the heavens. Alone. Lonely.

Despite the minuscule size of the canvas, it held an astounding amount of detail and emotion. With a single stroke here, or the brilliant curve of a line there, it told a compelling story.

A faint impression of the constellation Perseus lay at the center of the cascading meteors. He picked up a magnifying glass and drew closer. Not only was it remarkably—breathtakingly—beautiful, but it was scientifically precise as well. Well, relatively so. Perseus's shoulder was a bit too high.

His hand burned where the enamel rested in his palm.

His heart pounded to think how long it had lain there, unknown, mixed in with his papers.

He turned the painting over. On the back, painted in Celeste's tidy hand, were the tiny words, *My zenith doth depend upon a most auspicious star*. Marlowe? No, Shakespeare, if he wasn't mistaken, although literature had never been his strength.

She must have painted it after the meteor phenomenon and their rooftop kiss. Had thought of him as she worked. What did the inscription mean?

Did it matter? Where his path had been muddy and shadowed before, it was now clear. He knew what he had to do. She'd written the words, but it was as if his heart had spoken them.

CHAPTER THIRTY

HARRY RODE THROUGH THE NIGHT. The sun had risen over the Downs by the time he crested Bellamy Hill. Ashford's telescope waited patiently for darkness to illuminate the constellations once again, the wooden mount a dark skeleton silhouetted against the morning light.

Harry was struck by the irony. They'd spent weeks . . . months . . . to see further, deeper into the heavens, but he hadn't seen what was before him until it was too late. Was it too late? He'd been plagued these last hours by *what if.*

What if . . . she didn't love him?

What if . . . she'd already left?

What if . . . he wasn't enough?

And then he would remember their last weeks together. The sweet passion of her kiss. The inscription on her painting. He would remember, and his heart would settle.

Together, they were enough.

He tried to picture Celeste in Cairo. In the heat and dust and sand. And he found he . . . could. She had an adventurous spirit, and she would delight in exploring the unknown, but he wouldn't ask it of her. She planned to return to Paris, where she'd built a life around her painting. He would not take those dreams from her. But neither could he let her go.

There were enough questions in astronomy that he could do his research from anywhere. If he didn't join the Cairo expedition, there would be other avenues of study he could pursue from Paris. Or wherever she wanted to go, because that's where he wanted to be.

Remy was the wiser of the two of them. *So long as Odette's with me, it matters not where we are.*

His horse rounded the curve in the lane, and the drive leading to Redstone Hall appeared. The house sat regally in the burlap pillows of the surrounding hills. It was unapologetically red in the morning sunlight, a ruby nestled in a poor jeweler's box.

He slowed, working up his courage, and watched the coachman pull the St. James traveling coach to the front entrance. The large double doors opened, and Celeste appeared, cloaked in a rich, plum wool pelisse.

Then he noted the trunk at the foot of the steps. His heart stuttered then began to race.

She was leaving?

She was leaving!

He kicked his horse into a canter then a gallop. She looked up at the sound, mouth rounded and brows raised. He stopped before her and dismounted. He reached up to remove his hat, but it had come off during his race down the hill, and he dropped his hand.

"Harry?"

He tried to think of something to say. Something brilliant or pithy. Despite the hours he'd spent in the saddle planning an elegant speech, words deserted him. All he could think, all he could say, was, "Don't go."

She looked at him in confusion and he rallied his brain. "You asked me what I'm seeking." He swallowed, willing her to hear the earnestness in his voice. "I will always seek to understand the world around me. I love the sun and the moon and the stars and all the ... magic ... that governs them. That won't change. But I'm *in love* with you. You, Celeste, are what I'm seeking."

Her mouth formed a small O, and he continued in the language he knew she would understand.

"Everything was shades of grey before. But with you, I see all the colors of the spectrum. Every glorious color, even the sad and angry ones. I'm not going to Cairo."

She studied him for a brace of heartbeats, her eyes wide.

He drew a breath. "Please say something."

She looked at her trunk lying on the ground beside the carriage. Looked back at the house, to where a curtain twitched in the front bow window. She turned to him and smiled. Smiling was good, wasn't it?

"I was coming to *you*, Harry. I'm tired of watching you ride away from me. And don't you dare say you're not going to Cairo. I've become much too excited about the adventure. I even bought a new paint called Desert Sand."

His heart soared. "Are you proposing to me then?" he asked.

"No! You're proposing to me. And poorly, I might add."

Was she—did she say yes? "Is that a 'yes' then? Will you marry me?"

"If you're asking, then yes. Yes, Harry! Now kiss me." Her grin was blinding.

"But what about Paris, and your painting?"

"Harry, I can paint anywhere. But wherever you go is where I want to be. Now—"

He stopped her with a bruising kiss, hands cradling her face, mouth angled over hers. She plunged her hands into his hair. Her fingers were cool against his scalp, twisting and pulling. His hands moved to her waist, and he pressed her closer. When he pulled away and touched his forehead to hers, his voice was hoarse.

"Darling, your mother is watching from the window." Indeed, he counted no less than three curtains twitching in the windows.

CHAPTER THIRTY-ONE

THREE WEEKS LATER

"I, CELESTE VENUS ST. JAMES, take thee, Horatio William Corbyn . . ." Harry smiled. *Venus.* It was no wonder she'd refused to share her second name with him all those months before. He had to credit Ashford—he was nothing if not consistent in his devotion to astronomy.

His bride was radiant. A brilliant, shimmering excitement lit her blue-green eyes as she recited her vows. She glowed in a gown of soft white silk, like a beam of moonlight casting her luminous shimmer on him, and he felt . . . fizzy.

He was used to studying the unknown. He believed, philosophically, that everything was knowable. All the questions of the universe had answers, if only they had a bright enough torch to shine into the abyss. But how Celeste had become his . . . He couldn't wrap his mind around it. Surely that was one question without answer.

Lady Ashford had arranged an elaborate wedding breakfast following the ceremony, and Ashford began the celebration with a toast to the married couple. He looked at Harry and grinned. "May your own children give you as many heart-stopping moments as mine did."

"Hear, hear!"

"Just be sure to secure the door to the rooftop, my boy," —Harry's neck heated— "lest they try to fly from it."

―――

CELESTE LOOKED TO HER FATHER at the head of the long table. He grinned at the assembled guests, clearly pleased with recent events, not the least of which was the acquisition of his new astronomer-in-law.

Harry sat beside her. If his hand occasionally tangled with hers below the table, the guests were polite enough to forgo comment. She noticed with a smile that Harry had added two Bath buns to the top of her already full plate. She nibbled at one, although she was too excited and distracted to enjoy it properly.

Her heart swelled with love for him. She watched his mouth, remembering their shared kisses, and she fanned herself, despite the chilled October air.

Harry lifted an eyebrow as he stroked the back of

her hand. He knew what he was doing, the wretch.

She counted the minutes until they could leave for London. They would spend their remaining week at Mivart's Hotel before sailing for Cairo. She savored the bubbling anticipation for the adventures before them. Although, if she were honest, she was less enthusiastic about the ocean travel.

As they settled in their coach for the drive to London, Harry wrapped his hand around hers. A small smile lit his face.

"What are you thinking, husband?"

"I find myself pondering what we should name our children."

She squeezed his hand, thinking of little Harry replicas until he continued.

"Perhaps . . . Mercury. Or Jupiter?"

She swatted his arm. "Absolutely not."

He looked at her, and the heat of his gaze wrapped her in its embrace. She sat straighter and twined a curl about her finger, thrilled as his eyes followed her movements. She felt a wondrous sense of power. She—who had no talent for flirting—was flirting with her husband. Rather successfully, she thought. She could get used to this.

"Harry?"

"Yes?"

"Kiss me."

He complied with astonishing speed and

thoroughness. Celeste marveled at how much had changed that day with a few simple words before Vicar Pitt. She was married. To Harry, her auspicious star.

EPILOGUE

FIVE YEARS LATER
REDSTONE HALL

LILY ST. JAMES EYED THE ladies' morning room critically. There were several tasks still to be done and re-done, as they were not to her exacting standards. The walls were finished in a silvery not-quite-green, not-quite-grey tone that reflected light from the bow windows. The ceiling plaster had been embellished with more acanthus leaves and rosettes. Elegant and tasteful. A new Aubusson rug filled the space with rich blues and greens, bordered by a burnished rust floral motif. But the window dressings . . . something still wasn't right.

"Charles, please ask Monsieur Perkins to bring his drapery swatches." Charles was a poor substitute for Remy, but he did try.

Her favorite footman had secured a position in London with a firm of engineers. According to Remy's letters, they were now designing a replacement for London Bridge called New London Bridge. Lily thought they surely could have devised a more imaginative name. Still, while she missed the man, she was happy for him. His role as footman had played itself out.

While Charles didn't have Remy's charm, he was pleasing to the eye. Lily had learned the best thing about asking Remy to perform a task was watching him leave the room. The man positively filled out a swallow-tail coat and knee pants. Charles was no different. Perhaps she should ask him to move that chair again . . .

The tap-step-tap of a cane on marble signaled Edmund's approach. She reluctantly pulled her eyes from the footman as he left to find Mr. Perkins.

"Lily," Edmund sighed when he entered the room. He crossed to stand next to her. "I don't understand why you must redecorate this room. It was perfectly fine the last time you did it. And the time before that," he grumbled.

"Edmund, dearest, that was *ages* ago. I can explain it to you, but I can't understand it for you." Lily waved a hand as she spoke, then her attention caught on the paper in Edmund's hand. "What is that?"

"We've received a letter from our daughter. Shall

we read it together?"

He handed the folded pages to Lily, and they crossed to the sofa. Lily arranged her skirts while Edmund settled his cane. Although he'd long since recovered from his illness, he still used his cane for the occasional weakness left by his fever. She suspected he also enjoyed the air of sophistication and gravitas it lent. Her husband, despite his arguments to the contrary, did enjoy a bit of drama.

Lily unfolded the letter and read to herself, deliberately keeping Edmund in suspense. Partway through the first paragraph, she gasped softly with delight.

"Lily!" Edmund admonished.

"They're returning to England! At last!" She read the letter aloud then. Celeste and Harry would leave Cairo within the month and settle at Denton Manor.

"And look, dearest. Aster has included one of her drawings." She passed the pages to her husband.

The illustration had been done in a four-year-old's bold and imaginative strokes. It depicted Harry holding baby Helen, while Aster held her mother's hand.

"What's that on Celeste's dress?" Edmund asked. They bent their heads together and squinted at the drawing.

"Is that —?"

"It is! *C'est un bebe!*" Lily squealed. "Aster has

drawn a baby in Celeste's belly. Oh!" She pressed her hands to her cheeks and glanced around the room. "I must get back to work. There are rooms to redecorate, and a ball to plan, and —"

"A ball?"

"Yes, we must plan a grand event to welcome them home. *Comme c'est merveilleux!*" she breathed.

Edmund's eyebrows lifted then lowered in thought, and a determined look settled on his face. "Indeed, indeed. I must finish my improvements in the observatory. Harry will be keen to see the new mechanics I've installed, and I'd like his opinion on how to solve my tracking dilemma."

Edmund had been corresponding with Monsieur Louis Daguerre. He hoped to use the man's photographic process to capture images of the stars, but he needed a way to track them with his telescope during the prolonged exposure. His expression took on that faraway, eyes-on-the-heavens look she'd come to accept.

Lily marveled at the change in their marriage. She felt a quiet acceptance—of Edmund, of herself and of their unique bond—that could only have come with time. Like a fine French wine, their love had needed time to mature. The pile of letters he'd written all those years before, professing his love and begging for her return, hadn't hurt, either.

Edmund grabbed his cane and tap-step-tapped

out of the room, intent on his observatory.

"Charles!" Lily called.

———

MUQATTAM HILLS
SOUTHEAST OF CAIRO, EGYPT

HARRY HELD CELESTE'S HAND AS she lowered herself to the thin carpet he'd spread for their star-gazing picnic. Her fair skin and the simple cut of her dress were stark counterpoints to the rich, exotic patterns in the rug. Sometimes he wished he were the artist so he might preserve moments like this.

Settling next to her, he stretched his legs before him as she nibbled a date. She favored him with a brief kiss, and he savored the earthy sweetness on her lips.

The sun had fallen below the horizon, and pinpoints of starlight began to wink overhead. Behind them, a stand of ancient sycamore trees cast shadows in the dusk, and the medieval silhouette of the Citadel of Salah ad-Din, with its distinctive domes and minarets, lay to their left.

He was content. No, more than content. That wasn't the right word. He was *fulfilled*. Fulfillment, punctuated with frequent moments of joy, wonder and serenity. That's what he was feeling.

That's not to say he and Celeste hadn't had rows in the past five years. Both of them were passionate—about each other but also about their own hearts' desires—so the occasional disagreement was bound to occur. But their love for one another grew each day in small, unexpected ways.

Shortly after arriving in Egypt, Celeste had published her first illustrated account of the transit expedition. That had led to a serial publication which gained a sizable readership. She had a talent for bringing the dry, staid details of scientific study to life, and her illustrations appealed to the imagination of scientists and non-scientists alike. She may have been surprised that her journals were so well-received, but he wasn't. She poured her soul and passion into her work.

She also continued to paint and refine her craft. She still hoped to exhibit at the Paris Salon, or the Royal Academy in London. But, as she'd explained to him, those were merely coach stops along the way in a broader journey of discovery.

But things were about to change.

Soon, they would sail to London, where Harry and Lord Porter were organizing a society for astronomical study. Harry had agreed, grudgingly, to serve as the inaugural president. He didn't relish the administrative tasks such a position was bound to require, but now was the right time for more formal recognition of the discipline. He hoped to persuade Ashford to join them as well.

But that wasn't all, not by half. He gazed at his wife's rounded belly and smiled.

"What's put that smug expression on your face?" she asked with a raised brow.

"Smug? I'm merely gazing at my wife—who is absolutely radiant, by the way—and our unborn child."

"Who is absolutely restless, by the way." She pressed a hand where he was certain she was being kicked by their acrobatic daughter.

Harry was certain she was a *she*. Again. Celeste was equally certain he was a *he*. Harry had accurately predicted the gender of both of their children, so he was confident he would soon have a third daughter.

Two-year-old Helen curled at their feet with her thumb in her mouth, cinnamon curls framing her face. An angel in repose, she was somewhat . . . less angelic . . . when awake.

"What you mistake for smugness is . . . Well, maybe I am a little smug. But any man with a wife and daughters as lovely as mine has a right to be."

He grunted as four-year-old Aster landed on him. Her knees and elbows dug in before she settled on her father's lap. Her dark braid was coming undone—again—and spiraling tendrils tickled his chin. She gave a wide yawn then pointed a chubby finger at the stars, naming the constellations. "Hydra, Ursa Major. Leo. Why do the stars twinkle, Papa?"

Harry thought about how best to explain the phenomenon of light refraction, and the combined effects of atmospheric winds, density and temperature. In the end, he settled for a simple truth. "The stars are winking as they smile down on little girls."

Celeste smiled at him in approval, and Aster wriggled, grinding an elbow into his rib as she settled. He wrapped an arm around her to hold her in place.

"Did you know," he began. "If you count seven stars for seven nights, the first person you see on the eighth day will be your true love?" He directed the words to Aster, but he linked his fingers with his wife's as he spoke.

"Truly, Papa?" She lifted her head to look at him and wrinkled her nose in confusion. "But what if the first person I see is you?"

"Then you'll know it's true." And he vowed to be the first face she saw.

THE END

WHAT ABOUT REMY?

Thanks for reading! Be sure to subscribe at klynsmithauthor.com/allbooks to claim your FREE short story. *The Footman's Tale* is a quick, 30-minute read (i.e., perfect for a soak in the tub). It tells how Remy came to be a footman in Lady Ashford's household and how his love story with Odette began.

> ★★★★★ *"Oh, Remy! I had no idea! You are a man with a large, loyal heart."*

Aster Corbyn is all grown up in *Star of Wonder*, a Victorian holiday novella, and Harry Corbyn is fit to be tied with the antics of his friend's son, Captain Andrew Grey.

Alexandre Marchand returns for his own happily ever after in *The Artist's Redemption*, and irreverent physician **Julian Grey** finds love with a female surgeon in *The Physician's Dilemma*.

And **Miss Anna Pepper** finds herself—and more—in *Jilting Jory*.

You can find all of these and more on Amazon.

BOOK CLUB QUESTIONS

Ten questions for your next book club gathering:

1. Harry believes everything is knowable. "If we look hard enough and shine a bright enough torch, we can see the answers." Do you agree?

2. What do you think Harry would make of today's understanding of the universe?

3. Comment on Celeste's perspective on art exhibits: "Separating ladies from the general Salon only diminishes the importance of their work."

4. Lord Ashford gambled one child's future for another's on what he thought was a sure thing. Do you think the risk was worth it?

5. What was your favorite line?

6. In what ways did Harry and Celeste show their love for one another?

7. Was there a part of the story that made you laugh? Cry?

8. Who or what was the astronomer's "obsession"?

9. Was Harry and Celeste's love believable?

10. How did Celeste change and grow throughout the story? How did Harry change and grow throughout the story?

AUTHOR'S NOTE

I create a mood board of the visual references I use when writing. If you would like to see my inspiration for Celeste, Harry, Redstone Hall, the telescope and more, check out my Pinterest board at www.pinterest.com/klynsmithauthor/_saved/ for all my boards.

The Astronomer's Obsession is a book of fiction based loosely on historical events and attitudes. Below are just a few. I took creative liberties with certain events for purposes of the story. History and astronomy enthusiasts may recognize some of these twists.

Many **19th century astronomers** were "gentleman astronomers" rather than professionals. Several early scientific societies originated as dining or social clubs. The Royal Astronomical Society was conceived in 1820 by fourteen astronomers at such a gathering. At the time the RAS was founded, there was strong opposition to a specialized society for astronomy.

A **transit of Venus** is a rare astronomical event that occurs when Venus passes across the face of the sun. An 1874 account from the *Illustrated London News* describes its size relative to the sun as "that of a pea on a cheese-plate." The transit usually lasts several hours and occurs in pairs separated by eight years. Each pair is separated by more than a century. Transit pairs occurred in 1874/1882 and 2004/2012. The next pair won't happen until 2117/2125. There was not a transit at the time of The Astronomer's Obsession.

Harry's **Cairo expedition** is loosely based on the 1874 expeditions, when the Royal Observatory sent teams to nine stations around the globe. Over the centuries, expeditions have been historically important as they helped form the first realistic estimates of the size of the solar system, using the principles of **parallax**. The Mokkatem Heights, above the citadel of Cairo, was chosen for the primary observing station in 1874. However, the timing of Harry's expedition is different from the actual expedition, and I've fictionalized the selection Commission. I can't fail to acknowledge Captain Orde Brown, who was the real-life lead astronomer for the 1874 Cairo expedition.

Lord Ashford's telescope design is based on Sir William Herschel's Great Forty-Foot Telescope, with the added fictional benefit of improved, more precise mirrors. Herschel's telescope was constructed between 1785 and 1789 in Slough, England. Although it was the largest telescope in the world for 50 years, it was unwieldy, and the images were not a significant improvement over Herschel's smaller instruments. Long-range telescopes didn't become practical until much later when manufacturing precision was improved.

The **meteor event** and Celeste's miniature painting of it are derived from the annual Perseid meteor showers that occur in August each year, as well as the Leonid event of 1833. Google "the night the stars fell 1833" — the first-hand accounts and illustrations are amazing.

At the time of Lord Ashford's Round Table gatherings, there were **eleven named planets**: Mercury, Venus, Earth, Mars, Jupiter, Saturn, Uranus, Ceres, Pallas, Juno and Vesta. The last four were reclassified as asteroids by 1854. As of this writing, there are eight identified planets in our solar system. However ... scientists have identified, through mathematical modeling and computer simulations, a giant ninth planet in our outer solar system. Planet Nine has not yet been observed directly.

While **Lunar Towns** and **Bat-winged People** do not actually exist (that we know of), stories of such oddities did.

Gericault's *Raft of Medusa* was not actually exhibited at the Salon until 1819, one year after The Astronomer's Obsession.

Celeste's emotional colors may be a form of synesthesia, which is a neurological condition in which stimulation of one sense activates another, unrelated sense. A person may hear colors, see sounds, taste numbers and so on. It's estimated that about four percent of people have some form of synesthesia.

BOOKS BY K. LYN SMITH

Something Wonderful
The Astronomer's Obsession
The Footman's Tale (Short Story)*
The Artist's Redemption
The Physician's Dilemma

Hearts of Cornwall
Discovering Wynne*
Jilting Jory
Matching Miss Moon
Driving Miss Darling
Kissing Kate

Love's Journey
Star of Wonder
Light of a Nile Moon

* Subscribe for updates at klynsmithauthor.com
and receive these free bonuses!

NEXT IN THE SERIES

THE *Artist's* REDEMPTION

A runaway countess must learn to trust an impoverished artist in Book 2 of the Something Wonderful series.

Here's what readers are saying:

> *"Still swoony over finishing this second book"*

> *"Quickly becoming one of my favorite Regency series!"*

> *"Exquisite!... I cannot recommend a book more heartily. "*

A problem-plagued painter

Problems are piling up for Alexandre Marchand. His last courtship ended in failure, he can't concentrate on his painting, and someone is selling forgeries of his work. He's running dangerously low on funds and sets out to find a wealthy widow or a biddable heiress. Instead, he encounters Regina Townsend. He has no wish to play the hero, but if anyone ever needed one, it's Regina.

A rogue-resistant runaway
Regina Townsend will protect her daughter and unborn child at any cost. With nowhere else to turn to escape her greedy brother-in-law, she flees to an abandoned cottage on England's southern coast. She has a plan to secure her future. One that doesn't require help from any man. Certainly not a silver-tongued, golden-haired, lying rogue.

When danger and Alex's past catch up with them, can Regina distinguish truth from lies and learn to trust again?

Get *The Artist's Redemption* and escape to a world of charming rogues and swoony romance!

ABOUT THE AUTHOR

K. Lyn Smith lives in Birmingham, Alabama, where she writes sweet historical romance about ordinary people finding extraordinary love. When she's not reading or writing, you can find her with family, traveling and watching period dramas. And space documentaries. Weird, right?

Visit www.klynsmithauthor.com, where you can subscribe for new release updates and access to exclusive bonus content.

Made in the USA
Columbia, SC
22 March 2024

33481690R00226